THE ACCIDENTAL KISS

HEATHERLY BELL

HEATHERLY BELL BOOKS

For my oldest son, a first responder. I love you, and I'm extremely proud of you.

1

"If you're afraid of butter, use cream." ~ Julia Child

Through the large picture window of the restaurant situated on Valencia Street, Charley Young caught sight of the man waiting inside for her. She recognized him from the photo on his Facebook page. Good-looking enough. Short, cropped sun-bleached hair matched a well-manicured beard. A relaxed smile on his lips, he perused the menu and casually chatted with the waitress.

Poor sap. He obviously had no idea that his entire life's trajectory might change in a matter of minutes.

Charley almost felt sorry for him.

But the thing is he'd want to know. Charley was certain of this. She hopped off her moped, removed her helmet, and walked inside to the sounds of couples chatting and children laughing. The smells of rich coffee, espresso, and mocha lingered in the air. She wanted a slice of chocolate cake but would instead have a double shot espresso because that seemed like the type of drink to have when delivering someone life-changing news.

Peter Adair looked up when Charley approached the table. He gave her a friendly smile. "You must be Charley."

Charley took a seat across from him and set the helmet to her side. "It's nice to meet you."

"Pleasure's all mine." He waved the waitress over and Charley ordered a double shot.

"Is that all? Nothing to eat?" Peter asked. "It's on me."

"I'm fine."

Charley mentally cracked her knuckles. No point in idle conversation. Get right to the point and get it over with. Like ripping off a Band-Aid.

"Thank you for meeting me. I don't believe in wasting any of your time, so I'll get right to the point." She cleared her throat. "I believe my friend is having your baby, and I was sure you'd want to know."

Milly, the "friend," was actually Charley's foster sister, but they were as close as biological sisters. She figured it might be best if Peter didn't know that. Charley was simply going by recent history. She'd tracked down another dude a few days ago. Robert Tramarco, one of the few prospects Charley had narrowed down as possible fathers, had become agitated and quite defensive when Charley said the words: "I think you knocked my sister up."

Weird.

He'd had a little bit of a hissy fit and thrown her out of his North Beach condo, declaring he'd dated Milly *once* and if Charley was going to make ridiculous statements like that, she had better come with a court order for a DNA test next time. Charley had made a mental note to look into DNA paternity tests should it come to that. Later that night, she'd pilfered a beer bottle from the uppity Mr. Tramarco's trash cans. *Just* in case it came to that.

She'd decided from then on that it might be best to set aside the familial ties and simply sound like someone honestly trying to help. Not as though she was searching for a guilty man to string up by his balls. No. Because Charley was definitely not trying to do *that*. Probably not, anyway. She was aware it took two to tango. Oh, yes sir. All she wanted was for the father to know that he'd planted his seed. And where. That his seed was growing. And where. Milly would thank Charley later, when her baby had a daddy and Milly had regular child support checks. Right now, her hormones were holding her brain hostage and there could be no other explanation. For reasons Charley still couldn't understand, Milly refused to reveal the name of the father.

Milly claimed they'd broken up, he wasn't daddy material, and that was the end of the story. She wouldn't be telling him because there was no need. She'd raise the baby on her own. What she really meant, of course, is that she and *Charley* would raise the baby. Because Milly couldn't possibly think in a million years that Charley would leave her alone to raise a child. And since Charley was a traveling sous chef and had her next job coming up in a week, she couldn't stay in the city and help Milly. Hence, she had to find the father and pronto.

The mission, for the next two weeks as Charley was caring for Milly while she was on bedrest, was to find the right man. That pursuit had led to her making a list of all the likely um...culprits. Frankly, there weren't all that many suspects. But Peter's name was near the top of the (very) short list. Milly didn't date much and hooked up even less. It only took once, but definitely at least *once*.

Uh-oh. Peter's eyes had now gone as big as two full moons.

He tugged at his shirt collar and coughed. Sputtered, actually. "*Excuse* me?"

Here's the thing. She'd decided to take this "shock and awe" approach to avoid men readily lying and skating on fatherly duties. If she asked, that gave him an opportunity to lie. If he couldn't be the father, they'd find out soon enough as Tramarco had maintained by oh-so-helpfully playing the DNA card. Truthfully, she didn't mind scaring a few men here and there anyway. It was kind of fun.

"She's due this August. I thought you'd want to know."

Peter rubbed his chest but didn't speak, so Charley continued. "I know you'll do the right thing by her and the baby."

"W-why didn't she tell me herself?"

Bingo! He wasn't even going to bother to deny it. This could very well be Milly's baby daddy. All the signs were there.

"She was a little worried at how you'd react. Consider-ing...you know, everything." Charley was reaching here and hoped he'd fill in the blanks.

Peter's hand shook as he picked up his coffee cup. "That makes sense. Our break-up was so difficult. But I've always wanted to be father."

While that was noble and inspiring, Charley couldn't help notice that his forehead had broken out in a sweat. Although it was early summer, *no one* in San Francisco sweated without at least running first. The weather just wasn't sweating weather. Ever. If you wanted to sweat from the heat, you'd have to drive further south. Like Palo Alto, or San Jose.

Peter gulped his coffee down, which must have hurt, then pounded his chest with a fist. "Is it hot in here?"

Charley shook her head. "No. I'm fine. But you did slam that coffee down pretty fast. Listen, I can't speak for my sis— friend, but I think you can probably be as involved or uninvolved as you want."

"I-I do want to be involved." His hand continued to tremble as he mopped his brow. Streaks of water, which Charley assumed had to be sweat, leaked down the sides of his face. "I-I think I'm having a heart attack."

Oh, brother. Talk about an overreaction. She'd seen plenty of commitment phobes in her life but this one took the prize. He was going to have a heart attack to avoid paying child support. If this didn't beat all.

"I doubt that. You're just shocked." Unfortunately, he was beginning to resemble the color of a bleached white sheet and she got a little bit worried. "I mean, c'mon. You're too young for a heart attack. How old are you?"

Peter clutched his chest. "Forty-five, but that doesn't matter."

Charley stood. "Forty-five? You're *forty-five*?"

Milly was twenty-eight like Charley, and Peter didn't *look* forty-five. A couple of patrons stared in their direction now. One of them took out his phone and appeared to be dialing. Good thing, because Charley had been about to do the same. One could never be too careful.

"Somebody call 911," Peter said, sliding down the seat. "I think I'm a goner."

"Peter! Please," Charley went to his side and stroked his back gently. "Calm down. I mean, how bad can it be, right? It's just a little baby."

Peter fisted his hands in Charley's blouse. "If I don't make it, tell Debbie that I love her. I always will."

"Debbie? Who's *Debbie*?" Please don't tell Charley this dude was *married* on top of everything else.

"She's having my baby."

Wait. He had another woman pregnant? But Charley's hands were the ones shaking now. She had a really bad feeling. It was unfortunately possible that...oh boy, she might have the wrong dude again. It's not like Milly had made this easy or anything when she refused to give Charley the smallest clue. But maybe, just maybe, Peter had been a terrible mistake. Even if Milly had scribbled a bunch of hearts next to his name.

He was *probably* the father of her baby. Maybe Milly didn't want Charley to know because he was so much older. And God, please don't let him be married. Also, please don't let him *die*. She was about to be in so much trouble and not just because of what Milly would do to Charley if she heard about this. *When* she heard about this.

They were coming. *Dylan* was coming.

She took Peter's sweaty hand in her own and spoke softly. "I'm so sorry, but I lied to you. My 'friend' is actually my sister. Milly Monroe. Do you know Milly?"

He scrunched up his eyebrows. "Milly? Yes, yes, I'm her accountant."

With that, he closed his eyes and slid the rest of the way down his seat.

ONCE THE AMBULANCE arrived in record time with the fire truck, ladder truck, and the whole enchilada, it was quickly determined by the paramedics that Peter Adair had suffered a massive...anxiety attack. So, he would be fine. Peachy. On the good news front, he and Debbie were getting back together.

He'd called her the moment he realized he wasn't dying. Yay! Peter said it took his life flashing before his eyes to make him realize how much he still loved his ex, whom he'd interestingly last seen about six months ago. He'd actually *thanked* Charley.

Gee, what a great guy.

"I'm happy for you," Charley said, as the EMTs loaded the stretcher onto the ambulance for a quick check at the hospital. "This all happened for a reason. And I can't say it enough...I'm really, really, *really* sorry."

"Easy mistake," he said kindly, lowering his oxygen mask.

No, it wasn't.

As the EMTs drove the ambulance away Dylan Reyes, the Firehouse 50 lieutenant, turned to Charley, his square jaw tight. As was her luck her best friend since high school days was six feet of prime male real estate. Full head of chocolate brown hair, sparkling dark eyes. When he smiled, one side of his mouth tipped up in a boyish half grin displaying a single dimple. Ridiculously handsome, he even had a cleft in his chin. The turn-out gear he wore did nothing to diminish his appeal.

Life was so unfair.

He faced Charley, arms crossed, and tipped his chin in the direction of the moving ambulance. "Why should you be sorry? I mean, he's a guy, right? He *could* be the father of Milly's baby. Isn't that your only qualification?"

"No! But I have so little to work with. His name is on my list."

"Is her dentist also on that list?"

She refused to answer that question on the grounds that it might incriminate her. The dentist wasn't on the list. She had already eliminated both the dentist and the veterinarian even though it wouldn't have been *impossible.* The vet was super cute and single, too.

"It's a very short list." She glared at Dylan. "Milly doesn't exactly get around."

"I'm going to tell you again. Let *her* decide if she wants to tell the father."

"I can't do that. You don't understand. I *know* Milly. She wants me to fix this."

"*She* wants you to fix it? Isn't that more like you want to fix this?"

"Wait and see. She'll thank me someday."

"And today is not that day."

"Well, no." Apparently not. Strike two.

"Reyes! Let's go," the engine truck driver said. "You two can catch up later."

"Stay out of trouble, Chuck, or you know I'll hear about it." Dylan strode away to the lieutenant's truck, climbed in, and drove away.

She sighed. While she would love to promise him that she would stay out of trouble that wasn't likely, and they both knew it.

2

"Life it too short for fake butter, cheese, or people." ~ meme

If not for the coffee, Charley would have to kill Milly.

But then again, if not for the coffee, a whole hell of a lot wouldn't be happening this morning. Charley wouldn't be up before dawn. Or at least not with her eyes wide open. She certainly wouldn't have enough presence of mind to work at the industrial-sized mixer in her family's bakery. And definitely not the patience to listen to Milly squawk out her instructions step by step over a baby intercom from her upstairs apartment as if Charley couldn't be trusted to follow a simple recipe.

Okay, so maybe she liked to wing it, but she understood baking was different. Cooking was all about creation and she didn't get to do enough of it as a sous chef. She loved traveling all over the United States working in different kitchens, and it was what she'd been doing for the last several years. But the dream was to one day be a chef, open her bistro, and call the shots. Right now, Milly called the shots. And lately, in some ways, she was no different than all the temperamental chefs Charley had worked with over the years.

At this point in her career, Charley had hoped to have already visited Paris to work, study and see all the sights where her idol, Julia Child, had lived and worked. Yet she was no closer this year than the last or the one before. The closest she would get to Paris was by way of New Orleans this July if her next job panned out. She'd had to tell Sean Hannigan, her friend and work contact, that she was headed home for at least a week because Milly needed her help at the family bakery.

When her foster mother, Coral Monroe, had died a few years ago, Charley had been shocked to learn that she'd left the bakery to both Milly and Charley. So, she was half owner in a bakery when she'd never been much of a baker and much preferred the main course. Sort of the way her life rolled.

Charley took another gulp of the magic bean potion. Not only was it early, but on top of all that it was Monday. Her least favorite M word. It had been far too many years since Charley had worked weekends at the bakery along with Milly, but she remembered two things: coffee was a necessity and baking an exact science.

"Did you scald the milk? That's super important because milk has an enzyme in it that won't allow the yeast to rise otherwise. Over," Milly said.

"For the love of God, I know this." She was going to pretend Milly's lack of faith in her wasn't insulting. "And you don't have to say over every single time. You're on a two-way baby monitor."

Milly hadn't heard about the "Peter crisis." Reason

number one she was still speaking to Charley. Numbers two and three were that she had no choice. Milly was eight months pregnant and on bed rest. Still, it wasn't as if Charley didn't know what she was doing in the bakery. She hadn't worked at SunRise Bakery in a few years, but it was all coming back to her.

If it made Milly feel better, Charley would let her give directions. As Milly instructed, Charley continued step by step. Measuring precisely because in baking there was no room for error. It was basic chemistry. Off by so much as a tablespoon of flour to butter ratio and you'll have flat cookies. Cakes that don't rise to the occasion. Been there, done that. Many times.

"Are you adding the ingredients with love?" Milly said. "I'm getting from Bean that you're not feeling the love today."

Milly, still unable to choose a name for the child she was certain was a girl, had taken to calling her baby "Bean" because the first ultrasound had looked like a little lima bean.

"Stop it. You are *not* psychic, and neither is the bean."

"Yes, we *are* psychic," Milly said through the baby monitor. "Since I got pregnant, I sense every disturbance in the universe. I'm feeling one right now and it's kind of bumming me out."

"And I'm thinking its gas."

"Stop it! I'm way too cool for gas." She cleared her throat. "Okay, butter is next."

Charley searched in the walk-in refrigerator. "You're out of butter. How can you be out of butter?"

"Lord of the flies!" Milly cursed. She'd recently told Charley that she was trying to clean up her language in advance of the baby and was forcing her to do the same. "Come upstairs. I've got a secret stash."

Charley rushed up the inner stairwell to the private apartment section above the bakery. This particular neighborhood in San Francisco not far from the Mission District had been nicknamed Miracle Bay by the locals, based on the legend of the sunset kiss. Kiss someone at sunset in Miracle Bay, the legend said, and you might find your true love. The legend was good for business, because every mid-July in a "kiss hello to summer," ritual, sailboats would launch at sunset boarding hopeful singles hoping to kiss and find their true love. It was a three-day event and all the rage in Miracle Bay.

Unfortunately, Charley knew from actual experience that the so-called legend didn't work for everyone.

Above the bakery there were two small apartments directly across from each other. One of them was where Milly now lived, and the other one had once belonged to Milly's mother, Coral. She'd been gone a few years now, but Coral had been Charley's mother too, or at least the last foster mother she'd had before she aged out of the system. The best one, and Charley's twenty-eight-year-old self could admit that now.

She threw open the unlocked door to Milly's apartment. She was still exactly where Charley had left her. Straight jet-black hair piled high on her head. On the plush purple couch in the main room were several hot pink, yellow, and bright orange pillows stuffed around her, Rufus the Siamese cat at her feet. He didn't even bother to lift his head and acknowledge Charley's presence. He was stuck-up that way.

"Who keeps a secret stash of butter?" Charley asked.

"Wise bakers. I buy it in bulk, but I won't put all of it in the walk-in. Why do I do that? Because sooner or later, something like this always happens. Someone who is not *me* forgets to make a note that we're low on butter."

Charley found butter in the vegetable crisper. Several pounds of it. No vegetables but plenty sticks of butter. Charley waved a stick at Milly. "I'm not going to call you weird or anything because you hoard butter."

Milly made a face. "Really, what *is* going on here? I'm getting that bummed-out feeling again."

"Could that bummed-out feeling have anything to do with the bed rest?"

"Why? I'm going to Netflix-binge for a week. This is like the best thing ever." As if she realized what she'd just said, Milly corrected herself. "I mean, though, I'm sorry about New Orleans."

"Sean said he'll talk to Chef Tati and see what he could do about stalling."

Either way, Charley's entire life had been one seismic change after another. By now she rolled with it. Milly needed her, and as the only family Charley had, there was no way she would let her down.

Milly pointed to her front door. "Now get back down there and bake with love!"

"Is there any other way?" Charley mumbled.

No sooner had Charley reached the bakery than the monitor squawked again. "One of the men from House 50 is coming by before we open, and I told them I'd have two dozen assorted donuts ready and waiting."

Milly knew that Charley and Dylan had argued. She just didn't know why. Dylan was still stewing over the fact that Charley wasn't listening to him and backing off. Lately, they'd had no late-night phone calls or text messages.

This was weird because they talked or texted every night when she was away from the city, long talks in which she'd carefully tell him every detail about her long day in whatever kitchen she'd been working in whatever city. He'd tell her about the crazy calls he'd run that day. The guy who'd taken too much Viagra and his girlfriend had to call 911. The three-alarm fire at a warehouse someone had been using to illegally rent out apartments.

Finally, a few hours later, the Sunrise bakery was filled with the smells of fresh baked bread, cinnamon, chocolate, and butter. Nothing quite hit home more than the smells of a bakery. And even if she'd chosen the main course over baking, she'd first found her place in the world here. Her purpose.

There was a sharp knock on the glass pane door.

Milly spoke through the baby monitor. "You better go let them in. Take me with you."

Charley sighed and picked up the monitor handset. "Really? I don't know, reception in that part of the store? Not good." She carried the monitor with her to the front of the store, smiling her evil grin. "Got...I...door...can't..."

"You're cutting out," Milly said. "I didn't get that. Over."

This micro-managing was getting out of control. Charley set the monitor on the counter and with a flick of her wrist shut it off. "Enough."

She pulled up the blinds that covered the bakery doors and found the figure of Dylan Reyes, hands shoved in the pockets of his blue SFFD jacket. As dawn broke outside, he stood framed by the fading gleam of a streetlight and a random ray of sunlight, like a beautifully dark fallen angel. Good Lord, he was perfect.

She hadn't realized quite how much she'd missed seeing him, despite the fact that he was proof incarnate the sunset legend seemed to work so well for other people and not *her*. Which made her special in a backward way she didn't want to be. What's more, being around him always caused all manner of physical reactions, from unexplainable tingles to more explainable deep affection. The affection she understood. The tingles not so much, though they weren't entirely unwelcome.

The moment his shimmering mocha eyes fixated on her, he quirked a brow.

She pointed to the "Closed" sign, then to him. Shook her head. Mouthed: *you're early*.

He mimed her opening the door. She shook her head, pressed her lips together, and crossed her arms.

He scowled and held up his wristwatch. Acted out hanging himself, ending with his tongue hanging out. And in spite of herself and her rolled-up tight resentment for a man who'd never see her as more than his buddy, he'd pulled a laugh out of her without saying a word. Charley removed the keys from her pink and yellow gingham Sunrise Bakery apron that was a size too large. She unlocked the door and stepped back. If he wanted to come in, he'd have to do the rest of the work himself. She gave him her back and the doorbell chimed as it opened. Heavy work boots thudded behind her.

"Since when do they send the LT to pick up donuts?" Charley said.

She stole a quick glance in his direction. A mistake. He had an amused look on his face, lips tilted into his classic one-tip smile. Edgy dark eyes not quite there. Typical. It was hard to get Dylan to smile on the best of days but when a smile reached all the way to his eyes you'd practically won the lottery.

He met her gaze. "Mad at me?"

"I'm not *mad*." Yep, she was mad.

"You haven't texted me."

"You haven't texted me, either."

"How's Milly doing today?"

"She's good." She broke eye contact first, as always.

Milly had given Charley a full report after the fact. Dylan and his crew had responded to the 911 call an anxious teenage Naomi, their part-time employee, had made when Milly collapsed at work. Charley had received a call later the same day and been en route the next morning to be with her sister.

According to Milly, Naomi had raved about how fast the response time had been when she'd dialed 911. Gone on and on about the hotter than hell firefighters. Dylan, the hottest of them all, of course, with a "swoony" bedside manner. He'd spoken so sweetly to Milly and reassured her, even held her hand. Naomi hadn't stopped going on about Dylan until Milly had given her the evil eye and told her that the bakery floor needing mopping.

No one needed to remind Charley that Dylan was swoony. She'd known that for what felt like forever but was in fact only thirteen years. Even now, she'd swear her entire body lit up and reacted to the heated awareness that he was only feet away from her. He, unfortunately, did not reciprocate said tingly feelings. This was a sad but true fact Charley had learned to live with. Mostly.

"How's the sleuthing going, Mrs. Marple?"

"We're so *not* talking about this."

Charley wished she had her butcher's knife in her hand right now, to stab it into her cutting board and make a point. Like all good chefs, she was learning to be temperamental. Instead, all she had was a little pink cardboard box to fold together. As she tucked edges in, she did so with a vengeance, with a lot of wrist action involved.

"Chuck, I don't want you chasing this guy—"

"You don't understand. She thinks she can do it all."

"Maybe she can. Let her decide how she wants to handle this situation."

"Nope, sorry, no can do. Milly needs my help. You know how she is."

"I know *you*. You're going to wind up in an uncomfortable position with someone on that ridiculous list you have."

"If I do, I can handle him."

"Whatever you say, Nancy Drew." He slid her his exaggerated look of patience and glanced at his watch. "Smitty called in a dozen donuts. I need to get going. Long shift ahead."

Box made up, Charley quickly grabbed the tongs. "What would you like?"

"Anything. Just fill it up."

"I *can't* just fill it up. I need your input. Or don't you care?"

"It's for the guys and they'll eat anything."

"Wow, what a compliment. Because we have scones, too. And cream puffs."

"Fill. It. Up."

"Alright, Bossy, then don't complain if you don't have what you like in it."

She sighed and threw in an old-fashioned raised, a raspberry crème-filled Danish, several sugar raised, and chocolate glazed donuts. Charley boxed up the donuts and taped the lid. While Dylan quietly waited on the other side of the register having obviously given up on arguing, she rang him up. And stole glances at him when he wasn't looking. His larger than life presence took up the space between them, stealing all the oxygen from the room. Filling up all the empty spaces. Calming her even while he managed to stir up every named and unnamed emotion. She hated when they argued, and it was true he had a lot of good points, but she couldn't budge on this one.

When he handed over his cash, their fingers bumped into each other eliciting a far too familiar tug of longing. The tug went straight from her fingers up her arm, where it gained speed and electricity, and found the quickest pathway to her heart. She knew from past experience that the ache would settle there.

His back already to her, he raised his arm in a half-hearted wave. "Text me later."

And they both knew she would. She'd text, and they'd fall back into old and familiar patterns. Best friends to the end. They were tomato and basil, bread and butter, chocolate and milk. Butter and cream.

But apparently, he wasn't her true love.

3

"I took the road less traveled and...now I don't know where I am. ~ meme

Dylan managed to hand over the box of donuts to his crew before he had to field his first question about Charley being back in the city. For how long was anyone's guess. No doubt she'd make herself scarce when Milly was officially on the mend. But he was used to her flitting in and out of his life, leaving a trail of smoke in her wake.

What was happening now felt different somehow.

"You still pissed at her? C'mon, it was almost funny." Smitty devoured a chocolate glazed donut in two bites. "Look at it this way. The guy's okay, and now he's probably engaged."

"How is that a good thing?" Marco, Dylan's younger brother, grimaced.

Smitty shrugged. "*He* seemed happy about it."

There was no excuse for the way Charley was making her way through the city, scaring men and putting herself in possible danger. He and Charley had a long history, so it was only natural that he worried. She had his back, and he had hers. Always. An argument here and there was to be expected between people who'd been friends for over a decade. Marco liked to joke they were like an old married couple who'd forgotten to get married.

And also, the sex. They'd forgotten that part, too.

They'd started a friendship at Mission High School, her the tiny but feisty girl who worked weekends in her foster mother's bakery. The girl he'd nicknamed "Chuck" because it fit. She had an extensive collection of Chuck Taylors and thought all designers of sexy women's shoes were closet misogynists.

"How long she staying this time?" This was from Tony, one of the old-timers at the station who'd worked with Dylan's dad.

"Figure she'll leave again once Milly is off best rest."

At least then she'd be forced to stop chasing prospective sperm donors down. After the scare over Milly's baby, he'd expected Charley to get herself back home. Charley Young was a lot of things. Beautiful and impulsive. Funny. Creative and honest. Wild. But even if he weren't her best friend, he'd made his mind up long ago that the last man she needed in her life was a firefighter. He'd always discouraged any man on his crew who'd wanted to ask her out. There had been plenty of them over the years, but he had to protect the girl who'd endured such loss and turmoil in her life.

He understood loss. His father, Emilio Reyes, had died in the line of duty eighteen years ago and Firehouse 50 had been like a second home to his mother Pepita, widow Alice, and three boys. Dylan had been the first to enter the field, but not before he'd studied fire science at San Francisco State. His brother Marco followed a couple of years later, getting in through an open call and some good old-fashioned nepotism.

But his youngest brother Joe was still the wild card. He had no interest in joining the family tradition of service to community and spent most of his time either on a surfboard or a skateboard. The twenty-four-year old's life was still one big party.

Later that morning, after they'd cleaned and checked all their equipment, Dylan locked himself in his office to take care of email and phone calls. One phone call in particular.

A call to Joe was long overdue. He'd made himself scarce for the past few months, which had greatly upset their mother and grandmother. When Joe finally answered, Dylan swore he heard seagulls in the background. Undoubtedly, the surf was up somewhere.

"Hey. Where are you?"

"Catching waves in Santa Cruz. You?"

"Where else? Work," Dylan ground out.

He would ask where Joe had been staying, but no doubt it was with a new girlfriend. His younger brother seemed to attract both women and friends like the Pied Piper. Hard work was another story. Last Dylan had heard, he was working as a surf instructor at a local board shop.

"Tight. Lots of business from the tourists."

"You coming up for Ma's anniversary party next week?"

"Wouldn't miss it."

Ten years cancer free. The good residents of Miracle Bay liked to call it just one of their many miracles. Dylan called it good health insurance and a whole lot of luck.

In the background, Dylan heard the sounds of waves crashing. He lived in San Francisco but couldn't remember the last time he'd been to the beach. Couldn't recall the last time he'd had fun with or without a woman. Somehow Joe managed to be where he wanted to be at all times. And they all, Dylan included, let him get away with it.

"Hey, any more thoughts on that EMT course we talked about?"

"Nah, you know I don't test well. I'll get through all the classes and I won't be able to pass the state licensing test."

Dylan sighed deeply and rubbed the back of his neck. "Giving up is easier than putting in the tough work."

He understood anything involving testing was rougher for Joe because of his late-diagnosed dyslexia. Dylan clearly remembered late nights spent helping Joe with his homework. The frustration he'd felt when it seemed Joe wouldn't even try. He'd been a good kid in school, funny, cute and entertaining, and the teachers adored him. He'd never had any behavior issues. Consequently, he'd received no real help despite dismal grades, until their mother had insisted he be tested. He'd wound up testing for a slew of learning disabilities, dyslexia included. Without any help, he'd slipped through the cracks.

"We don't all have to be first responders," Joe added. "Besides, I'm a certified lifeguard. That's good enough for me. You and Marco save the people from fires, I'll save them from too much water."

Dylan scrubbed a hand down his face. "Listen, I'll see you on the Fourth."

Dylan hung up and finished going through a slew of emails. It had been a slow day, but that afternoon, the first call turned out to be the usual medical response. Those were always the toughest because they were often dealing with the elderly, mentally ill, and homeless in the city. Today a homeless man had been spotted collapsed on the sidewalk in front of a law firm, but when they got to him, he reared up, ready to fight. He'd simply been sleeping.

"This is my spot!" The man came up swinging. "Fight you for it."

"Take it easy, man." Dylan ducked a punch. And another.

Growing up with two younger brothers, he had good reflexes he still employed to this day. They finally managed to calm the man down enough to ascertain that he was sleeping off a bender, and when he refused a ride to the county hospital they simply suggested he find another place to sleep it off besides the entryway of an upscale law firm.

Their second call involved a fire in a fraternity house. When they rushed upstairs, they found a pot in the hallway, flames rising out of it. Once they'd extinguished the fire, Dylan wanted to know who in the hell had dragged a pot of flaming hot oil into the hallway.

"Mummanshah." One of the students shrugged. He was chewing as he spoke, making it difficult to decipher what he was saying.

"Is that English?" Dylan asked Tony.

"Shaaat," the other one laughed. "Brooman!"

"Fried chicken." Marco nodded. "They were cooking fried chicken and the oil got too hot so they put it outside."

"How the hell did you understand all that?" Dylan asked.

Marco lifted a shoulder. "I guess I speak frat boy."

Their next call was to a "child struck by a truck" causing every one of the men break out in a cold sweat and respond as if their own child was on fire. But when they arrived at the four-plex residential area with lights and sirens, ambulance right behind them, an older woman sat on the sidewalk holding a rag to the head of a toddler.

"His brother hit him with the truck," she said with a heavy Spanish accent.

Dylan looked at the yellow metal Tonka toy truck she held, and a slightly older boy hiding behind a bush. He was so relieved he had to bite back a laugh. No one else on the crew was successful at holding back the laughter. Dylan examined the boy, whom he quickly determined didn't even need stitches. Cleaning the bloody area, he used what amounted to a Band-Aid on the kid.

"We can offer a ride to the hospital, but I don't think he needs one. That's all we can do, ma'am."

She wisely declined.

Dylan was in the rotation from hell. Either that, or God had a great sense of humor. The next call had involved a large and exotic bird stuck in a tree. Reluctantly, Dylan ordered Johnny up a ladder to get the $1,000 clipped-wing bird out of the tree. Part of him wanted to tell the owner that sure, he'd get the bird out of the tree. He'd dispatch his "sniper" immediately.

But that would be wrong.

On the way back to the station, Dylan caught site of something strange in the middle of the road that looked an awful lot like a...dildo.

"Did you see that?" he asked Smitty.

"I was just going to say something," Smitty said. "Was that what I think it is?"

Dylan and Smitty exchanged a look and in that swift moment a decision was made. They were going to have a little bit of fun with their probie, Johnny Fuller. Though he worked for the SFFD Johnny lived further south in Millbrae and didn't know much of Miracle Bay traditions. One of which, as with many fire departments, included a good hazing.

"We better check this out." Smitty turned the truck around.

"Could be important," Dylan said. Indeed there was a dildo in the middle of the road.

"What the hell is that?" Johnny asked, grimacing.

"What does it look like? It's a dildo." Dylan barely suppressed a laugh.

"Shame. Someone is going to be very unhappy." This came from Smitty.

"And it could be a road hazard." Dylan turned to Johnny. "We need to remove it. You've got this, right?"

"Me?" An utter look of horror crossed Johnny's face. "Why don't we just leave the thing there? Maybe they'll be back for it."

"It could cause an accident. Everyone stopping to look. We've got you covered. Smitty will block the road with the truck and we've got a minute or two."

Dylan had to give it to the guy. His jaw set and dialed to granite, Johnny carefully put on gloves, a mask, then bent on one knee to pick up the dildo, and as though the thing were nuclear waste, bagged it carefully. Dylan couldn't remember the last time he'd laughed so hard. It wasn't until then that Johnny realized he'd been had. Back at the station, after every dildo joke had been beaten into submission, they finished household chores.

It was Marco's turn to cook and he fed the crew ground turkey chili with black beans. The crew made their usual complaints about the noxious gas fumes they'd all have to endure. Marco reminded them beans were healthy, turkey was low-fat, and also that he'd brought along plenty of air freshener.

Dylan retired to his bunk that night exhausted. The men all shared a large room, four twin beds to a room. He usually bunked with Smitty and Tony and sometimes Marco. Best part of being with the old timers was the fact that they rarely wanted to chat about their day. Ear buds in place, he turned up the volume and folded his hands behind his neck. *Rage Against the Machine* blasted in his eardrums until he heard an incoming text. Holding his phone up, he read:

Chuck:

Sorry if I was mean today. I'm in a bad mood. I guess I've been in a bad mood for a while. Are we okay?

She added a sad emoticon.

Dylan smiled for the first time that day. His reply was short and sweet:

Always.

4

"I think my soulmate might be carbs." ~ meme

Charley sat behind the wheel of Coral's old sedan, dressed in black pants, black sweats, and a black knit cap. All the better to blend into the night if she had an opportunity to get out of the car and take care of business. She'd decided that Dylan couldn't give her advice on this because he didn't have a sister. Therefore, he couldn't give advice on the sanctity of the sisterhood. Enough said.

She'd brought along the cheap binoculars she'd purchased online and squinted through them to get a better view of what was going on inside the Victorian on Missouri Street. Through the window, she spotted her target: one Jim Mulvaney. An innocent sounding enough name but if Charley was to believe Naomi, and she did, he had been a regular at the bakery. He and Milly flirted constantly, according to Naomi, Charley's little informant.

Why did he suddenly stop coming to the bakery? Huh? Who knew? Very mysterious. He didn't even show up on Miracle Sunday where all pastries were buy one, get one free. Suspicious with a capital S. It wasn't like their product had changed. Seemed unlikely he'd go anywhere else for his donut fix unless...unless he was hiding out, worried he might be the father of Milly's baby.

Quite possible. But Dylan was correct in that Charley wasn't getting anywhere by confronting men. So, she'd simply fine-tuned her approach. From now on she was going the DNA way. All she had to do was collect DNA samples from the small pool of likely candidates (minus Peter, of course. Damn. Poor guy.) and save them in the bakery freezer until such time as Milly's baby was born. Then, Charley would announce she had collected the specimens, and Milly would cave. A side benefit of all this was that Dylan could stop bugging her and she could stop lying to him. Because she was not technically going after all these men to confront them. She was just going to collect their DNA, that's all. Easy-peasy.

She'd done her research and just needed a few hair strands, a cigarette butt, or a discarded cup or bottle. Going through someone's trash was the perfect way. And she didn't even think this was technically illegal. She should thank Mr. Tramarco for being such a regular beer drinker. Quite helpful. Unfortunately, from the recent surveillance she'd done, Jim wasn't much of a drinker. Or a smoker. Seemed like kind of a saint, actually.

Every evening around six he went out for a jog with his cute poodle. He'd be sweaty when he got back but in order to get sweat DNA, she'd have to jog after him, and offer him a towel to wipe up. That made her sound like a weirdo. Who goes around offering strange men a towel? Besides, sweat

DNA was unreliable. And there was all the jogging she'd have to do to catch up to him. Not going to happen.

Instead, she'd decided the trash route was the safest. Dressed in black she wouldn't attract attention. She'd parked two houses down so that when Jim brought out his cans and went for his jog, she could get to work. Like, clockwork, Jim left his residence at 5:55 pm, took out his cans and went for a jog. Charley ducked as he jogged past her, and when safe, climbed out the driver's side door and went for the trash.

And holy wow. Jim's trash was a thing of beauty. This guy should win a citizen's award. He probably used fruit peels and coffee grains to compost because there was nothing disgusting in his trash. She was forced to dig through his recycling bin where she found spring water bottles. Charley carefully lifted one with her gloved hand and put it in her plastic bag. Mission accomplished.

She had her hand on the door of the sedan when from behind her someone said, "What are you doing?"

Charley whipped around to confirm the reason for the tingle up her spine. Of course, it was Dylan. Jaw tight, eyes narrowed, brow creased. Arms crossed.

"None of your beeswax," she said, throwing the bag in the car.

He scowled. "This is getting out of control."

"You should be happy. I felt horrible about Peter, so I listened and I'm not confronting or scaring any more guys."

"You're just pilfering through their trash like a nut burger."

Whoa. Calling *her* a nut burger. Okay, this was kind of unusual behavior, but desperate times called for desperate measures. "What are you doing here, anyway? Are you *spying* on me?"

"Dropped by to see you and Milly said you went jogging." He shook his head. "Knew something was wrong."

"Why is it so *crazy* that I would take up jogging? Huh? Why?"

He stepped right into her and planked his arms on either side of the car, blocking her in. "You once said you wouldn't run if a grizzly bear was chasing you. Said you'd curl up in the fetal position and cry like a baby."

Charley's breath caught in her throat because he was so close that she could breathe in his wonderful scent of leather and whatever divine soap he used. All of this was a little distracting.

"T-that's what you're supposed to do. Besides, I couldn't possibly outrun a bear! Why should I even try?"

Hands coming down to her waist, he easily picked her up, moved her aside, and opened the driver's side door. "Get in the car and go home. Now. Before I have you arrested."

"*Seriously?*"

"May come as a shock to you but you can't go through people's trash. Maybe if you're a cop. But with all the iden-tify theft going around, you could be looking for sensitive information. And a man's DNA is about as sensitive as it gets."

Difficult to argue that point. She chewed on her lower lip and hung her head. "But I don't know what else to do."

He tipped her chin and in his eyes she saw a flash of sympathy for her in that shimmering dark gaze. "Sorry, but I'm with Milly on this one."

"If you were going to be a father, wouldn't you want to know?" She went for the big guns. Dylan would want to know without a doubt.

"I would, but that's not the point."

"The *point* is I can't stand the thought of Milly doing this alone. While I'm off in another state on another job or maybe even as far away as Paris, and I can't help with midnight feedings through a text or a phone call."

Neither Dylan nor Milly understood what it was like to have a wanderlust in one's blood. Because she'd never known her father and lived with her mother, Maggie, for only the first six years of her life, she couldn't be sure it was hereditary. She only knew that she wanted to see the world. In Paris, she'd learn French cuisine at the hands of a master chef the way Julia Child had. Absorb all the knowledge, all the secrets of the trade, and eventually open her unique bistro. She'd serve every kind of food in the world.

Dylan stood by the driver's side door holding it open for her. He waved her inside. "Go home."

When he didn't move aside enough for her to get by, she brushed up against the solid wall of male that was Dylan Reyes.

"I'm going home now, but this isn't over. I want it on the record that you didn't win this argument."

"We'll see about that."

His heated dark eyes caught a glint of the streetlight, and she didn't actually think she'd ever seen him this angry before. Unless...no, he was angry.

She wasn't going to read anything else into that sultry gaze.

5

I just don't want to look back and think, "I could have eaten that." ~ meme

C atching Charley in the act had been far easier than Dylan expected. Then again, he knew her too well. He was always two steps ahead of her. Of *course* she'd resort to collecting DNA specimens since Mr. "Helpful" Tramarco had practically gift wrapped her a new plan.

Charley could stick around and help raise Milly's baby, the right thing to do, but Dylan knew that was the problem. Charley didn't know how to be still. She craved adventure and travel, all things he couldn't give her. And then there was the fact that they were solidly friend zoned.

Sure, chump, just friends. That's why lately you're taking every opportunity to touch her.

He didn't know what had gotten into him but lately he'd caught himself *noticing* her. Noticing the curve of her ass.

Her toned legs. She'd always joked that he should never trust a skinny cook. And she wasn't skinny, but fleshy in all the right places. All things he shouldn't think about. After watching Charley reluctantly drive away in Coral's sedan he climbed in his truck and headed home. He was beat and looking for a few hours of downtime. Sleep for twenty-four hours sounded like a solid plan.

Pulling up to his restored Victorian on Texas Street, he noted it looked sharp, even if he said so himself. The home had been a rare find in the city. Dylan parked on the street in one of the few designated parking spots on his street. No driveway or garage but the home had everything else he needed. He spotted Marco's dark-colored truck parked nearby. They didn't always have concurrent shifts at the fire station, and whenever Marco was off duty he spent his time either at a girlfriend's house or working construction projects in the Bay Area, wherever he could find them. Dylan sometimes referred work to him that he didn't have the time to do.

He had been planning to flip this Victorian with his construction partner, Ty, but wound up buying him out. Ty agreed for the buy-out to be below market as long as Dylan agreed to help him out on a few future projects. Now that he'd put thousands of hours of sweat equity in, it was safe to say he wasn't selling. Not that he *could* leave the area even if he wanted to. He had too many responsibilities and commitments. Work. Family. Too much time and history invested in this community. And he was happy here, too. He was no longer the poor kid who'd lost his father in the line of duty.

Though Marco wanted his own place eventually, a houseboat he had his eye on, for now he lived with Dylan. Sharing expenses was convenient for both of them.

"Yo!" Dylan said as he opened the front door. Just to

make sure if Marco was indecent and had a woman with him, they'd both have a second to run for cover.

That's all Dylan gave him, though. A second.

"Yo," Marco yelled back from the kitchen.

"You alone?" Dylan threw his keys on the small table he kept by the door and went through his mail.

Please say yes. Dylan was in no mood to deal with Liz tonight. She was always so peppy and perky. Dylan could only take her in small doses.

"Yep. Bought a gourmet pizza. Too tired to cook."

"Seriously?" Dylan strode into the kitchen following the smells of tomato sauce, garlic and pepperoni.

This was most excellent. Marco was usually too concerned with his health to eat the dreaded carbohydrates. Dylan had no such concern. Like Charley, he believed he also might have been a carb in another life.

"And beer." Marco opened a bottle of beer and slid it across the counter.

"Holy shit." What a great night this had worked out to be. He'd caught Charley red- handed, re-directed, and now he was going to enjoy a good meal before sleeping like the dead.

"I'm celebrating," Marco said, holding up his beer. "Donna finally said she'd go out with me."

Dylan squinted. "Donna? What happened to Liz?"

"You gotta keep up. I haven't seen Liz for a week."

"A whole week."

"Yeah, she dropped me hard when I told her the truth."

Dylan took a slice right out of the pizza box. "What truth?"

"That I'd rather have my balls roasted over an open flame than go on a sailboat with her on Sunset Kiss."

"You're such a poet." Dylan took a swig of his beer and

gave Marco the side-eye. "You can't honestly believe in that legend."

"Nah, but why the hell take my chances? That's just bad juju."

"It's a silly fantasy. Nothing to it. A way to get laid."

Marco wiped his mouth on his shirt like a ten-year-old. "But what about Dom? Remember, he kissed Lisa Marie at sunset. Next thing you know, he's getting freaking married. I'm telling you, there's something to this thing."

"She was *pregnant*." Dylan quirked a brow.

"Yeah, but still. I mean, what kind of bad luck is that, you know?"

"The failed contraceptive kind?"

There was the sound of a knock at the front door and Dylan whipped around, then back to Marco. "You expecting anyone?"

He shook his head. "Not seeing Donna until Friday."

Dylan went to the front door and opened it to find the prodigal brother. Joe had grown a scruffy beard since Dylan had last seen him. He wore board shorts, flip-flops, a Santa Cruz Surf's Up windbreaker, and a smile.

"How's it hanging?"

Relieved to see him, Dylan grabbed his brother in a bear hug and hauled him inside. "Why didn't you tell me you were coming today?"

Joe fist pumped with Marco. "Pizza night? Do I have great timing or what?"

"Or what, little brother," Marco said, offering him a slice and a beer. "How's Santa Cruz?"

Mid-bite, Joe just nodded emphatically. "Took a few days off and came up early."

"Thought we'd see you on the Fourth," Dylan said.

"Can't I just come up to say hello to my favorite

brothers?"

He could. He just rarely did. Joe showed up for holidays and special occasions and also when he was in trouble. Or needed something. Dylan tensed, a Pavlovian response to Joe. He was forever conflicted when it came to his little brother. Help, or don't help? Let him figure it out on his own, or rescue him? And how many times?

There was no guidebook for this.

"How's Lilly? Or was it Layla?" Marco asked.

Since Joe had a different woman practically every other week, and juggled them as well, Marco couldn't really be blamed. His brothers were two of a kind in that way. Dylan could handle only one woman at a time. Right now, the only woman on his mind was Charley and he only wished he could stop thinking about her for ten minutes.

"They're all good," Joe said with a smirk. "I don't get any complaints."

With great restraint, Dylan kept from asking Joe what he needed now. Instead, for the next few hours he talked shit with his brothers, ate pizza and drank beer. Marco encouraged Joe to apply in an open call next month for a position in the fire department. Dylan kept his mouth shut as that was usually a short conversation with Joe. He'd never been interested. Eventually, all talk of the fire department, women, food and classic cars exhausted, they settled in to watch *Monster Trucks* and *Jay Leno's Garage*.

The next morning, Dylan woke, annoyed that it was ten o'clock and he was officially awake. He pounded his pillow into submission. His mind fully awake, he knew it was all downhill from there. Hitting the shower, he dressed and came out to the kitchen.

He found Joe asleep on the couch, laptop open, papers strewed about him.

"Hey," Dylan said and poked him. "Thought you were going to sleep in the spare bedroom."

Joe woke up with a start. He usually slept like the comatose and Dylan had prepared for a more aggressive wake-up call, but Joe sat up and rubbed his eyes.

He pinched the bridge of his nose and then quickly gathered up his papers. "Morning."

Dylan started coffee, then leaned his hip against the counter while he waited for it to be done percolating. Joe joined him, straddling a stool.

"What have you got planned today?" Dylan asked.

"Gonna drop by and see Mom, then swing by the bakery for Miracle Sunday."

"Good." Coffee ready, Dylan poured them each a mug.

Joe took a swallow of black coffee and winced. "Hey, is it alright if I crash here for a little while? Maybe until after the party on the Fourth. Might as well stay since I'm already here."

Every muscle in Dylan's jaw tensed to the consistency of marble. It didn't take a psychic to sense something was up. But if he brought it up now, Joe would be defensive. Dylan couldn't very well complain that his brother wanted to spend more time with family. Even if he strongly believed something else was up.

"Yeah, sure." Dylan grabbed the sugar bowl and creamer and slid it across the counter to Joe. "Everything okay?"

"It's cool." With that, he slammed down his coffee, stood and grabbed his skateboard. "Want something from the bakery?"

"Sure, get me a sugar raised and be sure to leave it where Marco can see it." He grinned. Nothing annoyed Marco more than the "garbage" Dylan occasionally used for fuel.

Joe smirked. "Will do."

6

"Stir things up." ~ kitchen magnet

On the first Miracle Sunday since she'd been back, Charley hit her alarm and rolled out of bed with a grunt. *Baker's hours.* She'd never been a morning person, and before winding up under the foster care of Coral Monroe, she'd considered 8 am to be way too early. By the time she graduated from high school, she'd gotten used to a 3 am wake-up time just as one grew accustomed to a wart. It was ugly but part of her life.

Charley's apartment whenever she was in the city was nothing fancy, but it still remained the nicest place she'd ever lived in. The window opened to a view where in the distance she could see a hint of the glimmering bay's port. She dressed, brushed her teeth, and used her key to check in on Milly across the hall. When she found her still asleep, Charley conveniently forgot to bring her half of the baby monitor down to the bakery.

Milly needed rest more than she needed another opportunity to micromanage Charley. All those early mornings helping out at the bakery on the weekends had come back to her. She and Milly didn't get to sleep in like other teenagers. Coral gave them a pass most weekday mornings because of school, which she believed far more important, but weekends were fair game.

A few hours and many coffee cups later flour was everywhere and on everything. It got in her hair, her eyelashes and on her nose. Good times. But the aroma of fresh baked donuts, scones and crusty bread wafted heavy in the air. That scent, even more so than the fog and the salty bay breezes, reminded her of home.

She rubbed her hands together, dispensing of the extra flour. Another morning handled.

The DNA situation, however, wasn't completely handled. If she listened to Dylan, she was done. She could find other ways. Maybe appeal to Milly's sense of duty. Or... use threats and intimidation. That was one approach she hadn't yet tried.

The phone rang, and Charley picked it up. "Good morning. Sunrise Bakery."

"Why didn't you wake me up?" Milly said.

"You need your sleep. You and Bean both. Don't worry, I've got this!"

"You do? *Really?*"

"Look, I'm going to pretend this isn't hurting my feelings. You need anything?"

"No. I'm good. Though you should know, last night I had another psychic impression."

"Oh boy."

"Hey, I'm on a roll. But today's not a bummed-out feeling. I'm feeling the love in the pastries. You're putting it there."

Charley sighed. "You are welcome."

She hung up and went to flip the Closed sign to Open. Maybe later, when Naomi came by to relieve her, Charley would take a box of pastries to Dylan and his crew. Just like she used to do even before Dylan was ever a part of Firehouse 50. She hated when they argued. It wasn't his fault that she had a ridiculous crush on him. The other night she'd have sworn there was a spark between them when he'd touched her. When he'd leaned in close. She'd hoped that the heat in his eyes wasn't anger but desire.

But she was likely imagining it all again.

The first customer of the day was Padre Suarez. He was from the Mission Catholic Church several blocks away and still regularly came in and blessed the donuts for the week. It was an arrangement he'd long ago made with Coral and was practically another Miracle Bay tradition.

He walked to the glass display case, his hands clasped. "Buenos Dias, Mija. I'm here to bless the donuts."

"And they're ready for you." Her hands swept over the case like the Vanna White of Miracle Bay.

Charley followed suit when Padre bent his head low and muttered a silent prayer, then made the sign of the cross.

"Two raspberry filled?" Charley reached for Padre's favorite.

"Aha, you remembered."

Donuts in hand, he shuffled over to one of the red Formica tables set against the one red brick wall of the shop. As the morning progressed, she served fresh baked croissants to Mrs. Luna and lemon scones for Mrs. Stephens.

"Are you back for good?" Mrs. Sorrento asked as she

paid for her pink box filled with donut holes for the senior citizen center.

"No. Just until Milly's back on her feet."

"Can we do anything to talk you into staying?" Mrs. Sorrento winked.

Get Dylan to see me as more than his best friend? Or in other words perform a real miracle, and despite what all the elders said about Miracle Bay being the place for it, the so-called sunset kiss hadn't "taken" for her and Dylan. No true love there. And all things considered, it was for the best that he never know about the kiss. Because if he ever found out what she'd done quite by accident, no doubt he wouldn't appreciate it. He might think she'd been trying to trap him somehow. No, he couldn't ever know.

"I'm going to say a rosary," Padre Suarez offered.

"Thank you, Padre!" Mrs. Sorrento paid and waved goodbye.

If nothing else, it was nice to be appreciated and wanted by the senior set and a man in constant communication with God. She filled orders and chatted with more friends she hadn't seen in some time. She wiped down tables, a lightness in her step. Tonight, she'd make Milly a pasta dish with her fabulous tomato cream sauce. They'd eat while watching the latest Netflix binge-worthy series. And then, when she had Milly fat and happy, she'd approach the subject of the baby daddy again.

After the morning rush, who should show up wearing a Santa Cruz beanie and his laidback surfer attitude than Joe Reyes. Little Joe Reyes who wasn't so "little" anymore. At six feet or more of hunky male, he had his share of women after him, too. All the Reyes brothers did.

"Hey," he said. "How's it hanging?"

"Hi, you. In town long?" She knew Joe to float in and out of the city almost as much as she did.

"Crashing with Dylan and Marc for a little while." He hovered over the glass counter, checking out her spread. "Gimme a couple of chocolate donuts with sprinkles and I'll just sit right over there and chill."

"Coming right up."

Charley rang him up. Joe gave her a genuine smile and winked. Incurable flirt. But that was Joe, a good-looking guy every woman, and even some girls, considered a prize. If you could catch him. Of all the Reyes brothers, he was the one voted least likely to settle down. As a consequence, most wise women stayed away unless all they wanted was a good time. Joe was not the marrying kind. She wondered how long that luck would last him, and if he'd ever accidentally kiss someone at sunset, fall in love, or wind up knocking some girl—oh. No.

No, it couldn't be. Right? Not *Joe*! Oh, Dylan would kill him. But it made sense. It had been staring her in the face the entire time. No wonder Milly wouldn't tell her. She, along with way over half of the female population in their neighborhood, thought Joe was sex on a stick. Joe no longer lived in the city, but he came by frequently, Charley happened to know. Had they hooked up one night, and Milly wanted to spare Charley and the Reyes family the embarrassment of knowing how careless they'd been? Or maybe she just wanted to save Joe from the responsibilities that he clearly wasn't prepared to face.

Yes, yes, that had to be it. Charley did the math. Joe was *always* home in November for Thanksgiving dinner. And that was exactly the month when Milly would have had to get knocked-up. Oh boy. This wasn't good.

Joe wiped at his chin. "Do I have chocolate on me?"

Great, she was staring at him. Probably with a look of shock and disgust.

"No, you're good." She swallowed hard. "Would you excuse me for a minute? It's slowed down and I'm going to go upstairs real quick and check on Milly."

"Say hi for me."

No reaction from Joe whatsoever to the mention of Milly. She ran up the steps to Milly's apartment and threw open the door to find Milly sitting on the futon, holding a mirror close to her face, Rufus curled up at her feet as usual.

"Everything people say about pregnancy is a bald-faced lie!" She held up the mirror and shook it. "I'm definitely *not* glowing!"

"Are you having a feeling right now? A psychic impression?"

Her forehead crinkled, and she rubbed her belly. "No. Why? Did something happen?"

"Joe is here," Charley said significantly. "Joe *Reyes*."

Rufus lifted his head up and hissed, as if the very sound of Joe's name made him mad.

"Oh, yeah? Say hi for me."

"Funny, that's just what he said. 'Say hi for me.'" Charley held up finger quotes. "He's downstairs. Right now. Having his *donuts*."

Milly went from wrinkled brow to wrinkled nose. "What else would he be doing on Miracle Sunday? Joe knows where to find a bargain."

"Is that all you're going to say about it?"

"About *what*?"

"Joe. I mean, he could easily come up here and eat his donuts with you. You two could talk. Maybe that would be the *right* thing to do." Charley went hands on hips.

"Don't take this the wrong way but you're being mega weird right now."

"Am I? Is it Joe? Is he the one?"

Milly threw the mirror to the side. "Wow. Just wow. You're going off the deep end. No, it's not Joe!"

"It's just that I remember you used to have a little thing for Joe."

"Please. I got over that crush years ago." She pointed to her belly. "And I'm a little busy here?"

Charley waved her hand dismissively. "Of course, of course. You've got a bean in there."

"Right."

Even though Charley couldn't read Joe, she certainly could read Milly. Her face, her eyes, everything about her choreographed, "business as usual." She wasn't lying. Clearly, he wasn't the father. She could easily collect his DNA sample just to be on the safe side. But thanks to Dylan, she felt guilty even thinking about it.

"I guess I better get back down there." Charley pointed. "Maybe talk to Joe a bit. We have a lot of catching up to do."

"O-kaay." Milly's tone said that she still believed Charley to be acting like a fool.

And she definitely...probably was, but c'mon! How else was she to find this magical woodland creature? Charley rushed back down the steps to find Joe behind the counter, arms splayed along the glass case, flirting with one of the customers.

"I've been staying in Santa Cruz," he said to a redhead Charley didn't recognize. "You should hit me up when you get back. We'll kick the surf."

The woman shamelessly batted her eyelashes and tossed her hair. "I will."

"*Excuse* me," Charley said, finding her place behind the counter and not so subtly shoving Joe out. "Can I help you?"

"You don't work here?" The woman said to Joe, as he joined her on the customer side.

"Just filling in." He grinned, winked, and hands in the pockets of his board shorts, strode back to his table.

"I heard this neighborhood is called Miracle Bay," the woman said to Charley. "And that if you kiss a guy at sunset, you might find your one true love."

Some people. But maybe sometimes your true love wasn't the one you actually wanted it to be. Life was funny that way. "That's right. And best of all, today is Miracle Sunday so every second pastry is free."

"Deal!"

Charley helped the woman to a dozen Miracle Sunday donuts, and then several more customers. Coral always said that she made her money back and then some by offering the second donut free. She'd been a marketing genius, her foster mother. But also way too strict, especially with Milly. She hadn't been allowed to date much at all, other than boys pre-approved far enough in advance. Charley had aged out of the system and left home at eighteen, tired of living by Coral's impossible rules.

But Milly had stayed and gone to college locally rather than leave the city. The dutiful daughter. The good sister and friend. She'd always been there for Charley, rarely asking for anything in return. Now Milly was in a jam. She would need the baby's father in the picture sooner rather than later. Whether she wanted to admit it or not, she needed Charley to fix this. She needed Charley to make sure she wouldn't raise this child alone.

The shop door chimed and in walked Charley's worst nightmare. Jenny Santana had been two years ahead of

Charley in school, but decades ahead in popularity. She'd been one of the mean girls in high school that taunted Charley. Today she rocked a pair of jeans that looked painted on her long legs. They tapered down to sexy ankle boots with four-inch heels. This made her look a bit like an Amazon, given the fact that she was already fashion model tall without the heels. The latest color of her hair, which seemed to change seasonally, was platinum blonde a la Marilyn Monroe.

But the worst thing about Jenny, hands down, was how she relentlessly went after Dylan. They'd gone out once in high school, and Jenny never seemed to tire of the idea that one day they'd get back together. One day she'd kiss him at sunset and find out they were each other's true love (Jenny wholeheartedly believed in the legend.) They'd get married, together forever, and make many Reyes babies. Charley only knew this because Jenny told everyone who would listen. Worse, she seemed to think that Charley could make this happen because of her influence on Dylan.

"Hey, Charley," Jenny said, sashaying to the counter.

Charley pasted on her customers-only fake and toothy smile. "The usual?"

"Let me have a coffee today. Black. I'm on a diet."

Charley wrinkled her nose. "Since when?"

"Since *Cosmo* said that a few extra pounds could kill your sexual mojo."

Charley tried not to snort at the mojo comment. Please. Jenny had enough sexual mojo to light up the west coast of the United States. If Charley could have half of her mojo, she'd be happy and satisfied. She served up a drip coffee, slapped on a lid, and rang Jenny up.

"So...Dylan. How's he doing?"

"I don't know, Jenny, you should tell me. I just got back."

Of course, they both knew Dylan didn't *talk* to Jenny so much as he slid her the same hot looks that every other living and breathing male did.

"Funny. Don't try to pretend you're not the ultimate 411 on Dylan Reyes."

True. She should not pretend that. "What do you want to know?"

"Is he dating anyone?" She leaned in close.

"Has that ever bothered you?"

"Catch me a break here. I'm just trying to gage my chances with him. Dylan always gives me the sultry, I-want-to-eat-you-alive looks, but he's never done anything about it."

Charley winced at the thought of Dylan giving Jenny those types of looks, which he'd never once given Charley, and threw a dishtowel over her shoulder. Glamour city here. "Let me get this straight. You want me to find out why Dylan hasn't asked you out?"

"Is he dating one of my friends? Or is there...something *wrong* with him?"

Charley's spine straightened in indignation at the suggestion there could be anything wrong with the dark and edgy dreamboat simply because he didn't want to hook up with Jenny.

Maybe he just wanted to be different.

Because Padre Suarez still sat nearby reading a book, infusing the bakery with a saintly aroma, Charley held back from cursing. Instead, she had a random thought so out of the blue that its deviousness scared her a little bit. But just for once, maybe if all the beauty contestants and model types would lay off Dylan, Charley might have a chance. A chance for what she didn't even know. Sunset kiss fail be damned. Maybe they wouldn't have true love, but how about a chance to find out whether there was even the slightest possibility they could ever be more than friends?

That could be the only reason, she told herself, that she said the next words percolating in her mind.

"He's getting married," she said in a hushed tone, less Padre Suarez overhear.

And oh God, she'd *said* it. She'd pranked Dylan many times before, once walking up to him in the middle of talking to a beautiful girl, only to ask him whether he'd taken the paternity test yet. All in good fun. He'd always get her back with a vengeance. Once he'd pilfered a set of hand-cuffs from his buddy in the SFPD and pretended to make a citizen's arrest in the middle of her dinner date. Her date had stared at her in horror and disgust. She wasn't going to lie, that one *had* been embarrassing.

"Married? *Dylan*?"

"Yep. He finally kissed a girl at sunset and apparently, it's true love. So...it's kind of a done deal." Charley wiped the counter top. "He doesn't want anyone to know yet. You'll keep your mouth shut, won't you?"

"Of course. Damn. Shows you how true the legend is! Someone finally caught him." Jenny whispered, "Who is she?"

"No one you would know. She's not from here and like forty-five or fifty or something." Once Charley got going, it was hard to stop.

"A cougar!" Jenny snapped her fingers.

"Well, I've seen pictures and she used to be really ugly, but she's had a lot of plastic surgery now so she's much prettier."

"Jesus, Mary and Joseph!" Jenny grabbed her coffee and took off at a near-run.

Padre Suarez stood, and his wise gaze followed Jenny out of the shop. "Where is she going in such a hurry?"

Charley bit back a laugh. "I don't know. Padre, how late is the confessional open?"

He blinked. "Aren't you a Baptist, dear?"

"No. Sort of a half-hearted Methodist." Mostly Coral's influence. "But just in case, I might need a miracle."

When Dylan found out, he was going to get her back and get her good. She would need all the help she could get.

Padre smiled. "You have come to the right place."

7

"Don't you wish people would mind their own business? Asking for a friend." ~ meme

L ate in the day, Charley took her mind off her latest disaster by cooking dinner for Milly as planned. She threw in a stick of butter and watched it melt and sizzle in the pan. Added a handful of chopped garlic cloves. Stirred, then added a handful of chopped basil and grape tomatoes, crushed bell tomatoes, and tomato sauce. The aroma in the room transformed Milly's apartment into an Italian eatery. Garlic, basil, and tomato smells rose in the air and tickled her nose. Charley added in whipping cream, guessing at the amount which she always happened to do just right, and stirred her favorite tomato cream sauce in the world. She finished off with a little cornstarch to thicken. Dipped her finger in for a taste. Oh, yeah. Just right.

Chopping, stirring, and butter always calmed her. That, and talking to Dylan, but she couldn't very well do that now.

She'd really screwed herself on that one. Now they would segue from one argument right into what would likely be another one. A new record for them. No maybe about it, she'd crossed the line on pranks. What excuse could she give him?

I didn't see any other way I'd get women to stop pining away for you for a minute. Maybe if there's no one else around, you'll finally notice me.

Blatantly obvious. Pathetic. She was so pathetic.

"Oh, that smells so good," Milly said. "Ever since I got pregnant, everything smells better. More intense."

"What about taste?"

"That, too. In fact, all of my senses including my sixth."

Charley rolled her eyes. "Sure, Miss San Francisco Medium."

If Milly really was psychic, she'd sense what was coming to her right after dinner.

"Keep on making fun of me, you'll see. Was I wrong about the love today?"

Milly hadn't been entirely off base. Today, Charley had let her stupid crush roam free and like a lost and wandering sheep fall off a cliff. She supposed that should have been an omen.

"Guess not."

"See, I told you." Milly rubbed her belly, satisfied.

Rufus meowed and rubbed against Charley's legs. Always so kind to her at dinnertime, the rat fiend. She quickly opened him a can of food and set his dish down, so he could eat at the same time. Charley drained the pasta and served herself and Milly in the bright colorful bowls Milly kept in the cupboard. This was Dylan's second favorite dish of Charley's, after the ratatouille she made and which they often ate straight out of the pan.

"Yum. So good." Milly closed her eyes in pleasure after her first bite. "How much garlic did you put in?"

"A handful."

Milly opened one eye. "Butter?"

"A stick."

"I just don't know how you do it."

"Trade secret." She lifted a shoulder. "I'm the food whisperer. It's a gift."

"Someday maybe you could write it all down. I'd like to make this for myself sometime."

"But this is *my* special dish. I make it for you when I'm home."

"I know, but..." Milly's voice trailed off. "You're gone so much."

Wait. Charley had something Milly wanted, so...seed planted. This could be easier than she'd thought. "I'm sorry, maybe I am being selfish. You can have the recipe since I've been away too much."

"Awesome!"

She glanced at Milly from under hooded eyes. "If you tell the father."

Milly scowled. "Still not giving up on this?"

Charley fixed her with a determined and steely gaze. "Never."

"You have to. Seriously, I don't want him to know and the reason I don't tell you is because you're going to take a big leap as you always do and *tell* him."

Basically, Milly didn't trust Charley which would be offensive were she not so correct in this case. "You can't raise a baby on your own. It's going to be too hard to run the bakery *and* raise a baby."

"I'll work it out. We Monroe women are strong, and we don't need a man."

Charley's eyes slid to Milly's belly and then up to her eyes. She had needed a man a few months ago.

"Well, for one thing. We need men for *one* thing."

After everything she'd been through, how could Milly not know what Charley was feeling? She'd spell it out for her. "What do you think it was like for me, never knowing my father?"

She frowned. Milly's parents had been divorced but she saw her father regularly until he moved to Oregon. "Not good, I guess. But you had me and Mama. We did okay, didn't we?"

"Yes, once I landed with you two. But there were many years when I didn't have anyone. Maggie left me, and I didn't even know my father. I had zero family. That's how I wound up in foster care."

"I'm sorry. I know that was rotten, but this is different." She patted her belly. "You'll see."

Charley went hands on hips. "Do you or do you not want my famous and fabulous recipe so you can make it for yourself when I'm not home?"

"Not enough for that."

Strike one hundred or so. Not sure. Charley had lost count since she'd been at this from the first day several months ago when Milly had called to give her the unexpected news. Charley would be an auntie. Bargaining had not worked. Begging and appealing to her sense of reason had not worked. But there was always fear and intimidation. Charley got up to return their dishes to the sink. She picked up her sharpest chef knife, stomped back and stood in front of Milly brandishing it with true skill.

"You better tell him." She said this as threateningly as she could, being that she was about five feet two and one hundred and twenty-five pounds of mostly sass.

Milly burst out laughing.

"That's not supposed to be funny!" Charley stomped her foot.

"I know, I know," she said through a wheeze, holding her stomach. "That's what makes it even funnier."

Charley was zero for one hundred and one (give or take) now. She was out of options and might actually have to go back to DNA stealing, possibly get arrested, and spend hard time at Folsom. She hoped Dylan would come to visit.

"I have to pee. Oh man, that was the funniest thing I've ever seen." She reached for Charley's hand to give her a boost. "You looked so serious."

"I *am*."

"Stop it! I might pee my pants." Milly waddled to the bathroom, near tears.

At least they were happy tears.

8

Diet, day one: I have removed all the fattening food from the house. It was delicious. ~ meme

The whole incident was an innocent enough mistake.

No, _really_.

Last summer, it had been just another simple evening in Miracle Bay. That particular Saturday in June had been a rare day off for Dylan, and Charley had met him at the home he'd renovated and decided to keep. She'd fed him (filet mignon in a reduction sauce with grilled asparagus shoots on the side) and afterward they'd watched the fifty-something showing of _Scarface_.

While Charley watched the bloody end through her splayed fingers, she dared to peek at Dylan, sacked out on the floor in front of her, head on a sofa pillow. He'd fallen asleep, his breathing slow and measured. She didn't know how long she'd been enduring this torture needlessly, so she shut off the movie. Dylan didn't move a single muscle.

He worked so hard, picking up extra work at the docks, occasionally doing odd handyman jobs at his mother's boarding house and now renovating this Victorian to flip. No wonder he'd fallen asleep during his favorite movie. It was all too much. Taking a folded blanket from the sofa, Charley draped it over his figure stretched out on the floor, one arm over his forehead, the other stretched out to the side. As long as she'd known Dylan, she couldn't say that she'd ever seen him *sleep*.

This was actual proof he wasn't superhuman and the knowledge settled into her, wrapping around her heart warm and cozy. He wasn't perfect.

Not entirely.

He didn't move as she tucked the blanket around him, not even when she dared to rake a fingernail across his jawline and the tough dark bristle there. If he woke up, she'd claim he had something stuck to his jaw. As his best friend, it was her duty to remove it. Here were a few new things to know about Dylan. He was a heavy sleeper if this was any indication. And there were many other things she didn't know about him, such as whether or not his full lips were soft. These were things she'd probably never know about him.

She studied his handsome face, relaxed and oddly vulnerable now in rest. For years, she'd used any excuse she could to touch him. Slapping his back if he ever coughed in front of her. Removing a little something he had on his face (there never was anything). Fist bumps. But she'd had to imagine threading her fingers through his thick dark hair. She did that now, surprised it was softer than it looked. Being this close to him, she felt an unexplainable heat and awareness of him. He'd always been attractive to her, but this moment felt different. Special. The air between them was charged and thick. And she was tempted.

A thought ran through her so wild and crazy that she pulled her hand back as if stung.

Because she could kiss him now. It wasn't cheating. He wasn't dating anyone, and neither was she. Plus, he'd never know. It wouldn't change anything. She wouldn't have to worry that he'd break her heart. That she'd somehow break his.

Just a kiss.

It wasn't going to be a great kiss, seeing as he wouldn't be a participant. This kiss would be chaste. Tender. And likely her only chance to kiss him. Ever. She bent lightly and carefully over him, so as not to make any sudden moves and wake him. Her lips brushed lightly over his full ones, pleasantly surprised at how soft they were. A tingle swept through her and she'd swear the room shimmered in a soft radiant glow.

"I love you," she whispered because it seemed that had always been true.

She stayed longer than she'd planned, lips feathering against his so lightly it was almost as if it hadn't happened. But it had. She'd kissed her best friend without his permission. Without his knowledge. Wrong. So wrong. She shot to her feet, terrified at what she'd done. They were friends and that was all she needed. All he wanted. All she wanted. Most of the time. In those other moments when he took her breath away just by giving her a lopsided smile, well, she'd get over that. Someday.

Blinking away tears of shame, she carried the popcorn bowls to the kitchen.

At least this small moment would always be hers. One

private moment in time she could keep locked in her heart as she traveled the country dealing with impersonal co-workers who never seemed to give a wit about her. Dates that never went anywhere. Someday, she'd laugh about this. Someday, she'd tell her husband about this and he'd say: "Baby, I'm so glad he didn't wake up during that kiss because if he had you and I might not be together." Someday, she wouldn't feel this aching emptiness, the sinking sense that as much as she had she had in life she had nothing if she didn't have him.

There was something wrong with her. She was selfish. That was the problem.

When she set the bowls on the counter of the kitchen, the sun was slipping down, a beautiful burst of orange, yellow and red. It was like a gift, a reward and acknowledge-ment that this pain and longing would pass someday. She'd be able to move on.

But like an unexpected slap or a sting, she hissed in a sharp breath at the realization that she'd *accidentally* kissed Dylan during the sunset. Fingers traced her mouth, remem-bering what she'd done. What she'd taken without permis-sion. If one believed in the legend of the sunset kiss, and she did, it meant he *could* be the one. True love. If this was real, Dylan would feel it too when he woke up. He'd look at her differently. He'd sense the same electricity between them that she had.

But one year later, not a thing between them was any different.

∽

DYLAN HAD the next forty-eight off from the station and used part of one day to finish the job he'd started on a yacht docked at the marina. He'd been hired to install some wood cabinets in the galley kitchen. He'd probably indulge in a couple of basketball games at the rec center. Sleep. Spend some time with Charley before she took off again. If he monopolized more of her time while she was here, she'd have less of it to try and intervene in Milly's life. Because he couldn't let her continue and if that meant putting a tail on her, well, he had friends at the SFPD.

But if she ever found out who the father was, no doubt Charley would try to arrange a sunset kiss for Milly and the man. Wouldn't surprise him. Charley was as much of a believer in the ridiculous legend as every other woman her age.

He wasn't a believer, and neither were half of the men he knew. Dylan knew a gimmick when he saw one. Sure, some men went along with it when they were seriously interested in a woman. Kissed them at sunset to up their game. True love. Ha! He could come up with the names of two relationships where the couples kissed at sunset, and though they were still together, they were also miserable. That wasn't true love. You couldn't build a life on a myth. A fantasy.

The legend of "true love" could be put to rest forever in his mind. He was generally suspicious of any woman who believed. Except for Charley, because her belief in the legend came from a deeper place than most. For Charley, it wasn't so much about a sunset kiss as it was about being the chosen one. Special. But since he'd appointed himself as the one who'd approve her "forevers," whether she liked it or not, he wasn't worried she'd wind up with the wrong man. A few months ago on a visit home, she'd briefly dated a dude from North Beach. Some loser type destined to break her heart. It was written all over the guy. Man whore. Player.

And even if it might get her to stay in the city permanently for a change, he couldn't sit by and allow her to get hurt on his watch. As usual, he'd taken it upon himself to break the news to her. He'd checked the guy out, and sure enough he'd been juggling three other women at the same time. But when he'd confronted Charley with the news, she hadn't been as grateful as he had expected.

"Did I *ask* you to do that?" she'd yelled.

"You didn't have to. Knew you'd want to know."

"Maybe I didn't, Dylan, did you ever think of that?"

"Why *wouldn't* you want to know? Do you want to live in denial? In a fantasy?"

Like all the other blind believers, he'd almost said out loud. True love and forever wasn't possible from what he'd witnessed. But if it was, it would start with reality. It would start with two people who were willing to work hard at keeping their love alive, like his parents had.

Charley had continued to yell. "I wasn't sleeping with the guy! What if he'd gradually stopped dating all the others and wound up with me?"

"Are you serious? Guys like that never settle down."

"What you mean is he'd never settle down with me!" She'd shoved him. "You just don't get it. I want to be happy, but you won't *let* me."

"How am I stopping you?"

She'd just stared at him for several long minutes and opened and closed her mouth several times, never saying a single word. There was something she wouldn't tell him. And that's when he got to call himself a hypocrite because he also kept plenty from her.

From the first time she'd leaned in front of him wearing a pair of tight jeans and he'd had a good look at her perfectly shaped ass, he'd had *ideas*. An attraction that he couldn't deny. Didn't mean he'd ever act on it. The friendship he had with Charley was solid, permanent, and he knew no matter how far she traveled she'd always be his best friend. That kind of physical distance wouldn't work in a serious relationship.

Later, he met most of the off-duty crew for drinks. Dylan took a swig of his Corona and glanced around Juan's, their usual hang-out. The owner kept it colorful and real. Huge sombreros hung from the rafters and tortilla chips and burn-your-tongue-off salsa were served up in Aztec orange and bright red painted bowls. His eye caught a few of the usual suspects in attendance tonight. Women like Jenny Santana, who were always up for a good time, no strings attached. The way he liked it and what he needed tonight. Find a woman, bury himself in her. Relax.

From across the room, he caught Jenny's eye and smiled at her. She quickly looked away. He'd mostly stayed away from her because of how much Charley disliked her. He couldn't see any chance at a relationship, even short term, when Charley couldn't stand to be around the woman. But for one night...who would know? He wondered if Jenny would be game for that, or if, as he feared, she'd be ready for a sailboat cruise at sunset and a marriage proposal shortly after.

Samantha Hill passed by giving him an odd look. No smile. Wouldn't meet his eyes. It was one of those curled upper lip "I don't even see you anymore" looks. What was up with that?

"9-11, dude. We have a situation here." Marco slapped a Corona on the counter top of the bar. "Charley got you big time. It's the prank to end all pranks."

"What did she do? Tell everyone I'm wanted in seven states for male prostitution again?" That *had* been a funny one. A little embarrassing to explain to his mother but otherwise most residents didn't believe it anyway.

Marco winced. "Apparently you kissed a woman at sunset, found true love, and are now officially engaged. To a 55-year-old woman from San Mateo. It's got Jenny Santana staying away from you, which is a nice bonus, but unfortunately she of the flapping jaws is telling everyone."

Suddenly the strange and off-putting looks made sense.

"This prank is just plain mean," Marco said. "What if I leave Charley's name and phone number on every men's room in the city?"

"Hell, no. Are you out of your mind? This is just another one of her pranks. It's been a while." He pulled out his phone and texted Charley all in caps.

Apparently, I'm engaged. Nice try. I'll get you back for this one. Count on it.

A minute later, she texted back.

Busy. Can't talk right now.

Yeah, right.

Ironic that she should pick the true love sunset at kiss crap to work a prank around. There was a first time for everything. The fact that Charley had pulled this prank said more about her skill as a storyteller than it did anything else. But it never ceased to amaze him how many women wanted to believe.

He'd take care of this in about two seconds flat. He turned to Marco. "Hold my beer."

Hoisting himself up, Dylan stood on the bar and clapped his hands. He hardly needed to do that to get anyone's attention. Even in the noisy bar, most were already staring at him, slack-jawed.

"Get down, you fool," the bartender said.

Dylan ignored that. "I'll say this once and only once: I'm

not engaged. Not to anyone. Didn't kiss anyone at sunset. Never will. I don't believe in the stupid legend."

A gasp from one of the women. Another covered her mouth. Jenny Santana simply glared, eyes narrowed to slits. Yeah, he'd once told her he might be convinced to believe in sunset kisses. He'd been a horny teenager at the time. Sue him.

"Look, there's no such thing as the legend of the sunset kiss." He held up air quotes. "It's good for tourism, but that's it."

"I can't believe you, Dylan Reyes!" Virginia Cruz said, waving a finger at him. "Maybe you don't believe, but that doesn't mean it isn't real. Don't ruin this for the rest of us. Why discourage everyone else from finding true love? Are you really *that* bitter?"

Bitter? Not him. He was realistic and sensible. Grounded. Dylan hopped off the bar, chugged the rest of his beer, and slammed it on the counter. "Later."

"Where you going?" Marco called.

"Somewhere I can plan an elaborate prank."

9

"Nevertheless she persisted." ~ meme

I t turned out, a prank of the magnitude Dylan was considering could take some time. A plan. Probably a cast of actors he'd need to hire. Not a problem. He could be patient. Stealthy. The best thing about this was going to be watching Charley worry and wonder when and where it would all be coming back to bite her. And how. She'd get jumpy every time anyone came up behind her. Because it might be today, or tomorrow. Maybe next year. But payback *would* be coming when she'd least expect it.

The next morning, he found himself at the bakery where he waited outside until the last of the morning customers rushed out, pink boxes in hand. When there was a slight lull in activity, he made his way inside. The doorbell dinged, and Charley turned to him.

"Hey, Chuck." He spread his hands, one on either side of

the glass display. Slid her a wicked grin. "How are we doing today?"

Her face already looked flushed. Wait till he got going.

"Are you still mad? Jenny was asking about you again, and...and I thought..."

"Yeah?"

"I thought maybe I could get her to finally leave you alone."

He felt a smile tugging at his lips and the fact that Charley's nose was dusted with flour might have had something to do with that. "And everyone else, too?"

"Um, well..." She fisted her apron and swiped at her nose.

"Know what? Let's forget it," he said, meaning no such thing.

"What? Really?"

"Yeah, I'm sure no one's going to believe it anyway. Marco and Joe will spread the word and they both know a lot of women."

"Oh, yeah. You're right." She bit her lower lip, looking disappointed.

"As long as you show me where the magic happens." He nudged his chin toward the back of the counter.

He'd never been allowed in the back nor was anyone else. One of Coral's many rules.

"Why?" she said, suspicion heavy in her tone, eyes narrowed. "Is this some kind of trick? Aha! You're going to prank me now right after you told me to forget about it. Well, good luck. I'm on to you."

Man, this was fun. "How long have we known each other? How long have I heard you complain about the old ovens, the heat, and the flour? How long have I been coming here to get donuts, but I've never been in the back?"

"Customers aren't allowed in the back," Charley said, crossing her arms and echoing Coral's mantra.

"I'm not *just* a customer." He rocked back on his heels. "I'm a friend of the family. Plus, you owe me. Thanks to you, I'm engaged."

"You never cared to see what happened back there before. You always send someone else for the fire safety inspection."

He simply stared and quirked a brow, knowing his silence had always worked for him.

"Oh, alright fine," Charley unhooked the partition door. "But don't tell Milly. She already thinks I'm going to break the bakery."

He followed her to the back and the large utility double ovens. There was a large walk-in type refrigerator. Jars of sugar, cinnamon, salt and other spices were shelved above the long wooden counter top. A huge sack of flour in a corner. Another one of sugar. Flour dusted everything.

"So." He nodded his approval. "This is it."

"Did you think you were going to find a unicorn back here? It's just a kitchen. A small hot kitchen." She wiped at her brow.

For reasons he could not explain, his gaze slid to her lips, plump and pink. Then, force of habit made him correct himself and instead he tucked a loose hair behind her ear. A few stragglers had fallen from the ponytail she always worked in. He was just helping. No other reason. She stared at him for a moment. Opened her mouth, then shut it. The air seemed electric between them, the tension and heat thick. Dylan hadn't planned on flirting when he made his way back here. This was *Charley*.

He'd simply wanted her jittery, wondering if the prank

return was coming, and he'd succeeded. It was time to go now. Mission accomplished. Instead, he kept staring like he'd never seen her before. Her eyes were a deep hazel with flecks of gold. Had he never been close enough to notice that before? He took in her dark blonde hair, wavy and unmanageable most of the time. It was the type of thick hair a man loved to fist during a wild kiss. Whoa. Where had that come from?

The phone rang, and the moment was lost.

She blinked. "Be right back."

This was his exit opportunity. He could leave right now and catch up with her later. They could both pretend nothing had happened here. No moment in which they'd both locked gazes in a way they never had before. He didn't want to ask himself why his boots stayed rooted to the floor. Didn't want to question why he was wondering what color of panties Charley wore and if she matched them to her shirt the way she matched her ever-present Chuck Taylors. She had them in black and white checkers, black, white, blue, neon pink, purple and green.

"I'm handling this," Charley was saying from the phone behind the front counter. "Would you relax, already? You're giving me a complex!"

A few more moments of talk and then the entrance door chimed. Another customer. Charley was back several minutes later. He was still here. *Why am I still here?* The simple answer: no freaking idea.

Charley eyed him suspiciously again. Her gaze went to his hands. "What did you do back here while I was gone? Did you switch the sugar for the salt? No fair! The pranks can't risk our careers. We agreed."

"Please. Sugar for salt? That's amateur shit."

"Good, because I was going to check anyway." She

tugged on the back tie of her oversized apron. "I know you're going to get back at me sooner or later."

"In due time. All in due time."

"Okay," she sighed. "Just don't be too mean. Make it a funny one."

Dylan stepped into her, one booted foot on either side of hers. His rough and callused hands slid down her unbelievably silky soft arms and settled on her hips. "Why? Because my getting engaged was so funny?"

"Um..." She had the decency to find her shoes completely fascinating for a moment. "Yes?"

"Hilarious." He tipped her chin to meet his eyes, testing his boundaries. His thumb brushed across her nose and removed the smudge there. "Flour."

"It gets everywhere." She stared past his fingers, to his lips, and he'd swear there was an invitation in her eyes.

They were no longer arguing. No longer disagreeing. In that moment, Dylan understood he'd just crossed a self-imposed line with Charley. He had no idea why or how this had happened, but there it was. She'd burrowed deeply under his skin. Since the moment she'd come back, he'd known something was off. Different. He stopped thinking about when or how or why, and it seemed like the single most natural thing in the world to pull her to him and dip his head to meet her lips. The heat between them almost suffocated him with its power. It seemed to float between them and surround him like the city's fog. But unlike the fog it wasn't showing any sign of dissipating.

If he'd intended to kiss her at all, face it, he should have made the kiss sweet and chaste. To his credit, and he would take all the credit he could get right now, that noble intention lasted about ten whole seconds. Then he lost his head when electricity pulsed through him. The kiss was a long, wet, deep kiss that demanded entry. She parted her lips and let him inside, clutching at his shirt with both fists. He kept kissing, angling her head so he could go deeper. Clearly losing his mind. No chaste and tender kiss this one, nothing sweet and tender. She reciprocated, and before long, it wasn't just the ovens that were hot back here.

He hadn't seen that coming.

An attraction had obviously bubbled beneath the surface for years. Right? Good. Made sense. It was logic. This was the reason for the smoldering heat of this first kiss. Great. He felt better already.

Dylan pulled back and bent to press his forehead to hers, his breaths coming a bit ragged. "Sorry about that."

Charley gripped his shirt, fisting it tight. "No. You don't get to be sorry. I won't let you."

"Let's not argue, Chuck. Not now. I think we better take five."

"I know what this is. You think you can control what just happened between us, too. But sometimes things just... happen."

He shook his head. "No. Nothing just happens. We all make choices."

"Like *you*, choosing to kiss *me*?"

He rolled his shoulders. "Yeah. Like that."

"Was it just me or was that kiss...really amazing?" She studied him with luminous eyes.

He stared at the pink sensual tip of her lips. The mouth he'd nearly devoured not long ago. And he was...a little out of his element here. "It was."

"You felt something."

"I am obviously attracted to you. I just didn't know this before...that kiss." He cleared his throat. "Here's the thing.

I'm going to suggest that we forget about what just happened here and move on."

"Wow," Charley said. "Just...wow."

"What?"

"You're that afraid of me, are you?"

"The hell I am."

"No, you're right. You're not afraid." She shook her head. "You're *terrified*."

"Excuse me?"

"Big bad Dylan Reyes. Firefighter and rescuer. Hero to all. Afraid of a girl."

"Stop." He narrowed his eyes. "I'm not a hero and I'm sure not afraid of you."

"I can see that." She smirked, then crossed her arms. "Because you want to forget all about this."

"That doesn't mean I'm afraid. I've just had...better conversations."

"No doubt. Maybe ones where you get to win the argument, for instance."

"We're not arguing." He was starting to get annoyed. "No one here is winning or losing."

"Uh-huh. Spoken like someone who's losing. And anyway, what's *wrong* with kissing me?"

For the life of him, he couldn't think of a thing. It was... so damn unexpected. Unplanned. For someone who planned for everything, it was unnerving. "Nothing."

Her gaze softened. "Nothing at all."

"Except for the fact that you're working, this kitchen is hot and stuffy, I'm getting hot and sweaty, and I'm due at the boarding house to do some repairs, I can think of nothing."

"Oh." Her hands skimmed down the front of his shirt, resting on his abs. "So, it's not me, then? You don't want to take five because it's me you kissed?"

"No," he said, not happy to see that old flash of insecurity in Charley's gaze. "And don't do that."

When she'd left the city on her first culinary adventure, he'd thought she was running toward her future, confident in herself. But maybe Charley wasn't running to something so much as she was running away. She kept coming back, but never to stay.

Why was it so hard for her to stay?

"Okay. I'm sorry."

"The hell you are. I won't let you," he said, repeating her words.

She smiled a little. "But if you don't want me, it's okay. I understand."

"I want you." His temper almost got the better of him, and he tugged her by the elbows. "Listen. That kiss was hot. You're fucking beautiful. A knockout."

"No, you don't have to say that. I'm not—"

"To me, you are."

Neither one of them spoke for one long moment.

Charley broke the silence with the question that had been wrapping itself around his brain for the past several minutes. "What are we going to do?"

He had no freaking clue. Talking himself out of this explosive attraction before he wound up hurting her was his only idea and he already hated it. "Like I said. Take five."

She sighed. "Okay, Dylan. We'll do it your way."

10

"Always be nice to the chef." ~ Apron

Dylan headed over to the boarding house his mother and grandmother ran to take care of a few last-minute jobs before the celebration on the Fourth. He'd looked for Joe to get his help this morning, but his youngest brother wasn't anywhere to be found.

He and his brothers had grown up in the three-story Victorian that had been in the family for generations and that initially housed only their extended family until his father died. After that, his mother and grandmother had been forced to take in boarders, and he and his brothers learned to live with strangers. Learned to understand that everything and *every*one other than family was transient. Temporary.

Mom greeted him at the door. "Well, well. If it isn't my eldest come to pay his mother a visit."

"Been busy, but I'm here now." He stepped inside and followed Mom into the kitchen.

"Oh, busy. I'm not *familiar* with the term. But I can only *imagine* how busy you must be when you didn't have time to tell me you're engaged!"

Dylan winced. He shouldn't have been surprised, considering how many boarders came and went through here every day. It gave new meaning to the old telephone game. He was surprised this time they'd gotten the rumor right.

"And just who am I engaged to?"

"A sixty-five-year old widow from Walnut Creek. Dylan, really? Are you out of your mind? You didn't think this was important enough to come right over and tell me?"

Nope. The old telephone game again.

"We need to meet this woman of yours, Mijo." Abuelita stood at the kitchen stove and stirred a pot of what had to be arroz con pollo, given the welcome smells of tomato sauce, hamhock and onions wafting through the kitchen.

He kissed her cheek. "There's no woman."

"No woman? How else you going to marry and give us more Reyes boys?" She waved her spoon.

Certainly not with a sixty-five-year old woman. He face-palmed again, something members of his family had him doing too often. "Meaning that I'm not engaged."

"Oh no, not another one of Charley's—" his mother said.

"Pranks," Dylan interrupted. "And yes."

"I'll never understand the two of you and your little games," Mom said. "Is nothing sacred anymore?"

No surprise, his mother also believed in the sunset kiss. True love and all that crap. "Don't worry, I'm getting her back."

"For the love of God, just take the high road and forget

about these silly pranks. It's like you're in third grade pulling on her pigtail."

"Nope, sorry. Can't forget it. Especially when she expects it. Fair is fair." He headed toward the patio to fix the screen and Mom followed him.

"Actually, the screen is fixed," she said, a glint in her eyes. "I had Tutti do it. Come and see what we've done to the patio since you were here last."

The flamboyant local Elvis impersonator, Tutti Blazes was the longest running boarder at two years and counting. That meant he'd stayed twice as long as the previous long-timer. It would be sad to see him go, but he'd been working to get to play Las Vegas where an act like his would shine.

Dylan followed his mother toward the patio he'd re-paved a year ago. Since the home sat at an angle near the end of a hill and was built in 1910, it had endured some seis-mological changes over the years. As with so many homes in their neighborhood, the yard was narrow but deep, with a garden and sitting area for their guests.

Dylan opened the patio door for his mother, and in the next second, he noticed Ashley Banning sitting at an umbrella table. They'd dated for a short time over a year ago, but Mom had been excited because Ashley told everyone who would listen that she was ready to get married and start a family.

Which was part of the problem for him. A second face palm would have followed, but Ashley sat smiling expectantly at him.

"What's going on?"

He shouldn't be surprised at this because his mother was a matchmaker through and through. And every summer she tried to match Dylan up before Sunset Kiss weekend. Coincidence? He thought not.

"I had a feeling you weren't engaged to a sixty-five-year old. And anyway, I just thought I'd throw out another option for you if you were. Ashley is around your age and everything." Mom reached up to tap his shoulder. "Now don't you dare be rude. That's not the Reyes way. She asked after you and wanted to know how you were doing. I invited her over so you two could re-connect. "

Ashley stared at them, the smile gone, a furrow creasing in her brow.

"It's about time you settled down. You're going to be thirty this year."

"Mom, for the love of—"

She held up her hand. "You and I will talk later. You're being rude. Go say hello to Ashley."

"Don't go far," Dylan said, gently touching her elbow. "*We* need to talk."

His mother turned and went back inside, waving him away. He strode toward Ashley. "Hey," he said as he sat across from her.

"Dylan, I'm sorry," Ashley said. "She invited me, and I just couldn't say no to your mother. I adore her."

"She's tried to fix me up every summer before Sunset Kiss. Sorry she got you involved."

"I had a feeling you weren't actually engaged. Another one of Charley's pranks." Ashley laughed. "Doesn't your mother realize you're not a believer?"

"She conveniently ignores that pesky fact. It gets in the way."

"I'm sure she just wants you to be happy."

"I'd be *happy* if she gave up on me. I'm never going to indulge in that ridiculous fantasy."

"We're both people of science so it makes sense that

neither one of us believes. It's a nice idea, you have to admit."

"Great for tourism. Guess it doesn't hurt people to believe that something special happens in their own little part of the city."

Residents of Miracle Bay lived in a small pocket of San Francisco, away from downtown crowds and city life. Even the fog wasn't as thick here. It made it easier to believe in legends and to feel set apart somehow.

Ashley cleared her throat. "What about Charley? I heard she's back in town for a while. Does *she* have a date for Sunset Kiss?"

"I don't think so."

"You would know." She said this with such an air of confidence that it annoyed him.

"I am her best friend."

"Sure. That's what you've always said."

Ashley almost managed to make him feel guilty. She'd been, at least he'd thought at the time, unreasonably jealous of Charley. He'd explained over and over again that she was his only close female friend, and yes, it was possible to have a platonic relationship with a woman. True at the time. Now he wondered if deep down he'd always had a thing for Charley that he didn't even want to admit to himself.

"Because it was true."

"Was?"

He cleared his throat. "I mean, it *is* true."

"Right." She squeezed his forearm. "If you say so, I believe you."

Dylan might be missing something here because in his opinion they'd had little chemistry and he had a feeling she sensed that, too. When they'd parted ways, there were no painful recriminations, no drama or high emotion and he'd assumed both understood it had never been serious between them.

"I took some time off from dating after us. Realized I had my priorities out of whack. I wanted marriage and family so badly and I know that scared you off."

"It didn't help."

"But I had a feeling you weren't all in from the start."

He didn't speak but simply nodded.

"I would like us to be friends," she said.

"We are friends."

"If nothing else, when Charley leaves again, and you need a friend to hang out with, someone to keep all the women you're *not* interested in away, I'll be around."

When she leaves. He'd pushed that little fact to the back of his mind. But it didn't matter. He'd known all along that she would. He was taking this one day at a time. It had just been one kiss, he reminded himself.

One explosive and electric kiss.

After saying goodbye to Ashley, Dylan tried to find his mother. He did this every time she tried to fix him up, remind her that he didn't want to settle down and have children. Other people could do that, like either of his brothers. He'd noticed she never pulled his on either one of them, but this was likely because he was the oldest and she liked to go in order.

"She's showing a room to a new girl," Abuelita said.

Dylan found her on the third floor with a wisp of a woman who barely looked eighteen.

"We have the kitchen and two common rooms downstairs. Now, we're like a big family here so if you should ever need anything, just ask. Anything at all. Do you have family nearby?"

"Excuse me," Dylan interrupted. "We need to talk. You got a minute?"

"Not now, honey," she said. "I'm showing a room, and if she's interested, we'll have to sign a lease and then—"

"A background check," Dylan gently reminded his overly kind mother.

"I'll take it," the woman said.

"Oh, that's wonderful. You'll fit right in. I'll get the lease agreement and we'll go over it together."

Two hours from now, his mother *might* be available for a talk but more than likely she'd be trying to fix up this tenant with one of her single male tenants. Sunset Kiss was only a couple of weeks away, after all. Much to be done for the happiest little matchmaker in Miracle Bay. His mother.

"Okay, Ma, we need to talk later."

But she was already telling her new tenant about Miracle Bay and the legend of the sunset kiss, while the tenant nodded and smiled politely.

11

"Kiss the cook (if your name is Dylan Reyes.)" ~ Charley Young

C harley took Milly to her doctor's appointment and waited roughly a millennium to be seen. But it was worth it when they got to the ultrasound. A 3D video displayed the distinctive body of a baby. Head, eyes, nose, mouth, arms, hands. Fingers. Legs, stomach, butt. All parts present and accounted for. A real live *baby*. So, Milly was doing this. This was *happening*. The realization sunk in. It was one thing to witness Milly's large and unwieldy body, but what was life at the bakery going to be like with a newborn baby?

If Charley didn't find the father, she'd be forced to stop traveling and stay with Milly. Goodbye, Paris for eighteen years.

She hadn't talked to Dylan since they'd kissed in the bakery by the ovens. "Taking five" had turned into two days and they texted back and forth as if nothing had happened. As if the earth hadn't shifted.

After he'd gone, she'd stood for several minutes simply staring at the closed shop door, shocked to silence, wondering if she'd dreamed it all. Despite time, distance, and other relationships, what they had together never seemed to change. She'd waltz back into the city and they'd take up where they left off. Friends forever. There were those who didn't believe that she and Dylan had been nothing but friends for years. They'd obviously had to have been lovers at one time, but decided they'd be better off as friends. She'd heard the rumors. Even started one once.

The rumors were all untrue. It *was* possible to have a chaste and totally platonic relationship with a man. Unfortunately.

But now he'd called her beautiful. A knockout. Their kiss was hot.

"Oh my God, look!" Milly cried out. "Is that her little arm?"

"Holy wow," Charley said, staring at the monitor. "Look at that."

"I *told* you," Milly said. "I'm having a baby."

The technician laughed and continued the swipe of her wand over Milly's swollen stomach. Charley hadn't known a belly could stretch so much, and it looked ridiculous on thin Milly. As if she'd swallowed a basketball. When it was time for the physical check with the doctor, Charley stepped out of the office and waited in the lobby.

Milly finally lumbered out a few minutes later, walking as she did these days, like she had a load in her pants. She made an appointment with the receptionist and waddled to the elevator.

"I don't like that doctor," Milly said as Charley drove them down Portrero Avenue in Coral's old sedan.

"Why not?"

"She said I have an 'incompetent cervix.'"

Charley wrinkled her nose. "What's an incompetent cervix?"

"It's that thing where it's my fault that the baby is going to come too soon if I don't stay off my feet as much as possible."

"*More* bedrest? How much?"

"Modified bedrest. I need to take it easy until I'm at least 36 weeks."

Milly in bed unable to work in the bakery for another entire month or more. No baby daddy to be found. New Orleans began to look like a dot in the distance.

"What are we doing to do now?"

"*We*? Don't worry, I'll figure something out."

Ouch. Sure, Milly wanted to act like she didn't need Charley but she knew better. She'd had every intention of coming home right after the little bean was born. This just meant that she'd extend her visit longer than planned. It wasn't as if she was giving up Paris. Just New Orleans. It wasn't going anywhere.

"I'll stay a while longer. You need me."

"Until the baby comes?"

And what about after that? Maybe Milly would come to her senses before much longer and confess.

"What about Chef Tati and New Orleans?" Milly asked.

A job in the French Quarter. She had the chance to cook authentic Cajun food under the tutelage of the famous Chef Tati of *La Bonne Nourriture*. Not Paris, but still a good opportunity.

"I'll just tell Sean that I can't take the job."

"You would do that for me?"

She'd do anything for Milly and it was surprising she didn't already know that. When Charley had wound up in a foster home with Milly and Coral, she'd already lived in approximately a home every year since age six. And she'd been ready to run away from Miracle Bay by day four. Coral was strict. She insisted on a regular nine o'clock bedtime even though Charley and Milly were both fifteen. She demanded homework be done every afternoon before anything else would take place. Smoking, drinking, or boys were not permitted for "her daughters." Out of the question. Charley figured it was only a matter of time before she got kicked out anyway. But Milly was a good sister, who secretly commiserated with Charley even if publicly she toed the line with Coral.

Charley chose her words carefully. "Maybe you should tell the father now. Everything's changed. You're having a tough time of it here, having *his* baby."

"I think you mean *my* baby. We don't need him." Milly rubbed her belly.

We don't need him. The words caused a slight ringing in Charley's ears and a little twitch formed in her eye. Maybe *Milly* didn't need him but someday her unborn baby just might. "Isn't that shortsighted? You might want some help. It's just going to be you and the baby."

"And our entire neighborhood. All of our friends."

"Okay, yeah, but who's going to take turns walking her in the middle of the night when she's got colic? Do you think the Padre or Mrs. Luna are up to two in the morning feedings?"

"You don't think I know what I'm getting into? I've read

all the books." As they rolled to a stoplight, Milly slid Charley a significant look. "I can handle it."

Stubborn woman. It was as if obstinate was in the air, drifting through like fog. The real miracle would be if her sister stopped behaving like a brick wall. Charley dropped off Milly in front of the bakery, and she lifted her body out of the car as if she was a crane.

"Go lie down and I'll be up after I park."

She watched Milly waddle into the bakery, carefully maneuvered to the one-car garage situated right next to the bakery, then pulled out her cellphone to call Sean Hannigan.

"Hey, baby," he said smoothly. "How you doin', girl?"

It never failed to surprise her how she'd at first missed the blatant fact that Sean was a player. Call it lack of experience. "Hey Sean, I'm sorry, but I can't take the job with Chef Tati but thanks for the opportunity."

"Whoa. Now, that's kind of sudden. You sure?"

"It's *not* sudden. You knew my sister was in trouble. Now she's on bed rest for the rest of the pregnancy and she needs me here to run the bakery."

"Sorry to hear that."

"But I'm grateful you thought of me, and—"

"Look, baby, working with Chef Tati is a once-in-a-life-time opportunity. I've already put myself on the line for you. It's not a good time to make any quick decisions."

She heard the implication loud and clear. Maybe she owed Sean for this chance, but it didn't mean she had to follow through when circumstances had changed. Yet she hated the idea of being thought of as unreliable in her career, because being a chef was the only place where she excelled. The one place where she shined, and where her colleagues thought highly of her abilities. Her career, no matter where she traveled to, was the one place where no one knew that Charley had once been a foster kid. No one knew that she'd been kicked out of homes for being mouthy. For running away. No one knew that for a long time, no one had wanted her. Just the thought that Sean would be talking about her behind her back sent a cold shiver to wrap around her spine. She wanted and needed to be respected as a sous chef. Sean was a work contact she couldn't afford to alienate.

Turn your life around, Charley, or you'll wind up just like her.

That girl is going to wind up just like her mother, wait and see. Might not even be her fault. I hear addiction can be genetic.

More than one case worker or teacher had declared their lack of faith, either to her, or behind her back. She'd done her best not to live up to their expectations. She didn't touch alcohol just in case they were right about that hereditary stuff. Never smoked. She refused to be anything like Maggie.

"I wish it could be different. It goes without saying that I appreciate everything you've done for me."

Sean had been a sous chef longer than Charley and he had an entire network of connections. He also had an uncanny ability to bring out the worst in Charley. All the fears, suspicions, and worries she'd ever had that she'd never be good enough rose to the surface.

"Maybe next time then," Sean finally said after a long pause in which she swore she could hear him breathing. "I know of something coming up in September and I thought of you immediately. Paris."

Charley's breaths came in short pants. Surely by then Milly and Bean would be settled and maybe even with the father. "Paris? As in...*the* Paris? Not Paris, *Texas*."

"No," he chuckled. "Paris, France, baby. We could see the

city together like we always planned. You interested?"

The chance to work at the side of a master Parisian chef would be a dream come true. To walk the same streets that Julia had. Eat in the same bistros. Breathe the same air. No way could she ever turn Paris down.

"Of course, I'm interested. Thank you! Milly will have her baby by then, and I'm sure this will all be resolved."

Charley hung up, crossing her fingers she'd hear from Sean even when she'd flaked on New Orleans. But she had something far more important to do at home first.

When she had first come to Mission High School, she'd been teased relentlessly by the mean girls who made fun of her clothes and shoes. Milly had wanted to go to the principal about it, or at least tell Coral. But Charley hadn't wanted the extra attention. She'd begged Milly not to tell anyone. Mostly Charley had been worried that, as with previous experiences, telling those in authority only made a bad situation worse. As in the time a well-meaning adult had reported to Child Protective Services that six-year-old Charley had wandered the neighborhood asking for food.

People meant well, sure, but they weren't there to pick up the pieces. But not only had Milly gone behind Charley's back and told the principal, she'd also told Dylan. And Charley had been wrong that time. The bullying stopped almost overnight even if she'd never had many girlfriends after that.

Milly *thought* she didn't want the baby's father to know about Bean and take responsibility, but she was probably just scared and too proud. Worried the man would feel trapped and not want anything to do with her except out of obligation. It was easier not to tell him than to risk that kind of rejection. Charley understood. She'd spent a little time searching for her mother, but eventually Charley stopped looking for Maggie Young. She was terrified of being rejected all over again.

And that fear of rejection was the very reason she had to do this for Milly. Find the father and let him know. This way if he rejected anyone, he'd reject Charley, and not Milly.

Milly would never even have to know.

12

"Pregnancy is the happiest reason ever for feeling like crap." ~ Meme

Working on boats docked at the marina was usually one of Dylan's few happy places. He enjoyed the work on his rotation days off. Kept him busy and near the swell of the ocean waves. Usually the jobs weren't pressing or on a strict timeline and the owners loved his craftsmanship. The extra money didn't hurt, either. He'd been putting it aside for years along with the money he made from the occasional house flip.

But today rather than peaceful at being near the sea, he'd slipped into the dangerous vortex of "dinner texting" with Charley. He should have known better. Not like this was the first time or anything.

Dylan:
Dinner tonight?
Chuck:

Okay. Where?

Dylan:

Wherever you want. Italian?

Chuck:

No. You know I'm picky.

Dylan:

You decide then.

Seriously. Sometimes this relationship of theirs was a bit like being married but without all the perks. Five or six messages later, with him suggesting and her knocking down, Charley texted him:

I'm actually not that hungry.

At that point he wanted to throw his phone into the cold waters of the bay. Hell. It shouldn't be this hard for two people to decide on dinner. He considered what she meant by "I'm not hungry." Was that code for "you jerk" or could she possibly mean she wasn't *hungry*? Was she mad he hadn't talked to her about the kiss? He finally texted:

What about Juan's?

Chuck:

Fine.

Dylan wasn't sure if that was a good fine or you're an asshole "fine." Yes, he'd been avoiding her. The reason? He realized he was in trouble here and didn't know what to do about it. She'd be leaving again before long, and he didn't see the point in starting anything up. What was he going to do? Have sex with her like he'd been fantasizing, or take the high road? And how painful would this high road be? Would she get that he was trying to prevent a likely disastrous break-up, or would she take it as a rejection and hate him? He was in a no-win scenario and he avoided those like candle-lit dinners.

At least a decision had been made about dinner. He

shoved a hand through his hair, uncomfortable. This was odd. It wasn't natural to second guess himself with her. He did *not* want that to change. But he'd done a lot of thinking about what he'd started. It would have been far better to find out that kissing her was like kissing his sister. Or a wall. Or a plasma TV set after the Giants won the pennant. But no, it had to be the most erotic experience of his life. In the back of a hot bakery.

And then he'd remembered something he'd nearly forgotten.

A year ago, he'd fallen asleep watching a movie with Charley at home and had a strange dream. In that dream, she had covered him with a blanket, kissed him, rubbed his jawline, and whispered that she loved him. Later that night, when he'd woken to his dark and quiet house, Charley had already gone, leaving him a note:

I watched several minutes of *Scarface* before I realized you were asleep. Now you have to watch *Letters from Juliet* with me, and I don't want any crap from you. ~ C

Had she still been there he might have told her about the dream. Whatever. But probably not, because one of the more compelling aspects of the dream was how enticing the fantasy had been. How soft her lips had felt against his, how she'd revved him up without even trying. A dream so real it took weeks to get it out of his head.

Dylan heard footsteps on the pier coming in his direction and looked up to see Ron Hiroshimo walking toward the yacht Dylan had just finished. He met him halfway down the pier.

Originally from Seattle, Ron was one of the original investors in a little company called Microsoft. Twenty years ago, he'd retired at forty and bought himself a small fleet of yachts.

"Hey," Ron said. "Done with that job?"

"Yeah," Dylan said. "Got something else for me?"

"I have a proposition for you," Ron said. "One of those deals that falls into my lap from time to time. A timely investment."

Dylan followed him down several boat slips to a sailboat named *Miracle One.* How about that. Someone apparently numbered their miracles. Dylan would be happy to stop at one. But if he were in the bargain for miracle wielding, he'd want Joe to settle his ass down. What his younger brother needed was to be in a service-oriented career. Something to give him purpose and direction. Dylan still didn't know what was going on with Joe, who'd been hanging around the house for days now. It wasn't like him. When he was at home, he seemed to be spending a great deal of time on his laptop, his brow creased in concentration. Whenever Dylan asked, Joe claimed he was charting the swell of the waves.

He was lying.

"My latest fixer-upper." Ron grinned. "And I see nothing but possibilities."

"Looking for a buyer?"

"Not exactly. Help me clean and polish her up, and I'll split the profits with you on Sunset Kiss."

There were usually dozens of sailboats doting the bay for three days. So much so that interested parties had to book a sailboat months in advance.

"You know I don't like to indulge in that stupid legend."

"What's the harm? We could make a killing. All the boats are already booked with a wait list. We'll get twice the going rate and split it."

True, he wasn't one to walk away from an opportunity. Even though mom and abuelita were able to support themselves by renting out rooms, he more than most people understood they were one more major medical catastrophe away from bankruptcy.

Sunset had broken over the bay, a splash of orange and muted yellow. The salty air stung his nose and the sounds of the seagulls squawking echoed. He hunched his shoulders against a cool Pacific Ocean breeze and shoved hands in the pockets of his jacket.

"Just some sweat equity?"

"Exactly."

It might take him a few of his free days to clean her up, but the return on investment was nothing but his time. Ron was being more than generous.

"Deal."

"RACK 'EM UP," Smitty called out. "I'm going to kick your ass, Dylan."

"Yeah, yeah."

As usual the guys had congregated at the pool table near the back of Juan's. Joe had joined them, and even if Dylan had his suspicions Joe wasn't being perfectly honest with him about his reason for being back home, it was good to have his younger brother around for a change.

Charley waltzed in a few minutes after he'd arrived, dressed in her usual jeans and a long-sleeved black tee that read, "My kitchen. My rules." in neon pink. She wore her pink Chuck Taylors tonight. Her long hair was pulled into a ponytail and as usual she looked like she put zero effort into her appearance. He appreciated being able to count on her being practical and that had made it easier not to fantasize about her. But tonight, she looked...radiant was the only word that came to mind. Was that shirt tighter than normal?

Did she always wear jeans that hugged her butt, or was he only now noticing this?

Marco picked her up and swung her in the air like she was a rag doll. "Hey, look who it is!"

"Put me down!" she squeaked and pounded his chest.

He set her down, but because he apparently had a death wish he only handed her over to Joe. But once Joe set Charley down, he was summarily distracted away by a blonde crooking her finger at him.

"BRB."

"Look at that," Marco said. "One pretty blonde and suddenly he's an only child. Whatever happened to the brotherhood?"

"We're about to rack 'em up again in a minute because Dylan is going to miss a shot at some point," Smitty said, holding his cue stick.

"The hell I am." Dylan leaned over the table, easing his hip against the edge.

"Dylan never misses," Charley said.

He met her eyes. "Black ball, corner pocket."

Made the shot handily if he did say so himself.

"Damn! She's always been his lucky charm," Smitty said. "Did you have to show up right now?"

Charley whistled. "Don't be a sore loser."

"Next round it's me and Marco against Dylan and Charley," Smitty said.

"Are you new here?" Marco slapped Smitty's shoulder. "What the hell is wrong with you? Put those two together and nobody wins against them. No, no. It's me and Charley against you and Dylan."

"I'll take it!" Smitty racked them up.

"I want in on some of that action," Johnny said, tipping his beer bottle.

They proceeded to play, with Dylan and Smitty ahead at first until Charley, with little help from Marco, easily caught up with them. Dylan kicked back when his chicken wings arrived. The waitress, who obviously hadn't heard of his fake engagement, brushed her breasts against his arm. She was pretty and smelled good but didn't do a thing for him. While Smitty was taking his shot, Dylan pulled out his wallet, paid, and then nodded to Charley. Pointed at the wings.

Have some, he mouthed.

No thanks, I'm about to beat your ass, she answered.

He rolled his eyes and took a bite out of a wing. She looked pissed, as if she had any right to be. He was the one supposedly engaged thanks to her.

"How long you going to be around?" Marco asked, lining up his shot.

"Until Milly has her baby or until I find the baby's father." She hit the ball with her usual finesse and easily made the shot. "Whichever comes first. She has to be on bedrest for the rest of the pregnancy."

Dylan thought Charley would be headed off to New Orleans. "What's wrong? Is she dilated?"

She glanced at Dylan. "Yeah. How bad is that?"

"It can mean a premature baby, so she should follow doctor's orders."

Personally, Dylan understood why Charley would never be able to leave Milly with a newborn baby. Which is the reason why, he assumed, she'd become a little irrational in her attempts to find the father. She was like a hamster in a cage, dying to get out, ready to move on to her next adventure. Someday she'd get to Paris like she'd dreamed, and Paris was a long way from San Francisco.

On Charley's turn at the table, she lined up and quietly

made the shot. Dylan made his too. Before long, they were tied.

Donna walked in the room and rubbed against Marco, causing him to lose his shot. "Damn it, babe."

"Outta my way." Charley hip checked Johnny, made her shot and then the next, recovering Marco's loss.

This made him smile. She didn't like to lose. Ever. But a few more shots back and forth later and oh, look at that. Dylan and Smitty handily won the game.

"Hey, baby doll." A man who looked three sheets to the wind sidled up to Charley. "Can I buy you a drink?"

A white-hot streak of anger shot through Dylan, which he couldn't explain if he were given a million years to do so. Charley could take care of herself. She'd told him so, countless of times. Still, he moved to her side.

"Go home, sober up, and I'll reconsider," Charley said.

"You don't want this badger cat, man," Smitty put his arm around Charley's shoulders. "She's too hot to handle."

The guy backed up slowly, palms out. "Can't blame me for trying."

Dylan smiled, unreasonably happy the man gave up. Because if she found someone else, someone worthy, of course, that would certainly make this whole ordeal easier for him. But damn if he didn't want that, either. Which meant he didn't *want* easy. Someone order him a brain scan because that didn't sound like him at all.

The others had left to congregate at the bar and he was following when Charley's phone rang. She pulled it out of her back pocket and casually glanced at it. Her eyes widened, and she chewed her lower lip.

"Bad news?" he asked.

She held up her phone, a panicked gaze in her eyes, and showed Dylan the text message from Milly:

What did you do????? Peter Adair called me today. We need to talk! Now!

He did not say, "I told you so" but it took nearly biting his tongue in half. Dylan pulled on his jacket. "C'mon. I'll walk over with you."

Dylan called out a goodbye, then steered a jumpy Charley out of Juan's, his hand on the small of her back. Had he ever had his hand on the small of her back? Given by the surge of desire that pulsed through him, he'd have to say no. He hadn't. Because he would have remembered this. The kind of heat he usually felt when he'd done a whole lot more with a woman than simply have his hand on her back. At the door he held it open for her, and when he closed it behind him, all of the loud sounds from inside were hollowed out. The sounds of the big screen TV set to the baseball game, the sound of the balls racked up in the pool room, were all muffled and distant.

Outside, a perfect July night surrounded them. The fog had descended, giving everything from the streetlights to the older Victorian homes lining the street a filmy glow. And all he could think about was another bone-melting kiss. This was fairly self-centered of him, he understood, because Charley was about to be skewered over fiery hot coals by Milly. His only job was to be her support system.

They reached the bakery, the doorbell outside still covered with taped piece of faded paper in Coral's precise cursive handwriting: *Bell for upstairs residence only. Please do not ring during business hours.*

"Want me to run interference for you?" He'd done so for the sisters in the past, though it had never gone over well with Milly.

"No," she said on a sigh. "This is on me. I'll explain. I'm pretty sure she'll understand."

He highly doubted that. Charley's optimism was inspiring if a little misguided. Peter Adair had wound up in the hospital. That wasn't easy for anyone to forget, no matter how great and forgiving the dude.

"I'll come with you."

"No, Dylan. It's okay. She'll just get madder if you're with me."

"I'm coming anyway." His tone left no room for disagreement. No way was he letting Charley upstairs without some moral support.

She pushed on his chest. "Fine! But you wait next door. This is between Milly and me."

"Whatever you say."

13

"Count the memories, not the calories." ~ meme

C harley stood just outside Milly's apartment door, alternating between pants and deep breaths. Somewhere she'd read that deep breathing helped with anxiety. But it didn't help Charley much now as she pictured having to explain what she'd done. Explain how she'd lied. Why. All the DNA stuff. Would she really have to go there, too? Oh, God. She'd need to explain how she'd sent poor Peter to the ER with a massive anxiety attack.

Charley was about to have one now as she clutched her chest.

Big deal, though, you know? How bad could it be? Milly was her *sister*. If not by blood, then in every other way. They were compadres. Buddies. Yeah, Milly would forgive Charley. But it might take her a few minutes. She opened the door to find Milly covered by a blanket, an episode of

Dateline playing on the TV screen. Rufus lay on a chair nearby, looking bored. He lifted his head as if to ask: *you again?*

"If you're going to watch that show, at least listen to their warning. You're not supposed to watch alone." Charley picked up the remote control and flicked the TV set off.

"Stop trying to control my life!" Milly shrieked. Rufus jumped off the chair at a near run, and Charley jumped back, too. "What do you think you're doing?"

Charley knew very well what she meant, but she stalled. "That s-show. It always scares you."

She stood up, hands on hips. "What about poor Peter? Do you *care* that you nearly gave him a heart attack? I heard he was taken to the hospital!"

"In my defense, because of what happened, he's now back together with the love of his life. He thanked me. So, yeah, that happened."

"He *would* thank you. Peter Adair is a prince!"

And probably the reason for all those hearts next to his name. Charley couldn't argue there. The guy really was wonderful. "Again, in my defense—"

"You have no defense, Charlotte Rae Young! You're a menace. You can't keep out of things that don't concern you. I asked you to stay out of it, and you didn't."

"But...but you're my sister and what happens to you does concern me."

"I've kept *your* secrets. I covered for you with Mama so many times I lost count. You got to have a life, and I didn't. Did I ever tell Dylan about your stolen kiss? Did I? Why can't you ever be happy or satisfied with what you have?"

Charley resisted the urge to shush her. These walls were thin. "Now wait a minute. I—"

"When are you going to get it through your thick skull that this, for once, is really *none* of your business?"

"You mean like it wasn't your business when I was being bullied and didn't want you to report it?"

"Ancient history. And I did that for your own good." Milly crossed her arms over her big belly.

"And I'm doing this for your own good. Look, I can see you're in a bad mood. Pregnancy hormones and all. I'm sure it's way worse than PMS. We can talk about this later."

Charley had her hand on the doorknob when a pillow hit the back of her head. She turned, annoyed as hell. "What was that for?"

"To get your attention."

"Sugar Honey Iced Tea," Charley spit out, picked up the pillow, and brought it back to her. "I'm just trying to give you some space."

"Face it, you didn't want to come home. You don't want to stay. And right now, I'd just as soon you leave."

"That's not fair. I'm here for you, but Bean needs a father. And what are you going to put on the birth certificate? Unknown?"

A mother who claimed not to know who her baby's father was…that wasn't Milly. It was Maggie. Maggie also said they'd never need anyone else, but one day Charley did. And she didn't have anyone. For years. Not until Coral and Milly showed up in her life. Charley knew better than most what it was like to grow up without a family. Not to have any real roots or sense of permanence. No security. No soft place to fall.

Milly blew out a breath, and for the first time Charley saw uncertainty in her eyes. "I haven't figured that out yet."

"You do know *who* it is?"

"Of course I do!"

"You don't have much time left." She took a strangled breath that passed through her lungs like a stone. "You *can't* do this on your own."

"I can, I will, and I don't need you, either."

Charley pushed back her own tears, swallowing until she could get past the ball of raw pain in her throat. "You don't mean it."

"Stop trying to fix me and fix yourself. You're always chasing after something you think is going to change your life in some way. Make you special. Paris. New Orleans. New York City. You already have everything you could have ever dreamed of right here, but you just can't see it."

"You don't know what it's like to be moved from one home to another, nobody wanting me, for years."

"*We* wanted you! But that wasn't good enough."

"Of course it was...I—"

How had Milly managed to turn this entire conversation around to Charley's issues, of which, admittedly, there were many? But none of them had anything to do with this conversation.

"You did it again! Turned it back to me. Oh, you're talented."

"Well, Coral was my mother so I guess I learned from the expert. She always wanted to be your mother, too. Did you ever think about her and what it did to her to know she wasn't enough for you? You always thought Maggie would be back for you and she loved you too much to take that away from you. She loved you like you were her own daughter."

Charley couldn't breathe. Her throat was closed up so tight it had become difficult to talk.

Milly was having no such issue with all of the talking. "You *don't* want to stay. Mama and I...we were never enough for you. Go ahead and take your job in New Orleans. I don't want you here!"

"But you need my help. You're on bed rest." Charley fought back tears. Milly had never been this irate before.

"I'll get Naomi to help more."

Naomi was just a girl, and she wasn't Milly's sister so she didn't care as much as Charley did. She saw Milly in a frosty haze through wet lashes. "If that's what you want. I'll leave."

"It's what you do." Milly rose from the couch, walked to her bedroom and slammed the door shut.

Charley let herself out the front door and banged it shut. That last statement was so unfair. Charley didn't always leave. Even if she did, the point was that she always came back. That counted for something. When she stepped inside her apartment, she caught Dylan standing by the opened refrigerator door apparently searching for something to eat.

He took one look at Charley, and his brow creased in concern. "What?"

Without a word, she launched herself at him. He had stepped forward, so that the impact of their two bodies colliding was jarring to her senses. He caught her tightly to him, his hands at her waist. She pushed her face into his chest, the cotton of his shirt smelling fresh and warm. The tears came easily then.

"Tell me," he said as strong arms wrapped around her, holding her close.

"S-sorry. You were right," she managed through ragged breaths. "I s-should have minded my own business."

"She's mad."

"Mad?" She pushed back and tilted her head to meet his eyes. "I've never seen her like this. S-she told me to leave!"

"She doesn't mean it."

"You warned me. I never listen, do I?" Oh boy, the tears were coming harder and faster. The dreaded ugly cry.

"Stop—"

"No. You were right." Her eyelashes were wet. No holding back.

"You know I didn't want to be right about this. I hoped Milly would cut you some slack. She knows you love her. She knows that you mean well."

She also knows that I didn't have a father. I barely had a mother until Coral. But this wasn't Charley's baby to love and do right by. That was up to Milly. Charley should have realized she didn't have control over this anymore than she'd had control over Maggie's life choices.

She reluctantly pulled out of Dylan's arms and laid on the couch, drawing her legs up to her chest and assuming the fetal position. "Go home. I'm going to lie here and regret all my life decisions until I finally fall asleep."

"No way." Dylan crouched beside her, balancing on the balls of his feet. "I'm not leaving you like this."

"I'm not good company."

"Don't care. You didn't eat."

"So? Who needs to eat?"

Okay, she was scaring herself now.

Everyone needed to eat and eat a lot. Rich and delicious food. Butter. Cream. Red meat. Screw the calories. She'd skipped the buffalo wings at Juan's because...please. She *had* planned to cook for Milly tonight but now she just wanted to shrink up and die. Milly wanted her to go. Charley didn't know what to do next. Maybe she could take the job with Chef Tati in New Orleans if it wasn't too late now. As usual, nobody wanted her. Not even Milly.

When she heard rustling in the kitchen, she sat up to find Dylan next to a pan on the stove. Oh no. He was going to *cook* for her. It would be an unmitigated disaster and she would have to eat it because...the "best friend card." And her face was so expressive she could never conceal when she hated a dish. It hadn't made her many friends in the culinary world, except for excellent cooks who didn't have a thing to worry about in the first place.

She heard the sizzle of butter. She'd recognize that sound anywhere. It was like hugging an old friend. "Dylan? What are you doing?"

"Making you an omelet. You're going to eat." He said this as if there was no debating the subject.

She prayed for him because there was nothing worse than eggs that were either undercooked or heaven forbid overcooked. But she told herself that if she resented Milly micromanaging in the bakery, surely she could stop herself from doing the same with Dylan.

"Any advice for me? I'm going in." His sleeves were rolled up to his elbows, displaying those muscular forearms.

"Um, no."

He chuckled. "This must be tough for you."

Oh, he had no idea. No one cooked for her. No one! The only thing she'd let someone *else* make her for dinner was reservations. But this was so sweet of Dylan and she watched him silently as he chopped basil and grape tomatoes, the muscles of his back and forearms bunching. A few minutes later he brought the dish to her on one of her blue and orange ceramic plates. He'd garnished it with a sprig of basil. He'd even plated the meal.

He slid an easy smile and her heart flopped around in her chest, not knowing what hit it.

"You've been watching me," she said in awe. "All these years. Can you really cook, Dylan Reyes?"

"To quote one of my favorite movies, 'Anyone can cook' but I guess you're about to find out." He sat next to her.

"*Ratatouille* is not one of your favorite movies. It's one of mine."

"I've watched it with you enough times. Believe me, I can cook. I take my turn in the station's kitchen." He lifted a shoulder. "No one's died yet."

"High praise." Charley prepared to take a bite, breaking off a small piece with the fork. She brought it to her lips, inspecting it. Hazard of the trade.

"You're scared." He studied her, his grin widening.

"No, no. I'm just...I'm...eating this."

In her mouth, the bite dissolved into a combination of fluffy eggs cooked to perfection, melted goat cheese and the always noteworthy combo of her favorite standbys, tomato and basil. Her taste buds leapt for joy.

"This is...this is good." She took another bite. Then another.

"You're *that* surprised. Afraid of the competition?"

"Please." She rolled her eyes, then nearly licked her plate clean.

"Uh-huh."

"You're a good cook. A promising one. I'd teach you. Take you under my wing. It could happen."

"Yeah?" He folded his hands behind his neck and leaned back. "That would mean you'd have to stick around. And teach me."

She hitched a breath, afraid to breathe. Her next question was so significant she was almost too afraid to ask it. But she wanted an answer. Especially after that smoldering kiss in the bakery.

"Do you want me to stay?"

14

"I love you more than cupcakes." ~ *meme*

n interminable second later, Dylan answered. His soft gaze met hers, then he reached to squeeze her hand. "Stay."

Oh. My. God. He'd honestly never asked her to stay. Well, he hadn't asked this time, either, she reminded herself. But he'd confirmed it to be what he wanted, and she'd run with it.

"About that kiss..."

"This isn't about the kiss. It's about you and Milly. You can't leave her like this. You'll regret it and so will she."

Her stomach churned with regret. "Oh. That's it? You haven't thought about us...you and me...together?"

"I didn't say that."

"Because I've thought about us."

"I know," he said.

"Wow, okay then. Just because you're handsome, you know, that doesn't mean—"

"It was in the way you kissed me."

"You kissed *me*."

"Well, you kissed back."

"Look, I don't want to argue about who's right. You can be right this time." She moved the plate aside. "And because you asked, I'll stay."

"That's all it takes? Asking? Because *that* would be a first."

"There's a first time for everything."

Taking her chances, she moved to climb on his lap and straddle him, threading fingers through his thick dark hair. His eyes immediately heated as his hands skimmed down her spine. Shy and fixated on his sensual mouth, already tipping up in a half smirk, she sent him a wordless invitation.

He certainly got the message and took her mouth in a soul-ripping kiss, consuming her just like she'd devoured his eggs. Pulling her closer. Tighter. She met his hot tongue as it explored. Plunged. He tasted like seduction. Like the sweetest of sins. When his hands lowered and settled on her hips, she kicked things up a notch and gyrated hips over him. He let out a low hiss. The pattern of his breathing changed and matched her short and panting breaths. They were moving fast but she didn't give it a second thought and hoped that he wouldn't.

He stopped kissing her and hand on the nape of her neck, pulled back to meet her gaze. "This could be danger-ous. You and me. Here. Alone together."

The words sent a shiver of sweet and intense pleasure up her legs, and warmth grew heavy between her thighs. Danger and Dylan were two words that never went together for her. But there was another side of him she'd never seen, and she liked edgy Dylan.

"Dangerous?" She kissed the rough light stubble of his jaw. "How? Are we talking I'm going to need a safe word kind of danger?"

He sent her a wicked smile and his teeth dragged over his lower lip. "There are a whole lot of steps between making out and needing a safe word."

A tingle curled up her spine. "I know that."

"But maybe you should pick a safe word anyway."

"Okay," she said, enjoying this game. "My safe word is 'pineapple.' How's that?"

"*Pineapple*?" His eyes narrowed.

"I've decided that it's my favorite fruit. It's just so...regal."

"Stop thinking in terms of food, chef." He squeezed her behind. "Try again."

When he touched her like that, she would do anything he asked. "Then I think I'll choose 'please' as my safe word."

"See, that could be taken both ways."

"As in 'please stop' and 'please don't stop?'"

A muscle in his jaw twitched. "Exactly."

"Well, I like my safe word and I think I'll keep it. But you need one, too. I can be kind of dangerous. What makes *you* think you don't need one?"

"The fact that you picked pineapple as your safe word."

His fingers trailed from her thighs to the back of her knees and caused an electrical current in her belly.

"Stop teasing me," she said, gazing first at his trailing fingers, then meeting his eyes.

The teasing was familiar, but the heat in his eyes...not so much.

"Never." His deep voice was almost a whisper as his gaze slid to her lips.

The muscles in his shoulders tensed and bunched. She sensed a momentary hesitation as his hands settled on her ass, tightening. He kissed her with a heartfelt, wet and deep kiss that had her head spinning. She could hear her heart-beat loud enough to wake the comatose and swore she smelled fresh crisp apples. Tasted the mint of his toothpaste, but that might be because she was doing her utmost to inhale him. He was so male, so strong, so hard and firm beneath her touch. Not like any other man she'd ever kissed before. Just...more.

More of everything.

Her hands slid up and down his strong back, coming to rest on the waistband of his jeans. He made a very male, deep sound in his throat. The growling was good. Then he fisted her hair and broke the kiss. She was about to protest, when he reached with one hand to swiftly remove his gray hoodie. Underneath he had on a dark blue long-sleeved tee stretched tight across his wide shoulders. It read: *Just Do it Already and Stop Whining*.

She smiled. *Yes, please. Let's just do it.*

"You're trembling," he said.

His deep voice, husky and gravelly near her earlobe, scraped at her tender pink parts and had her nearly coming with the sound. She shook at the sensation of his warm breath against her skin. His hands slid down her arms to cuff her wrists. She was actually shaking. How embarrassing. He'd barely touched her, but the anticipation was killing her slowly.

"Tell me." He tipped her chin to meet his eyes. "You scared?"

"No. Not with you."

He cocked his head and his smile tipped up on one side in that boyish smirk she adored.

"Alright, I'm a *little* bit scared."

"We're not doing anything you don't want to do. You're safe here with me, you know that, right?"

"I know. I've always known."

One emotion she'd never felt around Dylan was fear. He'd been her protector for so long that she'd taken at least that part for granted. When she'd gone out into the big bad world as an adult, she'd received a real education. Most men *wanted* something from her. Sex. Money. She'd only known one man who for as long as she'd known him had never asked anything of her.

Including asking her to stay. "It's just that you and I...we never."

"I know."

"So why does it feel so natural?"

"Because it's going to be good."

She had no doubt *he'd* be good, but she didn't know that she would be. And she hated to let him down. This was *Dylan*. Everything mattered in an epic way. She couldn't bear to disappoint him.

"H-how do you know?"

His brow furrowed in confusion. "It's you and me. *Us*. And believe me, this kind of chemistry doesn't come around every day."

"I know."

"You're so beautiful, Charley. So damn beautiful. Believe that." He kissed her long, deep and hard.

No wonder she'd loved him for half her life. It wasn't just the dark and brooding Reyes looks. It was the way he looked at her, as if *she* was the most precious thing in this world. As if she was the prize. It was in the way he'd always had her back. In the way he'd die before he ever let *anyone* hurt her.

She stood, wordlessly led him to her bedroom and tentatively shut the door. He kissed her again, and this time the kiss went on and on and got a little bit wild as they clutched at each other. She fisted his tee like he was her anchor. He had his hands up her shirt and then under her bra cup, tweaking her nipple. The move sent a shiver that wrapped around the back of her knees. A few seconds later she no longer had a shirt on and neither did he. Their clothes were discarded piecemeal as they moved, grasping for each other and careening towards the bed, occasionally bumping into walls. The dresser. A lamp which fell to the floor with a thump.

Dylan laughed and settled the lamp on her nightstand. Then he turned to her. She wore nothing but her bra, panties, and what she was certain had to be a quivering smile.

He'd seen her in a two-piece bathing suit plenty of times, but from the look on his face now, he'd never really *seen* her. Not like this. And it wasn't as if her bathing suits had ever been the slightest bit revealing. She'd have never been allowed to wear anything skimpy when Coral Monroe had anything to do with it. Smutty underwear was also forbidden. To hear Coral tell it, all teenage boys had X-ray vision. But from the day Charley moved out of Coral's home, she'd taken to stocking up on racy panties whenever there was a sale.

She had quite a collection.

"Nice." He whistled.

Wearing nothing but his close-fitting boxer briefs, he took a step toward her but then stopped as if he wanted to get the full view.

"Like it?" This matching bra and panty set was hot pink with a velvet red heart right over her happy place.

"I like it so much it's coming off in two seconds." He

closed the distance between them and true to his word had her bra unhooked in seconds.

Her breasts fell into his hands like they'd been waiting for him. He kissed each one tenderly, then backed her up to the bed. She fell in a heap of heat, lust and hormones. This was happening. Her wildest fantasy come to life.

But first. "I need to tell you something."

"I'm listening." But he'd also sunk his teeth on her earlobe while tweaking her nipple. Man of many talents. Multi-tasking like a boss.

"Um, I—"

Why was she so nervous about telling him this? This was *her* Dylan. She could tell him almost anything, even something she'd never shared with another human being before. Certainly not a man. It was private. Sensitive. But if anyone would understand this about her, wouldn't judge, it would be Dylan. And she *had* to tell him because he of all people would see right through her otherwise. He knew her too well.

"It's just that I don't—"

"Don't worry, I have a condom."

He slid off her panties and suddenly she was bare and completely exposed to him with nothing but a breath between them.

He cursed under his breath. "Soft and so beautiful."

She jerked on his arm. "Dylan!"

He finally heard the urgency in her voice, braced himself above her and met her eyes. "What is it?"

"You don't know this about me, because why should you? But I think it must take me a long time to, um, *you* know. Please be patient. It's just....me."

"Uh-huh." He studied her. "Haven't you ever had an orgasm?"

"Ha!" She snorted. "What do you take me for? Have I ever? Well, you know...I guess not."

"You *guess* not?"

"At least I don't *think* so."

"You would know it if you had."

She blew out a breath because of course she'd known that. For a long time. "Then, no. I haven't. Not with...anyone else around."

"Got it." He gave her a slow easy smile. "Do you remember that time we all drove down to the Santa Cruz Boardwalk?"

"Yeah?"

"The bumper cars. You were so good at driving yours that no one could ever catch you. Later you said that was the best time you'd ever had."

She smiled at the memory. "Such a good day."

"And *this* is going to be about a thousand times better."

15

"I'm just a girl, standing in front of a salad, asking it to be a donut." ~ meme

When Dylan removed his boxers, discarding them to the side, Charley had a view she'd never seen before and it was...spectacular. She swallowed hard. After all the anticipation, after all the fantasies over the years, she was not at all disappointed. He was every bit as gorgeous as she'd imagined, all hard planes and inherently male angles. Beautiful olive skin.

He'd just promised her the best time of her life. If she were to go by his slow grin, and the easy and confident way that he moved in his own skin, she had no doubts that he'd deliver. He covered her with his warm, hard body and she felt something else that was incredibly...hard.

"Hi," she said inanely, from the most wonderful place on earth. Under him.

Giving her a wicked grin, he found the racing pulse at

her throat and traced it gently, then followed with his mouth. Wanting to touch him, anywhere and everywhere, she threaded her fingers through his thick dark hair. She stroked up his back and back down again, resting at the gorgeous curve of his ass. His fingers skimmed over her breast and his mouth followed their path.

He reached between her thighs and stroked the sensitive area there, touching and teasing her folds. Her skin was too tight. This was unlike anything she'd experienced before, and she felt her control slide away. An intense wave of pleasure rippled and rolled through her body. Everything else in the world slipped away. This might be too good. Too much.

"Is it supposed to feel this way? I don't know, I—"

"How do you feel?" he asked, then nipped at her earlobe.

"L-like I might explode."

"Good." He pressed his forehead to hers. "I'm going to watch you come apart, and then I'm going to put you back together again."

Lord, his voice. It was so gravelly deep. Sexy. Not wanting to be a slouch and fall behind, she took the opportunity to reach for him and wrap her hand around his shaft. She stroked him, gratified when he hissed between his teeth.

"Wait." He removed her hand after a few minutes. "I want this to last."

"And I want you inside me."

"We'll get there."

Not soon enough for her. Dylan's palms skimmed down her bare skin, creating an intoxicating sensation. He dipped his head again and then his tongue was where his fingers had been minutes ago. When he touched her right in the middle of all her heat and desire, she fisted the sheets in both hands and undulated her hips in rhythm with the exquisite caresses of his warm tongue.

Like the tide, her desire rose slowly and methodically until her entire body shook and she came in a rush of lust and pleasure. Boneless and liquid, she was mildly aware of the sound of plastic ripping open. Dylan thrust into her and her body woke up again. To everything under the sun. To every sound and every tantalizing smell. She heard the sound the bed made as it creaked beneath them. Dylan groaning as he pushed inside her, filling her so completely. He moved slowly, pulling out and then back in again. Even her hands on his ass, urging him to go faster for her didn't sway him. But each time he drove into her he did so harder and a little faster, the pressure building inside her.

She didn't know how long it was, hours or minutes or days, because she lost all sense of herself and time. When it seemed as though the tide took her under the tow, she shuddered and came again, clutching on to his shoulders. Dylan pumped faster and harder, locking eyes with hers when he followed her over.

A few minutes later, when she stopped panting like an animal in heat and came back down to earth, she opened her eyes to find Dylan smiling. "You okay?"

"Um, yeah. Sure. I'm...fine."

Not just fine. She was more than fine. She was a word that hadn't been invented yet. Because who knew sex could be like this? But maybe sex was different when you could trust a man completely. Trust him enough with your body to let yourself go. She wouldn't know because until now that had never happened.

He rolled on his back and took her with him. Splayed on top of Dylan's chiseled hard chest, she didn't think she'd never seen a more breathtaking sight. And she'd once watched a five-star dessert chef create a white chocolate and raspberry truffle in the shape of a Faberge egg. That dessert had been a work of art.

So was Dylan.

"Look at me," he said.

"I am looking at you." Oh, maybe he meant his eyes.

Those eyes were now crinkled with the start of a smile. He threaded his fingers through hers. "This thing here between you and me. I won't let it change us. No matter what happens."

There went the ache again. Her heart felt too big in her chest, her skin too tight. "Friends forever."

He kissed her, a long deep kiss with a heat she felt all the way to her heart. "Naked friends."

DYLAN WAITED for guilt to cut to slam into him, slicing through his gut. Taking advantage of Charley when she needed him to be nothing more than a comforting friend? Guilty as charged, your honor. Enjoying the feel of her soft legs wrapped around him, of being inside her, giving it to her hard and loving how much she wanted him? *I confess. Put me under the jail.*

But guilt didn't arrive. Guilt was MIA.

Instead, there was surprise and shock rocking him, making him wonder why he'd never seen this connection before. Why he'd never acted on it. Maybe because, first, she'd never given him any indication of the depth of her feelings until now. Second, because they began as friends and grew to be best friends. He never wanted to mess with that. Third, because...

Because she leaves.

Yeah. But maybe...since I asked her to stay, she will. He didn't know what it said about him that he was letting his thoughts run in this direction. It was time to enjoy her. Enjoy this incredible connection and forget about tomorrow.

Live in the moment. Don't think so much.

Charley rolled and stretched her naked body to his like a cat. "I know what you need."

She rolled away from him and kicked the sheets off. But that was the wrong direction for what he had in mind. He caught her elbow when one leg was off the bed. "What I need is for you to stay right here."

"You're not going anywhere for a while, so I need to feed you, and you can keep up your strength for me."

"Good idea. I'll eat you again. You liked that, didn't you?"

Her cheeks pinked adorably. "You know I did."

"Yeah." He'd guessed that from her gyrating hips while he went down on her. It was erotic as hell.

He folded hands behind his neck and watched as she pulled his T-shirt on. It fell to her knees and damn if he didn't think she was the sexiest thing he'd ever seen. "What are you cooking?"

"It's a surprise."

Wondering why the big mystery, he had his answer a few minutes later when Charley carried a pot into the bedroom, two forks inside. "I think this is the best batch I've ever made."

His favorite dish. The pasta carbonara she often made for him. He smelled the enticing flavors of garlic and pancetta. Melted cheese. She made it the way he liked it best. Simple. The purist's version, she called it. They'd often eaten it straight out of the pan while hanging out watching a movie. This time would be quite different.

She curled next to him under the sheets, the pan between them.

He took a fork and ate a mouthful. As always, the best he'd ever had. "Why does this taste so much better? What's different?"

"We're eating it in bed together." She licked her lips. "Naked."

"No doubt." Less interested in her food than he'd probably ever been, he tugged her close. "We should have done this a long time ago."

"I have to say that I agree with you there." She took a few more bites, then had a wistful look in her eyes. "You know, maybe we should run away together."

Stomach tightening, Dylan paused with his fork midway to his mouth. "Run away?"

"Yeah, I mean get away for a while. Leave everything behind. Just the two of us."

She always wanted to run. All the bright and shiny of a new and intriguing city was too much to ignore.

When he finally spoke his voice had a rough edge to it he couldn't help. "Your thoughts always go to leaving."

"What? I meant you and me running away *together*."

"So that makes it better?"

Her eyes went wide. "I didn't really mean it. Just a fantasy."

"Right." Dylan climbed out of bed and pulled on his boxers. "A fantasy."

Like the fantasy of the sunset kiss legend. More of the same. He should have expected this from her. And while he wanted real, Charley wanted a dream. He could never give her that. Dammit, now he was irritated. Frustrated with her, when he had no cause to be. It wasn't her fault. The problem was all up in his own head. His issues, not hers. *Calm down.*

You knew what you were getting into and you still don't regret this.

Not for a minute.

She followed him, still dressed only in his "Just Do It" tee. It was going to be impossible to stay mad. She was irresistible.

"You can't walk away from me when we're fighting." Her hair was adorably disheveled, and she looked so tiny in his T-shirt. Small and confused. He'd already hurt her. Good going, Einstein. His chest pinched uncomfortably.

"We're *not* fighting." He rolled his shoulders.

He was used to people coming and going in his life because he'd grown up in a boarding house. Many of their tenants had been kind people he'd enjoyed getting to know, people he often came to love like family. He'd had to get used to the feeling of being left behind when one after another they moved out. Moved on. The delineations became clear even as a young kid. Only family stayed.

He should be used to that by now.

"Yes, we are." Her voice was shaky.

She stayed a few feet behind him. It wasn't as if she hadn't seen him shut down before. On the anniversary of his father's death every year. On bad days when he hadn't managed to save someone's life despite Herculean efforts. His feelings of loss and abandonment were not her problem. They were his to own and handle. He was certain she had enough of her own memories that clouded and influenced her decisions.

"C'mere." He reached behind and hauled her into his arms. "You're cold."

"That's because we left a window open and I'm not a penguin." She wrapped her arms around his waist and buried her face in his chest. "Why aren't *you* cold?"

"I'm too tough to be cold."

"I'm sorry, Dylan," she whispered.

"No, I'm the one who's sorry." His hands rubbed up and down her back creating friction and warmth. "You were trying to be romantic. I'm an idiot."

"Aw, but you're my idiot." She squeezed him tighter.

"Yeah." He framed her face and tipped her up to lock eyes with his. "And this idiot is not sharing you. With anyone else."

"I'm not sharing you, either."

"You know what? I got that, because of the whole fake engagement thing."

She closed her eyes. "I'm so bad."

"Yes, you are." His lips grazed the curve of her jaw. "But you're right. We should go away together sometime. Just the two of us."

"You're not joking. Really?" She smiled up at him. "I'd love that."

But while he was thinking of Lake Tahoe or Napa Valley, he'd wager she was imagining Paris.

Hell, maybe, if he got really lucky, they could meet in the middle.

THE NEXT DAY, Dylan tried to concentrate at the station. With the emphasis on *tried.* He schooled his expression into "LT means business" for the sake of the guys, but his mind kept wandering back to Charley. And last night. Christ. Last night. Who knew it could be like that with her?

He'd started the rotation at the station in the usual way, assigning the crew their household chores. Later they responded to a slew of medical calls, picking up a woman at a local restaurant who had complained of chest pains and shortness of breath, and checking on an elderly man who had fallen at his nursing home. Since medical was about fifty percent of their runs it was a typical morning. He ran a training exercise for the men using some of their new hydraulic rescue tools since some of the crew had little experience with them. Slow times were a perfect opportunity to work on skills.

Dylan had Johnny run the hose from the truck a few times and stretch the line. He was not only new to Miracle Bay, he'd also had no experience with structural fires. It showed, too, and that concerned Dylan. He preferred to minimize the risks to his men by allowing experience to take root. Later in the afternoon, having completed a presentation on blood-borne pathogens, Dylan headed to the room where they kept the weights. After a few minutes on the bench, Marco joined him.

"Hey, spot me." Dylan said.

He bench-pressed seventy-five pounds. He grunted and put the barbell down after ten reps. "More weight."

Marco added more weight. "What's up with you?"

"Nothing. But *something* is going on with Joe. You notice?"

"Notice what?"

"Seems preoccupied. And he asked to crash with us for a while. That's not like him." Dylan mopped his brow.

"Maybe he missed home. Thought you'd be happy about that. Ma certainly is."

"Yeah, of course she would be."

"He says he loves his job and all's good."

"Then it's something else."

"A woman?"

"Could be."

Given the situation in his own backyard with Milly,

Dylan couldn't help but imagine that Joe may have knocked someone up. And holy crap, Dylan hoped he wasn't running from the situation. From the responsibility. Because if that's what he was doing, Dylan would have to kill him.

"Either way, whatever it is I'm going to assume he's handling it since he hasn't asked for our help. And he needs to grow up and decide what he wants to do with his life."

Dylan sat up and reached for the towel before going for another rep. "Talk to him any more about the open call?"

"Until his eyes glazed over," Marco said. "He's not interested. You need to accept it."

"Reyes!" one of the crew shouted.

"Yeah?" Both Dylan and Marco answered at the same time, and then laughed.

"And you really want there to be *three* of us?" Marco smirked.

"Joe's here," someone else called out.

"Speak of the devil," Marco said and when Dylan stood from the weight bench, he quickly took his place.

"Hey!" Dylan said.

"What? If he's here, I know you'll want to talk to him about the open call next month." Marco slid him an evil grin.

"Is that so wrong?"

"He has to want it," Marco said.

Marco was right. The problem was Dylan didn't understand why Joe wouldn't want to have some direction in his life. A purpose. He wouldn't have to be an EMT or firefighter forever if he didn't enjoy it. But it wasn't as if there was any other direction in his life. If there were Dylan would back off. Probably.

He found Joe in the kitchen surrounded by some of the

crew, including Smitty and Tony, who'd been around when Emilio Reyes had been part of the crew.

"Little Joey Reyes," Tony said, though Joe had a good six inches on him now. "What's it been? Six months?"

Smitty grabbed him a bear hug, as was the big man's way. "Missed you, son. Ought to come around more often."

"I've been living in Santa Cruz working as a surfing instructor and a part-time lifeguard. But the shop's being sold, so I got a little time off."

The news slid through Dylan with no small amount of relief. Joe wouldn't have come to see family if he wasn't thinking it might be time to move back. He was probably considering options.

"Hey, why don't you let Smitty show you the new rig?" Dylan said.

"Let me guess. It's red and super shiny." Joe grinned, tipping back on his heels.

"You should come out for the open call next month," Tony said.

"Guys, you all know I'm a surf bum."

"Even so, even so," Smitty said, arm hooked around Joe's shoulder, leading him to the bay. "Couldn't hurt to see this baby. You know, your dad used to love the beach, too. Did I ever tell you about the time he and I went fishing at Bodega Bay?"

Joe turned slightly and caught Dylan's eyes as if he wanted to be rescued. But Smitty was really proud of that new rig.

Dylan simply shrugged as he made his way to the kitchen to grab a post-work-out snack.

16

"Can't eat because of nausea. Nauseous because I can't eat. Well played, pregnancy. Well played." ~ *meme*

L ater that same evening, the rotation crew were all waiting for Tony to serve them spaghetti and his famous meatballs. Only Tony believed them famous. Charley would more be more inclined to call them infamous.

"Hey," Johnny said. "Is that girl that played pool with us the other night seeing anyone?"

"You mean Charley," Smitty answered for Dylan.

"Man, she's really cute," Johnny added. "Low maintenance. Just my type. Think I stand a chance?"

A hot spike of jealousy flared in Dylan. Johnny stood a chance over his dead body. *Mine.*

"She's sort of a sore subject 'round here," Tony said as he drained the pasta.

"Why?" Johnny pressed, clearly not aware of Dylan's

level of irritation.

"Because she's the one that got away." Smitty smiled with satisfaction.

Dylan groaned. These guys really could write a Hallmark movie of the week. He had no idea what they were talking about. She'd never been more than a good friend to him. But they were convinced he couldn't possibly be best friends with, of all things, a girl. But that's the way it had been for years. Still, what had recently developed was nobody's damn business. He was still coming to terms with it himself. For now, he wanted it to be his and his alone.

"Let me tell you something, Johnny-boy." Tony took a heaping serving of pasta and set it on a plate. "Our LT here could have any woman he wanted."

Dylan snorted. *Before or after the fake engagement?* Either way, not true.

"Must be nice," said Johnny, eyeing the plate as Tony piled on the sauce.

"And also, if anyone cares, not true," Dylan added.

"But he and Charley? Never quite happened," Smitty continued, shaking his head.

"And we always wondered why," Tony said. "She's perfect for him."

"Man, that looks delicious," Dylan said, re-directing.

"Oh, it is." Tony served them their generous plates right to the table. "Dig in, guys!"

Dylan had poised his fork above a meatball when the fire alarm's set of tones, growing in volume, resonated through the fire station.

"Two-alarm fire on 20th Street. Believed to be at least one child still trapped inside," the dispatch operator said over their loudspeaker.

There was one word Dylan never liked to hear on the

job: children. Everyone moved fast. They all met at the
housing bay, where their turn-out gear and boots were liter-
ally lined up next to the engine truck for them to step right
into. After gearing up, Dylan jumped in the truck next to
Tony, pulling on his comm headset and air harness.

"ETA is three minutes," he confirmed into his headset.
He turned to his crew. "Anyone know the closest fire
hydrant?"

"Got it," Tony said through his set.

Many times the guys used the headsets to talk to each
other on the way but there were few words spoken now.
Anyone trapped inside was always cause for concern but a
child...Dylan could only hope for the best-case scenario.
Maybe they'd get there in time. Before the toxic fumes of
smoke made the child pass out or worse.

Their unit was the first to arrive and went to work immediately. A crowd of onlookers and residents had gathered on
the sidewalk watching the black smoke billow from the
second-floor windows. Tony unfurled the hose on the smoldering building, and two men stretched the line, one of
them turning it on the house. The other stood behind him
as back-up.

As LT, it was up to Dylan to check around the structure
for any unknown hazards and for the best entry point. Craig
Lyons, LT from a second unit that had responded behind
them, approached Dylan as he was coming back around
from the side of the residence. "Kitchen fire. The residents
say the little girl was cooking and told them she'd started a
fire. She got one of her sisters out but the other one is still
missing."

"Anyone else trapped?" Dylan asked.

He frowned. "Neighbors are looking for the mother. It's
just her and the kids living here."

Dylan nodded. "Front door is our point of entry."

By now, Tony had stretched the line and one of the men was turning the powerful spray of water straight to the roof, where the flames leapt out. The rescue crew would be working with the line crew when they entered the residence.

Dylan joined Smitty at the front door with the thermal imaging camera. He gestured for Smitty to get behind. Dylan led the way through the front door, crawling under the smoke since they wouldn't be able to stand until the outside crew was finished ventilating the roof. For now, visibility in this smoke was less than zero. The camera would show him the differential heat between the heat of a human body and the heat in the residence, whose ceiling had to be getting close to two thousand degrees.

He continued to crawl, Smitty behind him, and as he approached the kitchen confirmed the fire had started there. A black hole had burned directly through the ceiling straight to the second floor. The missing child could be on the second floor, maybe hiding somewhere, terrified.

But with any luck, or maybe a miracle, still alive.

Dylan crawled up the steps. In the second room, the camera led him to a heat differential and under the twin bed he found the missing child. He couldn't see anything in the thick black smoke, but he could feel the small and limp body, grabbed the child in a bear hug, signaled to Smitty, and followed when he turned back to lead them out.

Give her air from your mask. Just rip it off and do it. Now.

But he couldn't. Couldn't break the rules and take off his air mask. The rules were there for a reason. Logic told him that if he couldn't breathe, if he burned out his lungs, he couldn't help anyone. The creaking of the roof told him this structure was about to cave. Swinging the child over this shoulder in a fireman's hold, he walked low to the ground.

Seeing an opening that was closer, and knowing the child needed oxygen immediately, he headed that way. Interminable seconds later that felt more like hours, he neared the exit.

He focused on process as he'd been taught, to avoid the sinking sensations curling through him now. Adrenaline, pure and powerful, flooded him. He might not get out of here alive. The crew might have to pull his charred remains out with God help him, this child in his arms. A large piece of the structure fell right in front of them and Dylan instinctively used his body to shield the child and take the hit. But the frame missed them both. In another minute, he was pulled out by a strong pair of arms.

"Close one," Smitty said.

Too close.

He ripped off his mask and gave the child some oxygen on his way to handing her over to the EMTs. It didn't happen often, but for what seemed like several minutes but was possibly only seconds, Dylan stood by watching them work. Unable to move. He wanted to be told the girl was going to be okay, but he knew it wouldn't be that simple. It was never that simple.

One of the ambulances left with her shortly after, sirens wailing. Hours later, after some of his men had ventilated the roof so that they had some visibility, and the fire was one hundred percent contained, the mother showed up. But by then CPS had arrived and taken the other two children into their custody.

"What happened?" She ran toward the house, screaming. "Where are my babies?"

"They took your kids and Angela went to the hospital. Where *were* you?" a neighbor yelled.

"I had to work!"

"*Work*? You're high, Kathy."

Dylan stopped listening and in the next seconds he was forced to sit down while an EMT from a second ambulance checked his vitals and listened to his lungs. He was going to be okay, this time. But he'd meant what he said to Smitty. That was too close for comfort. The roof had creaked, the wood had snapped. The fire, its fierceness and intensity, had humbled him. And reminded him that like his father he was simply...mortal.

"How you doing, LT?" Tony asked, as Dylan walked away from the ambulance.

"Hard to say," Dylan said because it was the simple truth. He couldn't quite put into words the feeling he had at the moment. His adrenaline levels still hadn't come down.

"I've seen this many times. Just don't be surprised if everything tastes better for a while," Tony went on. "Sex is going to be better. Nothing is going to piss you off. Too bad it doesn't last. Enjoy it while you can. You're lucky to be alive so enjoy every freaking minute of that."

"How long will this last?"

"It's different for everyone. Mine lasted a couple of weeks, but I'll tell you, once you've been that close to death, some part of that appreciation for life never goes away."

When they got back to the station, gear sooty and black, bodies exhausted, the spaghetti was cold. First, they had to face the task of cleaning their gear. After all that was completed and assessed, the spaghetti was frigid and bitchy. And Dylan was past the point of hunger. His stomach burned with another kind of intensity entirely. Adrenaline still riding high, he felt like running five miles. Climbing a mountain. Sailing at midnight.

Having sex with Charley all night long.

"I'll warm the spaghetti up. It's always better the second time around, anyway," Tony said.

"I'm starved," Johnny said.

"I'm so hungry I could eat my left arm," Smitty said.

Later, Dylan let the hot water pound his tired muscles in the shower, a stunning realization hitting him hard. He wondered why he'd never seen it before. The reason he hadn't noticed this spark with Charley was nothing more than fear. It was what had held him back from asking her out years ago, knowing that she'd already lost so much. Why give her the burden of being with someone in his profession, too?

But there was the thing. She was willing to risk it all. And suddenly it occurred to him that damn if he wasn't right there with her.

17

Cooking is love made edible." ~ Apron

"And *then*, Dylan carried the poor child right out of the house," Mrs. Perez said to Charley while ordering a loaf of French bread and a dozen donuts. "Too bad he's engaged. That's the kind of man I want *my* daughter to date, rather than these losers she keeps on picking."

"Um—" Confess now, or let the prank die a slow death?

The word was getting out slowly but surely given that Jenny knew the truth. Eventually Mrs. Perez would hear. Dylan wasn't engaged, but he was definitely otherwise occupied.

With her.

The bakery was humming by six a.m. when she opened the doors. Padre Suarez came in an hour later, blessed the pastries, and had his usual. When the morning rush slowed

Charley almost didn't notice the man who'd walked in and held the door open for Padre Suarez as he left.

Sean.

"Hey, baby." He whipped off his shades and gave her a toothy smile. "What's going on?"

"What are you doing here?"

"Knew that New Orleans wouldn't be the same without you. The next big thing is Paris anyway. And you're coming." He glanced around the shop. "But hey, look at you. Baking."

"Well, this *is* my family's bakery."

He waggled his brows. "And everything is rising to the occasion?"

"Yes, *Sean*. It all came back to me. Like riding a bicycle." She went back behind the counter. "What can I get for you?"

Sean was a bit of a snob when it came to anything sweet, since he believed he was God's gift to pastries. He lingered over the glass case, passing loafs of crusty bread, glazed donuts and scones and finally pointed. "What are those?"

"My special pastry puffs."

"I'll have one."

She batted her lashes at him. "Feeling brave today?"

"I guess you could say that." He pulled out his wallet.

Sean was such a mean critic that she didn't want him to sink her spirits. The puffs were something new she'd tried, mixing unexpected flavors but also sticking to some classics. They certainly weren't classic bakery fare but more like a gourmet artsy quiche.

"These are on the house. Just tell me what you think."

"You know I will."

Oh, she knew. His criticism had hurt her feelings more than once. More like daily. He'd once ever so helpfully told her that her jeans made her butt look too big. Looking back, it had spelled the beginning of the end for their short romantic relationship. After that, they'd gone back to just being work friends and Charley had never once looked back. But his opinion as a cook meant a lot to her because he had so much more experience than she did, working in his family's French restaurant and making connections in the culinary world early on.

Sean took a bite, closed his eyes and cocked his head as if meditating. She waited in suspense for his verdict, wishing she'd put a little cayenne pepper in for him. Just so there would be an excuse when he hated it.

He swallowed, coughed, and hit his chest. "What in God's name did you put in here?"

"Why?"

"Because...they're not *sweet*."

"They have butter. Lots of it. And the crust melts in your mouth. Does every pastry have to be sweet?"

"Why, yes, now that you mention it, at least in a bakery. It's all about expectations. Know your audience, baby. And then *deliver*."

"What if I want to be a little different? Maybe I'm trying something new. We're expanding, and I've got a lunch menu planned." Milly didn't know it yet, but they were, whether she liked it or not.

"Back to the drawing board with those," Sean said with a slight shake of his head.

That was possibly the nicest thing Sean had ever said about her cooking. "What are you doing here? You didn't just drop by to check up on me."

"You've talked about Miracle Bay so much, and it's been years since I last worked in San Francisco. When I was looking for somewhere else to land quickly, I checked it out. Working for a pop-up on Valencia Street. I start next week."

"Sorrel's?" She'd seen the signs. They were operating from a former storefront.

"That's the one."

But Sean didn't fit into this world. He was part of her other world, the world that never crossed lines with Miracle Bay. With Dylan.

Her safe place.

Sean would now infiltrate her world, reminding her that she'd been on a quest for years that hadn't led her anywhere. She wasn't a first-class chef, she hadn't been to Paris, she didn't have a bistro, and she wasn't in a committed relationship with anyone but her cutlery set. And damn it all, she wanted all of those things. A serious relationship with a man. Her own bistro someday where she would be the head chef. She'd paid her dues, almost ten years of dealing with irrational chefs and pompous men like Sean.

"Want to go out tonight? Check out some of the restaurants and make fun of them?"

Another thing about Sean? He had a mean streak a mile wide. Charley secretly believed it was his destiny to host a reality TV cooking show in which he yelled and belittled all of the contestants, all with a smile on his face.

"Sorry, but I'm busy."

The bakery's door jingled, and Jenny strode inside. Her face red, brows lowered over squinted eyes, there might as well be smoke coming out of her ears. She came up to the glass case, nearly shoulder-checking Sean.

"If you wanted him for yourself, all you had to do was say so!"

"Um, hi Jenny." Charley dug her hands inside her apron and wouldn't meet her eyes.

"Don't you 'hi' me. There's no sunset kiss or true love. No engagement for Dylan. You *lied* to me and made me look like a fool. I never did understand you and Dylan and your stupid little jokes. And by the way, half the neighborhood thinks you're already screwing and have been for years. So why not get on with it and *do* him so the rest of us can give up."

"Sorry, Jenny. I went too far that time with my prank."

Jenny went hand on hip and swiveled her neck. "You think?"

Sean, who had been checking out Jenny's goods the entire time she'd been yacking, spoke up. "Hello."

Jenny turned as if she'd just noticed him. She tossed her long dark hair, then appraised him from the top of his spiky blonde hair to the tips of his Birkenstocks. "Hey there."

"Jenny, this is my friend Sean Hannigan. Sean, this is Jenny," Charley said. "An old friend."

"Want to go out sometime?" Sean's gaze slid up Jenny's body without the slightest bit of covertness.

Slow was not in Sean's repertoire. No preamble, no big set-up. Just put it out there. Awkward for anyone that wasn't Mr. Sean Hannigan.

"Sure," Jenny said, her voice laced with honey and arsenic. "Any friend of Charley's is a friend of mine."

Charley wiped down the espresso machine and gave them some privacy. While there she took a moment to roll her eyes nearly right out of her head.

"I'll call you," Sean said.

When Charley turned back, he was alternating between typing into his phone and watching Jenny's behind as it wiggled away. Emphasis on the wiggle.

"She doesn't usually walk that way," Charley said. "Thought you should know."

"Even better. She must really like me. Looks like I'm going to be busy and not just at Sorrel's."

"Look, Sean. I should warn you—"

Jenny is predatory. She chews men up and spits them out before she's on to the next one. Run, don't walk, away from her. But then she flashed back to the day Sean had told her butt looked too big and later at work, that her torte needed a major overhaul. That if she ever wanted to be anything like Julia Child, be a chef or have her own bistro, she was going to have to up her game.

That sometimes he doubted she had it in her.

"Uh, never mind." She went back to wiping the espresso machine. "I was just going to say that she doesn't have a real appreciation of French cuisine. Just a heads-up. Where are you taking her?"

He braced an arm over the counter. "Figured I'd let her take me around."

"She does know the city."

"Don't worry, baby. You haven't completely missed your chance with me. Just say the word and we're on again." He winked.

Though their relationship was firmly in her rearview, lovely Sean liked to keep all options open. Occasionally he flirted and fooled himself into thinking that Charley might give him another chance. If neither one of them was married by age forty, he'd once suggested, they should get married to each other and open a bistro together. She was to be his consolation prize, and he was to be hers.

Flattering.

"I'm sure Jenny would be more than willing to help you drown your sorrows."

"Yeah, she's pretty but she's no Charley Young." He flashed his mega-watt smile.

"Stop it."

"Whatever you say, Princess."

Oh, yeah. The silly and cheesy nicknames. Like foreplay for Sean. "Princess?" How *original*.

Finally, she had another customer.

And by the time she'd filled two dozen special order boxes for the Chamber of Commerce meeting, Sean had gone.

18

"I'm pregnant, which means I'm sober, swollen and hungry. Approach with EXTREME caution." ~ meme

"What do you think about adding a lunch menu?" Charley asked Naomi.

Naomi shrugged. She wore a "Death to Capitalism" red tee over a long-sleeved black sweater, cut jeans and black combat boots. Her strawberry blonde hair was tinged with blue highlights, and she wore black nail polish. Charley wasn't sure she should ask for her opinion. After all, she strongly resembled Charley at age sixteen, and one thing that could be said of sixteen-year-old Charley was that she could not be trusted for a reliable opinion.

"I thought you said Milly didn't want to do that."

"Milly isn't here now, is she?"

"Dude, if you say so."

"What does that mean?"

"Milly keeps asking me if you've left yet. And how things

are going. I think she wants me to spy on you." She stage whispered. "See if you're doing a good job or screwing everything up."

"Still?" Seriously, this was insulting.

Naomi shrugged. "You two should just talk it out. That's what my mom always tells my brother and me."

"In order to talk it out, Milly would have to talk to me, too."

"I hear ya. My bro won't talk either. All he does is grunts. I hate guys."

"Uh-huh." Not something she could relate to at the moment. For once, her issues weren't with those of the male persuasion. Just with one stubborn sister.

After WWIII, Charley had made herself scarce as Milly had requested. No more hanging out watching Netflix or watching Scottish Highlander shows. (Milly's guilty pleasure, she loved men in kilts). No more pedicures and no more pampering. It gave Charley a lot of extra time during the work day to think. And plan. For years, she'd wondered why Coral had never wanted to expand the bakery into also offering lunch.

"Because I'm not greedy," she'd once told Charley.

Well, Charley wasn't greedy either, but she loved feeding people. Enjoyed watching their expressions when they tasted something new that she'd created. Something she'd prepared with her own two hands and her passion for food. She'd always wanted to expand palates beyond sugar, chocolate, cinnamon and flour. Yes, those were good (alright, fantastic) but there were so many more flavors under the sun. Smoked salmon, for instance, possibly her favorite. Sundried tomatoes and grape tomatoes. Basil. Goat cheese. Gruyere. Dill cream fraiche. Capers. Had she mentioned basil? Culinary school had opened her eyes to the wonder of cooking with every flavor under the sun and she'd never looked back.

Charley might have turned Sunrise Bakery into something quite different after Coral passed away. It would have become the Sunrise Bistro, offering not just the highest quality pastries but gourmet sandwiches and crepes. Quiche and soups. But even though Charley was technically half owner of the bakery, she'd never felt like it was hers.

After Coral was gone, Milly had managed the bakery and she hadn't changed a thing. But now, maybe for the short time when she had full reign and Milly was laid up, not currently speaking to Charley so none the wiser, she could try a few things. Experiment. She might expand their customers' tastes with what she did best. Not everyone had the money to enjoy gourmet food cooked by an outstanding sous chef quickly on her way to becoming a Michelin chef. Okay, maybe not quickly but someday.

Yesterday she'd experimented in her apartment kitchen, smoking salmon and making specialty panini sandwiches. Adding capers. Roasted peppers, wild mushrooms, and caramelized onions. Brie and prosciutto. Deliciously tantalizing. She was certain the smells were drifting out the crack of her doorway and wafting into Milly's apartment next door. But just in case they weren't, Charly had carried the pan of caramelized onions and held it under the slip of Milly's door.

No response, though she heard Rufus meow in obvious hunger. No wonder because this put the "D" in delicious.

And if Milly wanted some of this delicious food, she was going to have to *ask*.

～

WHEN DYLAN WENT home at the end of his shift, he was still riding on an adrenaline high. Maybe he'd test drive that sailboat at midnight tonight. Or talk Charley into an all-night sex marathon.

Joe sat on the couch, laptop at the ready, fingers flying, his face a mask of concentration. He didn't even look up when Dylan threw his keys on the counter. He hadn't seen Joe this involved in reading anything since *Catcher in the Rye* back in high school.

"What's up?" Dylan finally asked, by way of announcing he had walked into the room.

"Hey," Joe said, finally breaking away from the screen.

"That's impressive concentration," Dylan said, making his way to the fridge. "I haven't seen you this focused on something since you offered to take Mandy Kelly to the prom. She was a senior and you were in the eighth grade."

"Oh, yeah. Almost forgot about that. I had a plan." He closed the screen. "It would have worked, too, except for her boyfriend."

"Yeah, he was a little bit of an obstacle." Dylan handed Joe a beer, then plopped on the couch next to him. He nudged his chin in the direction of the laptop. "What's so fascinating?"

"Another one of my plans."

"Don't tell me it's a woman again."

"Nah," Joe said, twisting his bottle's top. "This one is a winner. Besides, I'm taking a breather from all women. They wear me out."

Dylan blinked. "What the hell is in the water in Santa Cruz?"

"I know I need to focus, and I finally have the chance to do something that matters to me." He opened his screen, typed into the keyboard, and turned it to Dylan.

Before him was a spreadsheet. Next, he flipped to a detailed business plan. There were charts and projections. More spreadsheets. Finally, a photo of a property. The Surf's Up shop.

"This is what you've been so secretive about?"

"Like I said, the shop is being sold. And I've been talking to my boss over the last few months about buying it."

"You? *Buying* it?"

"Before you tell me I'm crazy, I've already done my due diligence. And I've got a partner. Eddie Paxton is a surfer buddy and a graduate of Stanford who just moved down to Santa Cruz with his wife. He wants to go into business with me. I'm the salesman, he's the logistics."

"I don't know what to say." It was like stepping into another dimension. One in which Joe was focused and determined. Hell, practically a grown-up. "I'm...impressed."

"Thanks," Joe said. "I know you wanted me to go on the open call and if I'm honest, firefighting has always been my back-up plan. Like dad always said, it's honorable work, and I think you're all heroes."

"We're not he—"

"But I never knew how focused I could be once I found something that I want. A dream of my own."

Not someone else's dream.

"Where did you learn how to do all this?" Dylan flipped through the documents, more impressed with each one. The figures projected were solid and the forecast looked optimistic.

"Google," Joe said with a smirk. "And I'm only half joking. But I read books, researched, and taught myself."

"This is great. But it also looks like you'll need an influx of cash." He assumed his partner would be coming up with that because Joe wasn't exactly rolling in cash.

"Yesterday Eddie got the call from his lender. We're approved on a small business loan." Joe shut the screen again.

"So, this is happening." Dylan took a gulp of cold beer and tried to imagine Joe as a business owner.

It wasn't the craziest thing he'd ever heard.

"Hell, I know I haven't been the picture of responsibility. But I've also been enjoying my life. I know that's easier to do without a bunch of responsibilities, and I'm sorry if I kept you from doing the same."

"You were right, Joe. Life is short and we need to grab up the joy where we can."

Joe's eyes widened. "Right?"

'You're looking at the new Dylan Reyes. I'm not going to be such a killjoy anymore. Not going to worry about you, Mom, Abuelita, Marco, or anyone else."

"That sounds like something you'd say if you were mad and fed up with me. But you look happy."

"I am. Damn happy." He stretched his legs and leaned back, practicing a relaxation pose.

"Since I've got you at a good time, you've seen the numbers. How would you feel about investing as a silent partner?"

Dylan Reyes, silent owner in a surf shop. Stranger things had happened.

19

"I was told there would be glowing." ~ Maternity T-shirt

"Alright, cute entry number nine, I know I have to give you a name, but right now you're moving a little bit over here to make room for entry number ten."

Charley arranged the smoked salmon cheese encrusted panini next to the turkey and gruyere panini and slid in the grilled prosciutto. She made a note on the menu she was creating. All the years working at the bakery and all the years on the road, she'd never had a chance to create a menu. The idea was intoxicating. The creative control she had, and the license to do whatever she wanted. For now. It was a dream come true. No chef had ever given her a chance and listened to her ideas. After a while she'd begun to wonder if the past was written in invisible ink on her face and in her eyes.

Maybe everyone could somehow see where she came

from. She was Maggie Young's biological daughter. She didn't want to be anything like her, but one couldn't control the genes they'd inherited. The family history. But Charley hadn't gotten pregnant at sixteen like Maggie had. She'd never done drugs and her only vice was her annoying love of store-bought cookies. It was safe to say that she'd exorcised Maggie's influence, if not her genes.

She'd hit the foster kid lottery with Coral and Milly. Despite what Milly had said, Charley had adored Coral. Even after Charley had moved out, she'd visit Coral. She'd brought Coral candy and flowers on Mother's Day. Kept in touch on her progress at culinary school and made frequent test meals for both her and Milly.

She'd been devastated and cried in Dylan's arms when Coral died after a short battle with colon cancer.

Milly saying that Charley somehow hadn't loved her enough was both painful and unfair. It had caused Charley to question everything about her life. Her choices. Had her need for adventure driven away the people she loved most? She couldn't accept that. Unconditional love was just that...unconditional.

She'd like to think that Coral would be proud of her now. Charley had tried. In the long run, Coral had accepted that Charley was stronger willed than most, and once she'd even said out loud that this might be a good thing. At least she'd never follow the crowd, Charley had overheard her tell a friend. And Coral had been right.

Right. So yes, again, Charley was *nothing* like Maggie.
Glad we settled that.

She washed her hands and dried them on the dishtowel. There was a knock on her door and Charley's heart skipped. This was it. Milly had come to her senses and was finally apologizing. Maybe the apartment smelling like a gourmet eatery was more than she could take. Good. Whatever had brought her to her apartment door, Charley would take it and accept her apology with open arms.

"I forgive you!" She threw open the door.

Dylan's eyebrow quirked. "For?"

Charley poked her head out and searched the hallway. No Milly. Instead, from inside the thin walls of the apartment next to hers, Charley heard the loud and distinctive sound of dragons. Milly must already be through all the seasons of her Scottish Highlander show.

"I thought you were M—"

She didn't finish that sentence because she suddenly found herself airborne in Dylan's arms, carried into the apartment. He walked straight into her bedroom, still holding her, and deposited her on the bed.

"I hope you don't have any big plans tonight because I'm here to break them." He began unbuttoning his shirt.

"What have you got in mind?"

"If you behave yourself, I might let you sleep a little tonight."

"Who needs sleep? Sleep is overrated." She rushed to join him in losing her clothes since he was already ahead of her and half naked.

Her clothes went flying and she laughed when her bra hit Dylan in the face before it fell to the floor. Then he was on top of her, his warm hard body covering her. His mouth went to her breasts, his hot tongue sucking and coaxing each nipple to a crest. Her nipples hardened, and she was already wet between her thighs under his ministrations. He crawled down her body, kissing as he went, paying extra attention to her belly button ring. When he kissed between her thighs she nearly came apart right then and there.

"Get in me now," she gasped. "I need you."

"Love to hear that," he said, crawling back up her body. But then he froze and groaned.

"What is it?" She was dying here. "Why did you stop?"

"Charley, are you—"

"Am I ready? Dylan, I was ready yesterday! *Please*."

One half of his mouth tipped up in a smirk. "Are you on the pill? Because I forgot a condom."

They'd obviously never talked about this sort of thing. But it was high time. Weirdly, she almost responded with "none of your beeswax!" Jot another surreal moment down in the Charley and Dylan show.

"Yes," she said. "I am."

"Do you trust me?"

Now she was about to lose it. "Yes, I trust you. Now, shut up and do me!"

She didn't need to ask him twice. Almost as if he wanted to shut her up, he thrust into her, and they both moaned. No more words were spoken as she clung to him, her pleasure mounting as he drove into her. Not slow or tender this second time, but hard and fast strokes as if he'd lost control. It was everything she wanted and craved. She'd lost all control within minutes, writhing under him and matching his thrusts. Quickly reaching that precipice and coming apart just as he'd said she would.

CHARLEY LAY in Dylan's arms, clinging to him. Sated, he was playing with her hair, wrapping strands around his finger. She didn't want this night to end. This night, which he'd promised would go on as long as she wanted it to. On a high, she didn't think she'd ever need to sleep again. Sex could be amazing with the right person. Charley was still reeling from the knowledge of how good it could be.

But this man who was everything to her scared her sometimes even if she had total faith that he knew what he was doing. "I saw news coverage and the fire was horrible. The whole building destroyed. Why didn't you tell me how bad it was?"

"Hell, I don't *want* you to worry." He tugged on a lock of her hair.

"You can't do anything about it. I've always worried about you. I'm not going to stop now."

"Always?" He grimaced. "That's years of you worrying. I should have picked a different profession. Accountant maybe. Like Ma wanted."

But it almost seemed that Dylan had been born with a fire helmet welded to his head. She couldn't see him ever doing anything else with his life. She rolled to prop her chin on his chest, giving him an incredulous look. "You can't be serious."

"No. But I don't want you to worry. I'm okay. More than okay. Changes are coming. Looks like I'm going to be Joe's silent partner in a surf shop in Santa Cruz."

"Joe is going to own a *business*?"

"I wondered what he was doing all this time, keeping to himself, mostly on his laptop. It turned out he wasn't playing online video games. He has a business plan, and we might even make some money at this if all goes well."

"Wow. Joe Reyes, all grown up."

"And it's about time."

"Are you okay with this? I know you always wanted him to join you and Marco."

"He's never been interested. I should have known better. At least he's strong enough not to listen to me. He knows what he wants now. I'm glad he found it."

But the idea of Dylan owning part of a surf shop struck her as funny.

"And you're going to own a surf shop? Am I going to see you on a board, catching waves with all the other surfer dudes?" She laughed, rolled to her back, and flashed him the "hang 10" sign.

"It's time for me to do something fun for a change, right?" Taking full advantage of her current state, he was on top of her within seconds, flashing her that irresistible smile.

"You've always been fun."

"Liar." His hand drifted down one leg and up again, coming to rest at the apex of her thigh. "I know I've always been too up in my head. Too serious. But that's all changing. You and me, Lake Tahoe, as soon as you can leave Milly."

"Really?" Her heart swelled to the size of the moon. He wanted to go away with her. So romantic. "I'd love that."

"Fair warning. Once we book a room somewhere, you're going to have to be the one to drag me out of it every day. I wouldn't mind being locked up with you for an entire weekend. I would keep you busy."

"You're my favorite kind of busy." She framed his face in her hands.

"This thing between you and me? I'm in, Chuck. I'm all in."

"Me, too."

But then he rose from the bed, naked. "Wait. Where are you going?"

He swooped her off the bed once more. "Shower. You. Me."

Oh yeah. She could get used to this. She gripped her legs tight around his waist as he carried her to the bathroom.

Outside the shower stall, he set her down and kissed her,

and she parted her lips for his warm insistent tongue, her breaths shallow. Ragged. She broke the kiss, staring into his heated gaze. "Do you know how long I've waited for this? For you and me?"

"C'mere." He slid her a slow wicked smile and led her into the shower. "Show me."

And for the rest of the evening, that's exactly what she did.

～

IT WAS STILL dark outside when Dylan opened one eye, not sure if he had any feeling left in his right arm. Charley cuddled next to him, heavily asleep on his arm. Okay. So that explained the arm. And as memories of last night flooded back to him of last night, he remembered. Charley. All night long. First, she'd dropped to her knees in the shower and given him a blowjob worthy of a porn star. *The shower.* Just thinking about that got him hard and he wondered if he had time to wake Charley up before she was due to start baking.

She was definitely the best recipe for a man celebrating having another chance at life, after nearly having a roof fall on him. He was having the time of his life so far and last night was only the beginning. He carefully removed his dead arm from under her, and she rolled away from him onto her stomach. The sheets didn't go with her, revealing a perfectly shaped round butt that he wanted to bite like an apple. He dipped his head to do just that as his cellphone rang.

Caller ID read: Milly. Worried it could be an emergency, he picked it up. "Hey."

"Oh, hey, Dylan. Sorry to bother you. I just want to

remind Charley that she needs to start baking. I assume she's there?"

There went his fun wake-up call. His hand went instinctively to the back of her neck and skimmed down to the small of her back. "She's here."

"Uh-huh. That what I thought. She wasn't picking up her phone."

"She's still...sleeping." He winced, not sure how much Milly had heard about him and Charley if anything at all.

"Oh, well sorry to be trouble in paradise, but you know. The bakery waits for no one."

"I'll wake her up."

"Thanks." Milly hung up rather abruptly.

He pulled Charley to him, butt to nuts, and she sighed in her sleep. But before he could even say "baby" to wake her, he heard a buzzing sound coming from somewhere on the floor. Within seconds, the buzzing sound had risen in volume until it was a little something between the sound of a burglar alarm and a jet taking off.

"What?" Charley flailed in his arms. "Stop! Stop it!"

He decided it would be in his best interest to hold back the laughter that was threatening to break through.

"No, no, no." She dove off the bed and hit the floor. "Where is it?"

He could hear the sounds of her searching for her phone. A few seconds later the noise stopped, and from his position on the bed, hands clasped behind his head, he saw her slowly rise. Her morning hair was the definition of bedhead. Tousled and covering one eye completely.

God, she was beautiful.

"Sorry. Did I wake you up?" she asked, sleep thick in her voice, one eye open.

"No. I was just about to wake you up, but my way would have been a lot more fun than that alarm."

She sighed and half-smiled. "I have to start baking now."

"I know. Milly called me."

"She called *you*?"

"She said you didn't answer."

"But I have no missed calls." She scrolled through her phone and frowned. "What did you tell her?"

"That you were still sleeping. Because you were until that M80 went off."

"It's the only way I can get up this early. That plus coffee. Much coffee." She stood to pull panties, bra, and jeans on. "Milly still has no faith in me, or she wouldn't have called you and not me. Plus, you know what this means, don't you?"

"I have a feeling you're going to tell me."

"Milly hasn't called to remind me once since we had our fight. These walls are so damn thin that she must have heard us last night. It means that we shoved it in her face that we're sleeping together."

Charley tugged on her blouse and glanced at herself in the mirror, tracing the red love bite he'd left on her neck. "Dylan! What did you do?"

He winced, then smiled, remembering.

"I'm a teenager again." She turned to him, hands on hips. "You suck!"

"Yes, I do."

He wasn't going to apologize. At this point, he wanted everyone to know she was taken. He wanted to mark her, like she was his. Reluctantly, he rolled out of bed too.

He'd just pulled his shirt on when he caught Charley staring at him. "What?"

"I almost forgot. I-I need to tell you something."

"Go ahead."

"Later."

For the life of him, she looked guilty. He tried not to think the worst, but knowing her the way he did, this was difficult. "What did you do? Does this involve DNA?"

"No! I'll tell you everything tonight. It's kind of a long story but I think you're going to love it."

"I'm working at the marina, so come by when I knock off and we'll get dinner."

"It's a date." She went straight into his arms and he pulled her in tight. Buried his face in that tousled crazy hair and took a deep breath of her. "An actual date."

"Figured it was about time to make it official."

"You're my best friend," she said into his neck.

His chest tightened because he hadn't heard her say those four words to him in a while. It didn't mean they had ever stopped being true. "And nothing's ever going to change that."

"Promise me?"

His answer was to press his lips against hers, warm, wet and tender before she left. It was time for him to get to work on that sailboat.

There was money to be made and for once he was looking forward to Sunset Kiss.

20

"Bake the world a better place." ~ meme

I
t was time for Charley to tell Dylan all about their accidental kiss.

He'd always said that he didn't believe in the legend, but when she explained he'd have to change his mind. Why else would their connection have moved so seamlessly from friends to lovers? Because that's what they were now. Not casual, either. She'd known her share of players and that wasn't Dylan's way. He was far too serious a person for that. She could sense it in the way he'd made love to her last night. He'd seemed to lose all control.

And she'd loved it.

After making sure that Naomi had checked in on Milly one last time before she left for the day, Charley closed the bakery and went upstairs. She took a shower and then searched her closet for the shoes she'd found on clearance.

They were in the back behind her extensive collection of Chuck Taylors. Still in the box they'd come in.

"Aha! There you are, you beauties." These weren't painful contraptions designed by misogynists. They were soft tan leather ankle booties, and they were sexy as hell.

Just as she was, apparently.

They had a small heel and as she walked through the apartment looking for her keys and shutting off lights, she got accustomed somewhat to the elevation. She hopped on her moped and drove to the marina to meet Dylan. The Pacific Ocean sky was socked in, a dark and swirling color. Charley couldn't see the stars tonight, but they were there. Hiding.

Once after a particular bad day at school with the mean girls, Dylan had driven her to Yosemite in his uncle's Ranchero. Away from the city lights, the stars shined powerfully against a black velvet sky. Dylan had pulled her into his arms and whispered that the mean girls were full of shit. If they didn't like her, it was simply because they were jealous. And yes, Charley had silently agreed. Because though they might not be jealous of her unruly hair, her second-hand clothes or her shoes, they were over the fact that Dylan Reyes was her best friend. That their relationship seemed to take precedence over any of the many girls he'd dated.

That one memory had stayed with her long after he'd driven them back to the city. Never in her entire life had she had something so many others wanted. He'd always made her feel special. Unique. The seals barked as she approached the pier.

Hey there, girl! Where have you been? We missed you.

More than any other part of the city, the seals reminded

her that she was home. Now, they barked as if welcoming her.

Dylan had said to turn south at the entrance. Was that left? Or right? She spun in a circle, then continued to walk the dock south, or what seemed like it *could* be south. It was hard to tell because the sun had already set and there were only strings of fairy lights to guide her path. The marina next to the yacht club was filled with rows upon rows of all manner of watercraft. All these boats looked exactly the same to her. Motor boats, yachts, sailboats.

She got lost, walking down the different boat slips not seeing a single soul. If this was one of Dylan's pranks, his way of getting back at her for the fake engagement prank, she was going to kill him. Twice. She heard a whistle and turned. A few more steps in the direction of the whistle and she noticed a gleaming sailboat christened *Miracle One*. She sucked in a breath. Dylan had one foot braced on the edge of the boat as he watched her.

A sailboat. He was working on a *sailboat*.

"Don't tell me," he said with his half smile. "You got lost."

Giddy with the knowledge of what this sailboat could mean for their future, she grinned. "I've told you not to use words like 'south' and 'west' with me. Use my language, for instance, left and right."

"My mistake."

She rose her sexy booted foot to take another step in his direction and...couldn't move her right foot. Holy cheese-cake, the heel of her boot was stuck between two pier planks. How did she not see this coming?

She wiggled a little but nothing happened. And she did mean *nothing*.

"What's wrong?" Dylan's brow creased in concern.

"Um, nothing." She held on to her dignity since it was all she had going for her right now. "I might have...just..."

"I know you're not afraid of the water, so quit stalling and get over here." He beckoned her.

She made a jerky move and then stopped while she tried to absorb the humiliation of this moment. "I would. But I'm...stuck."

Dylan hopped over and the ease with which he moved his body was...admirable. She'd bet he'd never get stuck like this, heel or no heel. For just a moment, she yearned for her boyish Chucks which at least had never managed to get stuck between two wooden planks.

He squatted in front of her and his warm hand brushed against her ankle. "I see the problem."

Those beautiful mocha eyes gazed up at her with the hint of a smile twitching at his lips.

"Are you having fun down there? Please don't tell me we have to call the fire department."

"No problem," he said, straightening to his full height. "I have a pair of pliers inside."

"How humiliating." She covered her face.

"Would you rather me cut you out of the boot? I actually think that might be better. Hang on, don't go anywhere."

"Dylan, wait!" He turned and she caught the playful glint in his eyes.

True enough, he'd never stop messing with her. "I *really* like these boots."

His hot gaze slid up and down her legs and settled on the boots. "I like them, too."

She fisted her hands on her hips. "Get back here and let me use you as leverage!"

He strode back and planted his body in front of her. "Just what a man likes to hear."

"I told you to stop teasing me."

He met her gaze, his eyes shimmering. "And I told you I never would."

She gripped his waist, using him as an anchor, and wiggled her foot. She felt it give a little. Then she let her hands slowly drift down to his ass just because this was a good excuse to touch him.

"Oh good, this is working." She smiled up at him.

"Working for me." His hands slid to her hips and he pulled her close.

Everything inside her went flambé hot with his words, even with the sudden chill of an evening breeze. She wrenched her foot the rest of the way out and would have lost her balance if not for Dylan's grip on her.

"There!"

She moved her terribly sexy booted foot, deciding they were worth the agony after all, and angled her foot to the side to admire it. It seemed to have survived the night's humiliation intact.

"Okay?" He bent to inspect her ankle as if he thought she might have been injured.

"I'm good. Sometimes fashion is pain." That's what Milly always said, and now Charley believed her. True story.

He took her hand and led her to the boat.

She stopped at the slip to admire her future. Or what *could* be her future. "You're working on a sailboat."

He easily hopped on the boat, then held out his hand for her. In one swift move he hauled her on board by the waist.

"Ooph," Charley said when he knocked a little wind out of her. In the circle of his arms, her heart swelled with a powerful ache. This time the ache wasn't painful, but simply a warm and cozy feeling she couldn't name.

"What do you think?"

"Are we going somewhere?"

"No, but someone is." He waved to the bow. "My partner and I are going to make some serious coin come Sunset Kiss. We're going to rent it out. Three days of sailing at top dollar."

"Rent it out? To other couples?" She clutched at her chest, sure her heart had stopped beating.

"Why not? All the sailboats are rented out months in advance and he found this fixer upper. Asked me to clean it up. Figured we could make some quick money and split the profits. Couples will pay top dollar for the event."

Yes, she knew. Half of the women who dropped by the bakery had already been asked and there were always the singles who came from all over the city for the event. This year as with most, sailboats would dot the bay at sunset for all three days.

Dylan had always been the enterprising sort, and she understood that. But it was one thing to invest in a surf shop to help his brother out, quite another to take advantage of couples desperate for true love.

"Did I hear this right?" She pushed against Dylan's chest. "You're going to profit over a couple desperate to get a sail-boat? *Desperate* to declare their love for one another?"

He cocked his head. "You make that sound like a bad thing."

"It is! You're...you're..."

"Giving some couple the chance to indulge in a favorite fantasy." He shrugged.

"Taking advantage of something very...real."

"Chuck, it's not *real*. It's good for tourism and good for our community. And I'm on board with all of that."

"But you still don't believe."

"You know that better than anyone else."

She stuck out her bottom limp. "What happened to Fun Dylan?"

"Fun Dylan is alive and well. How's this? Do I believe in love? Yes. It just has nothing to do with the sunset."

21

"Don't be afraid to take whisks." ~ Apron

Damn, he was an idiot.

He should have known that Charley would see the sailboat and assume...things. Blame it on the fire and the new carefree attitude he owned. He hadn't thought this one through all the way. But he still refused to indulge her in a fantasy no matter how much he wanted the girl who believed. Even if it would, at least temporarily, make his life easier. Fun. Because this was *Charley*, and he did not lie to her. He did not sugarcoat anything and tell her only what she wanted to hear.

When they were both dating other people, it was easier to make fun of the legend. Now that he was the man in her bed, quite a different story. It he wanted to keep her, and he did, best to walk as if there were landmines every few feet.

"I'm sorry I didn't tell you about the sailboat." She

wouldn't look at him, so he pulled her to him and held on tight.

That's right, you fool. Hold her tight and don't let her go. Because the minute you turn your back, she'll be gone.

Only family stays.

"Never mind," she said, rather unconvincingly. "It's okay."

He took her by the shoulders, barely resisting the urge to shake her. "Believe in something real. Believe in yourself."

Frustration bubbled up as to why she felt the need to be special in some magical way.

"But what if it's real? What if a kiss at sunset *is* magic and suddenly you can see right in front of you who it is that you love? Who you've always loved?"

"That's a lot of what-ifs."

"What-ifs lead to what is." She tipped her chin. "Are you afraid to kiss me at sunset because you don't want to know that it *could* be me? Not for the long haul. Not...not forever."

She wasn't far from the truth. Though he didn't believe in magic, he wasn't sure he believed in forever love either. Forever friendships, sure, and that's what he already had with her. But that left him wondering about his relationship status with Charley. Friends forever, yes. For the rest he couldn't say. He knew what he wanted but what would actually happen no one could say for certain. Worse, she was forcing him to examine and evaluate when all he wanted to do was enjoy her and whatever time they'd have together.

As if she read his mind, she continued, "So what are we? Just friends? Lovers? Please don't say friends with bennies."

He flinched at the casual term. "You need a label for us? I want you more than I've ever wanted anyone. But it's always been one day at a time for me."

Another bay breeze kicked up, rolling over the waves, and she clung to him.

Hands fisted in her wild hair, he pulled her face close and forced her to look at him. "This is what we have. Here and now. Can you trust me?"

"I always have."

"Then let's go grab a clam chowder bread bowl, girl, because I'm a hungry man." He took her hand and pulled her in the direction of the wharf.

IT WAS FINALLY time for the Alice Reyes Fourth of July celebration and Charley wouldn't let anything ruin the C-word-free Celebration. Not the fact that she still wasn't really speaking to Milly. Not the fact that Dylan was possibly the most unromantic man on earth to consider overcharging couples for a sailboat on Sunset Kiss.

Today was a special day for more than one reason. Ten years ago, Alice Reyes had been given her remission news on the Fourth of July. The C-word took Coral Monroe and it almost took Alice Reyes. Charley and Milly had a pact never to say the word out loud again until the ugly beast was eradicated by modern medicine.

Alice called her remission a miracle. And if you wanted to claim a miracle, this would be the one. Charley firmly believed the "C" had been too afraid of the wrath of the beautiful boy who faithfully took his mother to her chemo appointments. Dylan had been studying fire science at the time, plus working at the marina. He took a break that semester and worked even harder to pay off the mounting medical bills. His brothers helped too, of course, but none more than Dylan. The residents of Miracle Bay rallied, organizing drives and crowdfunding to pay medical bills and keep up mortgage payments. Charley, Milly and Coral had visited often, delivering donuts, pastries and hugs. So, in a way, today was a celebration of all life's miracles, large and small.

There was only one matter that might go sideways.

On the morning of the Fourth, after she'd supervised Naomi baking, Charley ran upstairs, knocked on Milly's apartment door once and let herself in. This fight had gone on long enough and she would end it today.

"What are *you* doing here?" Milly said from the couch. "I asked Naomi to bring me a chocolate glazed donut."

"That's not healthy." Ignoring Milly's scowl, Charley went straight to the kitchen where she opened the cabinet door and pulled out a bowl. "Eggs are good for you and the bean. Protein."

She cracked three eggs, added milk, a handful of cheese, and whisked. She brought a plate of cooked eggs to Milly, but Charley didn't simply excuse herself and leave.

Milly took a bite and then studied Charley, her brow furrowed. "What is it?"

"Look." Charley took a deep breath. "I'm sorry, but I'm not leaving you. And I don't want you to be angry anymore."

"I'm sorry, too. I didn't really want you to go." Milly studied her plate. "And I'm sorry I yelled at you for giving Peter an anxiety attack."

"I totally deserved that." Charley plopped down beside Milly on the sofa, causing Rufus to hiss.

"The pregnancy hormones are making me too emotional." Milly rubbed her eyes. "If I'm not feeling homicidal then I'm crying during a kitty litter commercial."

"I've really missed you." Charley tried for a smile. "I'm coming in for a hug."

Like Coral, Milly wasn't given to spontaneous displays of affection. Charley could definitely relate. Given her past, she didn't trust hugs when they were sometimes followed by smacks. Even now, she had only a handful of people she hugged. Dylan, his family and...Milly. When she'd let her. Today all signs were clear for a landing in the arms of one very pregnant Milly. She opened arms wide and put on her little frown of acceptance, like this would be a big deal but she would allow it. It was a little awkward hugging with a huge baby bump between then, but Charley managed.

"And...I have a confession to make, but maybe your psychic wavelengths are picking up on this."

"You and Dylan? It's not the psychic waves picking it up, it's the thin walls." She made a face. "But hey, congratulations on all the orgasms."

"Um, thanks. But this is...something else."

"Huh." Milly quirked a brow. "Wait. I'm sensing...guilt. Which makes sense, because of Peter and all, but...no, that's not it. This is about *food*. That's not like you. Why are you feeling guilty about food? Are you sick or something? What's wrong with you?"

Maybe Milly *was* psychic. "You're close. I've been expanding our menu. Now, don't get mad, I can explain—"

"Why would I be mad?"

"You and Coral never wanted to do anything but pastries. This was always to be a bakery and nothing more." She stopped and spoke slowly in Coral's no-nonsense tone. "Don't want to get greedy, you know."

"But I kept everything the same after she died because I was too lazy to change anything. I might be my mother's daughter, but we don't do everything alike. I mean, just look at me." She pointed to her belly. "Can you even picture our mother knocked up and unmarried?"

They both laughed so hard that Rufus, highly annoyed, hopped off his perch and left the room.

"Honestly," Milly said, looking behind her. "When I first got pregnant, I half worried she'd come back to haunt me and scold me for the rest of my days."

"I know. I was really worried about you. The trouble you'd be in. It took me a minute to remember." Charley spoke slowly, hesitantly. "Sometimes...it feels like she's still here."

Milly nodded. "For me, too."

"Do you know why I looked for Maggie?" Charley asked.

"Because you wanted to know her, to see if you'd turn out just like her."

Charley opened her mouth, then closed it again. Of course, Milly would understand.

"I worry I'll be like my mom sometimes, too. Overprotective. Overbearing. Worried all the time. Afraid of men. A little afraid of life. Of course, the thing is, I hope I'll be all of the good things she was, too. Like loyal and compassionate. Kind. A good businesswoman. You and I both know no one is either all good or all bad. We're all made up of both nature and nurture. The good thing is we get to pick who we're going to be. Who we want to be. And I hope you agree that I may look like my mother, but I'm not like her. For instance, I'm taller than she was. I have bigger hips even if I don't want them. My hair is straighter. And I don't think all men are horrible creatures that only want to get in my pants. I wish! But I do wonder how I wound up with my Aunt Nancy's feet. Her feet are just like mine." Milly wiggled her toes. "Barney Rubble feet."

Charley hadn't ever given all that much thought to the obvious differences between Milly and Coral. Still, there were times when Milly said something or smiled a certain way, and Charley thought: *Coral.* Mother and daughter were linked to each other inevitably, both through DNA and love.

Charley had the biology with Maggie, but she'd never had the love. Or if she'd had it, it was the ghost of a memory now. Yet she couldn't forget her mother. Couldn't forget the way she'd brushed Charley's hair one hundred times until it shined. Or how beautiful she was all made up like a movie star. She'd been a goddess to Charley. Red lipstick, blonde hair long and wavy, wearing her high-heeled boots, leather jacket and jeans. Tossing her head back, laughing, telling Charley that one day they were going to live in a castle and have servants waiting on them. *Then* she'd buy Charley all the Barbies and ice cream she wanted.

But instead one day all the sparkle and shine that was Maggie was just gone. While the system, she understood now, had worked for family reunification, Maggie didn't hold up her end of the deal. And no other family had wanted Charley until Coral and Milly. Even though logically she now understood that as a child none of it could have been her fault, there remained one ridiculous part of her that believed with all her heart that nothing would have ever gone wrong if she'd simply been good enough.

"I loved Coral. And I stopped looking for Maggie. I was afraid that I'd get rejected by her all over again. And then finally one day I realized that it didn't matter anymore. I already had the mother I wanted. I didn't choose her, and I didn't deserve her either. But she chose me. You both did. And she never threw me away even if maybe...she should have. It would have been easier."

"If she'd even *tried* to kick you out, I would have stopped her."

"Aw."

"You were my sister from the moment you walked in that

door looking like the tomboy in *Some Kind of Wonderful*. You know I love shoes, the fancier the better, but somehow I've always wanted to rock a pair of Chucks the way you do."

"It's official. When I die, I'm leaving you every pair I own."

"Stop it. You're going to make me ugly cry."

"I'M TOO big to move. Just leave me here, and if I give birth while you're gone I'll try not to make a big mess." Milly hid behind a pillow, Rufus as usual in his perch above her as Cat Guard.

The party would start soon, and Milly still wasn't dressed.

"Sorry, no." Charley went hands on hips and Rufus hissed at her. "The doctor said *modified* bed rest. I've been letting you get away with this, but I looked it up. Modified means you can get up for a couple of hours every day. I'm not going without you. This is a big day. The C-free cele-bration—"

Milly smacked her forehead. "Oh crap, this means I have to get out of my yoga pants, doesn't it?"

"Wear the yoga pants. No one minds." Charley gave Milly a hand up.

"No, I want to look nice." Milly waddled to the bedroom. "You never know who I could meet. Maybe the man of my daydreams."

Charley snorted.

Milly turned back, rubbing her belly. "Kidding. I'm a little busy here."

Alice Reyes' three-story Victorian home was at the crest of one long and steep hill. It was several blocks from the bakery and a bit of a hike up the hill so for Milly's sake they drove the short distance. The house was already full to the brim when they arrived, but it usually was a full house anyway with all of Mrs. Reyes tenants.

The handsome Tutti, one of Charley's favorite boarders, opened the door. "Well, hello kids! Welcome to the fray! It's the cancer-free celebration and we're all atwitter."

"Actually, I think you mean Twitter," said Milly as she waddled past him.

Mrs. Reyes was right behind Tutti with hugs for everyone. Charley carried her paninis and followed Alice into the kitchen to set her plate down with the rest of the food. She kissed Abuelita, who leaned toward the stove and stirred a pot of soup as only an octogenarian could pull off without looking lazy. After saying hello to half a dozen people from the neighborhood and bakery regulars, Charley found Milly where Dylan had apparently deposited her. She was outside in a chaise chair parked near a tray of pretzels and chips.

"Have you seen Dylan?"

"I think he went looking for you, but I can't say I've seen him since he treated me like an invalid."

"Oh, c'mon, he was just trying to help."

"Wow. Kidding. Boy, you really don't get my sense of humor anymore." She waved her hands in a circular motion. "Hmm. I'm feeling a little upset in your aura."

Ashley Banning, one of Dylan's many exes walked toward Milly, a Corona in one hand. What was *she* doing here?

"Oh, okay," Milly said. "I see."

"Hey there, you two." She gave Milly a full appraisal. "Oh, you poor thing, look how *big* you are."

"I'm pregnant." Milly deadpanned. "Not *fat*."

Ashley laughed behind her hand. "You're so funny. I'm a

nurse, you know. Call me anytime if you have any questions."

"She's got a doctor," Charley said. "A good one."

"I'm only a phone call away."

"So is the doctor." Charley swallowed. "Does Dylan know you're here?"

"I hope so. He invited me. We're friends now. Kind of like you and he are. You know, besties."

Either it was Charley's imagination or there was a tone of smugness in her words. Ashley was never going to be friends with Dylan the way he'd been with Charley, so why did her entire body tense in response? Maybe it was because Ashley was eyeballing her like *Charley* had done something wrong. Like she'd been pretending to be his friend for thirteen *years*. Like maybe she'd broken the two of them up when she'd done no such thing. Dylan had dated a lot of women, and now...well, now it was Charley's turn.

"I'm going to go find Dylan," Charley said.

But she was stopped by Padre Suarez, Mrs. Sorrento, Marco and Donna before she finally found Dylan in the kitchen. He was forcing Abuelita to take a seat.

"I'm fine, mijo!" She waved arthritic fingers dismissively.

"Then why do you look like you're going to fall over?" He glanced up and made eye contact with Charley. "There you are."

"I was looking for you," Charley said.

After asking his Uncle Rick to watch out for his grandmother, Dylan pulled her out of the kitchen.

"Did you know Ashley is here?" Charley said.

"Yeah." He took her hand and led her out of the kitchen to the patio. "My mom invited her."

Right. That made sense. Alice was forever trying to get her oldest son married off.

The moment Charley stepped onto the brick patio floor, one of Alice's tenants used a spoon to ping against a glass. "Everyone! I've got an announcement to make."

Everyone turned to the tall and slender man holding his arm out wide.

"For those who don't know me, I'm Dan. As many of you know, I moved to San Francisco not knowing a single soul. I met Alice and Pepita Reyes and my entire world changed. I had a place to live and a family. Friends." He held up his glass in a toast. "This celebration is just one more day to enjoy life but Alice does that every day. Thank you, Alice. Because of you, I met my soulmate, Izzy."

A dark-haired woman next to him smiled and he pulled her into an embrace.

"She rented a room on the same floor, and we became friends right away. We spent time in the common area and helped cook meals together. Eventually that led to some dates, and...some other stuff."

Everyone laughed, Charley included. She reached for Dylan's hand and squeezed it.

"Yes, we took the sailboat last August and kissed at sunset! I would have waited a month, but because today is such a special day..." The man dropped to one knee and everyone gasped. "Izzy, would you marry me?"

Izzy was saying "yes" over and over again, kissing Dan and practically levitating. Everyone clapped, even Dylan. Charley's hands were too numb to clap.

Alice fanned her eyes, trying to hold back the waterworks. "He hasn't even told you the best part. They lived within a mile of each other where they grew up in Kansas City. Never even met until they both moved here. Everyone, this happened because they met here in Miracle Bay!

Another miracle, I'm telling you! This is the place for love and miracles."

More clapping.

Dylan snorted. "Okay, Ma."

Charley didn't clap. She didn't smile. One more sunset kiss miracle. How many did that make now?

She'd lost count.

22

"Sex is kinda like cooking. Everyone can do it, but only some can make it delicious."~ Apron

D ylan wanted to personally thank Dan on behalf of single men everywhere for making them all feel like chumps.

Seriously. *A miracle?* True love because of a stupid kiss at sunset? He had insider information on said miracle and if these two were together, it was largely due to the machinations of one Alice Ramona Reyes. He had a good guess how this miracle had happened. When she'd done their respective background checks for renting to them, it hadn't been that difficult to discover that they were both originally from the same area.

His mother then put Izzy on the same floor with Dan and introduced them. After that, he'd heard from Abuelita that she'd conspired to have them run into each other in the kitchen and the common areas. She somehow wound up with two tickets to a Giants game at the AT&T Park when neither one of them was busy and sent them on their way. She wasn't a horrible matchmaker, his mother.

The part about them living a mile from each other but never having met he hadn't heard before. Odd coincidence. But a miracle?

Charley stood next to him, holding his hand. She'd just watched a romantic proposal and for the first time he began to wonder if it was so crazy to indulge her. Maybe that was exactly what he should do. He simply refused to do it as a result of pressure, but the facts were that he wanted to make her happy. There should be no harm in going out on a sailboat next month with the rest of the suckers. It might even be fun.

Charley moved away from him when Milly waved her over, but she squeezed his hand before she left. For the next couple of hours, he tried to enjoy the party. Boarders, family, friends and neighbors were spilling out of the house. He tried to avoid his ex, Ashley, obviously invited by his overly kind mother. It meant leaving each room when she entered it. This meant he had to be hyper-aware of where she was at all times. Exhausting.

He found Milly sitting on a chaise lounge. "Seen Charley?"

"She went up to the balcony looking for you," Milly said. "You two should download the 'find your buddies app.' Saves you lots of time and walking."

The patio upstairs off the third floor was a quiet, out-of-the-way spot. A place he knew well. As a child he used to hide there after a favorite tenant had left. Some of them had children who had become his friends. Many had hung out with him on days when his brothers were too annoying, his mother was too busy, and his father was pulling a long shift at the station.

Charley stood with her back to him, against the backdrop of the cresting sunset, her golden hair shimmering in the last rays. She turned slightly and gave him a smile which made his chest tighten.

"Hey, you." He wrapped his arms around her waist and pulled her to him, dropping his head to her shoulder as she continued to watch the sun slip down.

"I couldn't find you, so I came up here to watch the sunset."

If he never heard the word *sunset* again it might be too soon. He took the high road. "Beautiful, isn't it?"

She turned in his arms, her hands coming to rest against his chest. "I-I have to tell you something—"

He had a feeling that something to do with what they'd heard a few minutes ago and while he might not be a sappy romantic, he had other skills. He covered her mouth with a kiss and shut her up. Her hands went to his spine and fingers drifted lightly up his back and down again leaving behind a trail of electricity. This was better than air. Better than forever. Because, and here was the truth, *this* was real. Charley moaned into his mouth and he smiled against her lips as he tugged her even closer pulling them hip to hip, belly to belly. She seemed ready to scale him like a monkey. And hell yeah, he would welcome that.

But just then a loud crash jolted him out of his lust, and he turned to see his mother.

23

"Today's mood is cranky with a touch of psycho." ~ *Pregnancy meme*

A shattered china teacup lay on the ground.

"I'm sorry to interrupt," his mother said. "I just didn't know...I...I...."

"It's okay, Mom," Dylan said. "Let's not have an aneurysm."

"But the two of you! I'm so delighted! Even if I didn't have anything to do with it." She bent to pick up the chipped pieces of ceramic off the floor.

"Don't." He stayed her hands. "You might cut yourself."

Yes, thank you, Dylan. Ever the safety nut, aren't you?

"I have to go check on Milly. You know how she is. She needs me." She moved so fast he only saw the back of her as she practically ran down the hall.

"Don't let me keep you," Mom called after Charley. "Leave that alone, Dylan. I'll get the broom in a minute."

"Let me take care of this." He started to brush by her on his way to get the broom when she grabbed a handful of his shirt.

"Not so fast."

Oh, good. His mother wanted to *talk*. "Yeah?"

"How long has this been going on between you and Charley and why didn't I know about it?"

"Sorry, I forgot to ask Marco to pass you a note during recess."

"Very funny, Dylan. I'm your mother and I should know who you're dating. If I'd known I could have saved you the embarrassment of having Ashley here tonight."

When she put it that way..."This is new. It just happened recently and I—"

"Didn't expect it." She nodded sagely.

He was about to say "so glad we had this talk" when she got a wistful look in her eyes and moved to the edge of the balcony that faced the port and gleaming bay in the distance. "Do you want to know why I came out here with my now broken cup of tea?"

Actually, he'd forgotten to ask, seeing as there were a few other things on his mind at the time, but it was interesting that she'd come to the balcony alone. In the middle of her celebration. For years, she'd been at the center of the celebration, always as happy as on the first day she'd received news of her remission.

"Why?"

"So glad you asked, son. I do this every year and no one notices I'm gone. It's just the way I want it." She turned to meet his eyes. "This party got out of hand a while ago."

"Why didn't you say something? We don't have to do this every year."

"I don't mind sharing my happiness and joy with family.

With my dear friends. And anyway, all I need is a few minutes to myself with my tea. I look out at the bay and count my blessings. I've survived losing a husband, and nearly losing my own life. I have three sons I adore, and a mother-in-law who thinks of me as a daughter." Her green eyes pierced his. "Do you think maybe I know a thing or two about life? About love?"

"Sure."

"I worry," she said, hardly missing a beat. "Two of my sons are firefighters and I have no control over that. You know that I support you, even though I wish you'd chosen careers as accountants."

He sighed because he'd heard that one before. A few hundred thousand times. This was why, if he had anything to do with it, she'd never hear about his close call.

"But when it comes to love, *that's* where I can give you some real advice."

He shoved a hand through his hair, knowing nothing would stop her now.

"You had a front row seat to how I fell apart after your father died. Yet you chose to go into the profession anyway. And you've never been serious about a woman. You won't allow yourself that happiness with someone because of how it hurt me to lose your father."

"It hurt us all."

"But that's the thing, honey. Instead of choosing another, safer profession, you chose to give up on love and a family someday. Did you ever ask yourself why?"

"Because being a firefighter is all I've ever wanted to do."

"I know. You take risks with your life, but you've never risked your heart."

She was right about one thing. Risking a heart was why he'd never wanted to be more than friends with Charley.

Fear had held him back. Not just fear that she would leave, but fear that he might someday leave her. But that was then. Life was short, and he was taking what he wanted.

And what he wanted was Charley.

"Don't worry about me. I promise, I've got everything under control. And I'm happy."

~

CHARLEY FOUND Milly asleep and Abuelita snoring peacefully beside her.

Charley cleared her throat.

Milly's eyes shot open. "Holy Ritz crackers, don't scare me like that."

"Sorry, but I was surprised to find you asleep. Are you that tired?"

She narrowed her gaze on Charley. "Am I tired? Or maybe I'd rather close my eyes while Abuelita gives me the third degree. I wasn't really sleeping. Just faking it so she'd stop asking me about the baby's father. And you know what? It worked because she got bored and fell asleep."

Charley's gaze went to Dan and Izzy, who were dancing in the moonlight without music. "Aw. Would you look at them?"

"They're really sweet. In a super sappy way."

"I want that," Charley said. "Super sappy and happy. Don't you?"

"I don't know. Maybe I could take some sap here and there. Someday."

"I want that for you." Charley squeezed Milly's arm.

"Yeah, me too," Milly said, and Charley was surprised by the admission.

"Move over." She squeezed in on the small space left next to Milly.

It was a beautiful night. The fairy lights strung through low branches of trees in the garden gave a warm glow to the evening. Heat lamps placed around the yard's perimeter did their duty. The first firework went up in the distance, a green flash of light that rose in the sky and exploded in a spectacular burst of brightness. The brash sound crackled into the night air and was followed by the soft awed sounds of onlookers. Then another firework followed, this one making a high-pitched whistle before it exploded like a million stars.

Charley sensed his heat before the saw him. She turned to see Dylan walking toward her. From the moment she locked on to his gaze, he did not break eye contact. He squatted next to her and possessively placed his hand on her thigh.

"Hey."

"Hey, Dylan," Milly said, then turned her gaze back to the fiery sky.

"You okay there? Not going into labor yet, are you?" Dylan said.

"Nah, I'm good," Milly said not taking her eyes off the display. "I'm glad I came. This was fun."

Dylan's warmth encircled Charley, chasing off the evening chill. Her heart feeling too large to fit in her chest, she glanced up at the display of lights and explosions.

When the last of the finale sparkles lit up the night, she closed her eyes and wished she could feel this happy and content...for just a little while longer.

24

"Where there's a whisk, there's a way." ~ Kitchen magnet

On the short drive back, Charley was forced to listen to Milly complain about how many people had fawned all over her tonight and treated her like she was helpless. Two women had the audacity to touch her stomach without permission. Another had offered the best names for both a boy or a girl. To hear Milly tell it, they might as well have suggested she name her baby after a dictator. Still another extolled the virtues of the "family bed," something called "attachment parenting," nursing, and baby-led weaning.

Good Lord, this baby business was so overwhelming. How was Milly ever going to...no. Milly could and would handle this. Charley would no longer intervene. She'd learned her lesson.

Milly unlocked her apartment door and turned to

Charley and Dylan. "You two mind if I fall asleep before you start going at it? I mean, thin walls and all."

Charley winced and nodded several times.

"Thirty minutes is all I need," Milly said, apparently enjoying herself. "I'm actually so sleepy it shouldn't take long."

She shut the door with a smirk, leaving Charley and Dylan in the hallway.

"That was embarrassing," Charley said.

"Wouldn't know. I'm not the noisy one." He waggled his eyebrows.

Dylan wore black jeans low on his hips and a long-sleeved gray tee pushed up to his elbows. His forearms were arm candy. And there again was that old pang of desire and longing for him rising up in her, so much a part of her life that she wouldn't know what to do without the feeling.

"What should we do for thirty minutes?" Charley asked.

"You can either kiss me or use the thirty minutes to tell me why you ran away earlier."

She should have guessed he of all people wouldn't buy into the Milly excuse. He knew her far too well.

"Okay. So, I was kind of embarrassed. It was a weird way for her to find out about us."

Dylan slid his arms around her waist and pulled her to him. "Don't run from me again, Chuck. Whatever it is, I need to know you're not going to take off when things get tough."

"I won't. I promise you." Tipping to the balls of her feet she kissed him right here in the hallway, long and lingering, the taste of him familiar and comforting but able to light her up like a cinder.

He broke the kiss and smiled at her from underneath

hooded lids. "If we go inside, it will be three seconds before I have you naked and about to be very happy."

"Ice cream," she suggested, knowing he was one hundred percent correct. "We haven't had ice cream since I got back."

"True," he said, tugging on her hand. "It's one thing that might cool me down."

In fact, all they needed to cool down on a summer evening in San Francisco was to simply step outside. But Charley, as a rule, never turned down an excuse for ice cream. Dylan held her hand as they walked the short block to Mr. and Mrs. Miscellaneous in the Dogpatch district.

She sat next to him with one hand on his jean-clad thigh, eating her cone one-handed. Over the years and through all the different restaurants she'd worked in, she'd watched couples sit together. Eventually she'd reached the point where she could pinpoint exactly when a couple had become intimate. It was in the body language. The way their bodies physically tilted toward each other, holding hands, touching hair, thighs, necks. Lips. Hot and pure envy had cut through her, nearly choking her with its strength.

And now she was the other half of one of those couples that she'd envied, with a man that meant more to her than the air she breathed. A man who would probably be upset with her when she told him about the accidental kiss. A sunset kiss. He might even feel a little betrayed. As if she'd been trying to trap him. But it had been an accident. He'd understand. Sure he would.

"What is it?" He tucked a stray hair behind her ear. "I can hear you thinking."

She choked on the ball of fear lodged in her throat and pointed to his chocolate ice cream. "I like chocolate, but there's nothing quite like a good French vanilla ice cream a la mode with warmed Dutch apple pie in a little hint of caramel. Sometimes it's good to get back to basics."

He smirked. "I never thought I'd hear *you* say that."

"Oh, yeah? Well, you're going to hear me say a lot of things you never heard me say before."

He quirked a brow. "Already have."

"Didn't mean *that*." She stuck out her tongue and he took full advantage of that by leaning forward to give it a love bite.

The storefront door opened, and a couple came in and headed to the counter. Jenny Santana and...Sean. Naturally.

"Who's that with Jenny?" Dylan asked casually. "I don't recognize him."

"Oh, that's...I meant to tell you. You remember Sean, the guy I work with sometimes? I guess it didn't work out in New Orleans, so he followed me out here and found a job at Sorrel's."

"He *followed* you here." Dylan scowled. "Sean *Hannigan*?"

While she'd never told Dylan the full extent of her relationship with Sean, Dylan most unfortunately happened to be the person she'd confided in the most. Whenever Sean ridiculed her soufflés or tortes, Dylan got an earful and more often a text full of devil emojis. Consequently, he wasn't the guy's biggest fan. And that Reyes machismo seemed to be rearing its head as Dylan stared bullet holes into Sean's back.

"Dylan." Charley squeezed his thigh. "Earth to Dylan."

"That guy's an asshole."

"I know that. But he's not my problem anymore, or yours." She turned him back to face her, framing his face.

Dylan's jaw twitched, and he gave the side-eye to Sean. "But that time you called me, crying, because he yelled at you in front of the entire staff? That's a problem for me."

"I think maybe we should go back now." Charley threaded her fingers through his thick hair. "It's been at least thirty minutes and now I just want to get you hot all over again."

She'd managed to distract him, and smoldering eyes met hers. "Yeah? What did you have in mind?"

"You'll find out." She stood and tugged on his hand.

"Hey, Charley!" Sean called out.

She might have ignored Sean, pretended she didn't hear him and kept walking, except for the fact that Dylan stood as still as a statue and about as difficult to move.

"Oh, yeah. Hi, Sean." She turned to Jenny. "Sean, this is Dylan."

"Heard so much about you." Sean stuck out his hand but Dylan did not accept it. He simply gave him quick, sharp nod.

Awkward.

Sean recovered and pulled Jenny close. She glued her body to his like a stamp to a letter. So...*that* had happened. Not that Charley had any doubt Sean would close the deal in a matter of days.

"Jenny is showing me around. I had wanted to catch the fireworks at the Pier, but she convinced me it's not worth the nightmare of parking."

"Newbie," Jenny said on a laugh.

"We're just walking around the Dogpatch trying a little bit of everything. Earlier we had the crepes at *Chez Maman*."

"Sean is *so* talented," Jenny said. "He really knows his food."

"Great. You must enjoy working with Charley, seeing as she's the best," Dylan said tightly.

Charley squeezed Dylan's hand. There was a bit of a dare in his bold statement. A challenge for Sean to deny it. But while Sean Hannigan was a lot of things, stupid was not one of them.

"Absolutely. Sure do."

"We have to go now. Nice seeing you." Charley pulled on Dylan's hand and thank God this time he moved.

"Charley," Sean said. "Forgot to tell you. I've recommended you for the job in Paris, so you should make your plans soon."

Charley froze, afraid to move. She could feel Dylan's entire body tense, and his hand was suddenly so still she half wondered if he still had a heartbeat.

Charley glared at Sean. "I didn't tell you that I wanted that job."

"Yes, you did. And it's Paris. How could you not? Every chef has to visit Paris at least once."

"You couldn't keep me away from Paris if I had half the chance," Jenny said, adding a shoulder shimmy. "Lucky you, Charley."

"Tell me about it. Charley and I used to lay awake at night in bed, dreaming of going to all the places Julia Child lived and worked."

And there it was. Sean's classy way of letting everyone within earshot know that he'd been with Charley. That she'd been with him. Not her proudest moment. Then, or now.

Jenny glared at Charley. "Seriously? I didn't know that."

"Charley and I dated for a while." He turned to Dylan, giving him a nod. "I'm sure you knew that."

Charley wanted a snappy comeback because it was in

her, somewhere, and she'd probably come up with the perfect zinger while lying in bed tonight. But for now, she had nothing.

Dylan led her out of the ice cream shop and they left without another word.

25

"It's not the pregnancy hormones. I've never liked you." ~
Maternity T-shirt

G ood thing Dylan had a decent walk ahead of
him up a hill in the brisk evening. He needed to
run some of his stress and anger off, but the
walk would have to do. Charley managed to keep up with
his long strides, clutching his hand, her palm sweaty. He
probably looked the picture of a jealous man and he wasn't
thrilled to hear about her and Sean. But the biggest
problem for him was knowing that she'd been with the
guy who used to make her feel like she was nothing. He'd
have put a stop to that if she'd been in the city, but he
couldn't very well protect her when she was far away
from him.

"Let me explain." She began to sound a little out of
breath as she half walked, half jogged to keep up with his
long strides. "Dylan."

Anger, hurt and frustration pulsed through his veins. "Not now."

Inside her apartment, she stood on her tiptoes, putting a hand on each of his shoulder. "I'm sorry I didn't tell you about Sean." Her eyes were watery.

"I didn't think you were a virgin, but seriously...*Sean*? You hated that guy. You had me hate him."

"I know." She covered her face with both hands, then lowered them. "I was lonely away from home. He wasn't always mean to me. And...I think maybe he was all I thought I deserved."

"Damn it, Chuck." He pulled her to him, till her head was flush against his chest. "I hate that you ever felt that way."

"That's because you're Dylan."

"No, it's because I know what you deserve. And apparently it's a lot more than you believe." Maybe now he could face some other truths. "I'm afraid I kept you away from all those other dudes who were never good enough in my eyes simply because...they weren't me."

She stared up at him. "You mean...you wanted me even then?"

"I never *let* myself want you. You would think I'd be used to people coming and going in my life. Just never thought it would be you, even as much as you talked about Paris and Julia Child. The first time you left slayed me."

"Dylan, if I'd only known—"

"Sean was right about one thing. Paris is the opportunity of a lifetime."

"I'm not going anywhere."

"I want to believe that."

"Then do. This thing between us? It means more to me than anything. Even...even food."

"C'mere." He hauled her into his arms holding on tight, fooling himself that he could always keep her close. There were warm tears against his neck. "We're done arguing about this."

"Oh, good. Because I actually really hate arguing with you." She licked his neck and sent a bolt of electricity straight to his groin. "But since this is confession night, I have something to confess. Something else that you don't know because I've never told you. And as long as we're talking about awkward stuff you didn't know..."

"Tell me."

She held up her index finger. "But first."

"Seriously?"

She sashayed to the kitchen and brought him back a cold beer. "For you."

"Trying to get me drunk and take advantage of me?" He winked.

"Ha ha." She led him to the couch and they both sat. "Now, I tell you."

"Whose DNA did you have processed?"

"Oh, no! It's not that. I told you I stopped, and I meant it." She took a breath. "This is something about us. You and me."

He took a gulp of the cold beer, letting the cool liquid slide down his throat. "Something *I* don't know about?"

She nodded. "You know that I care about you and I would never do anything to trick you, or hurt you, or in any way take advantage of you?"

Jesus. "What did you do?"

"Remember last year? When you fell asleep watching *Scarface* and I got irritated and left you that note?"

A night he wouldn't ever forget, since the next morning

he'd woken with the strange dream. "Yeah, of course. Still haven't seen *Letters from Juliet*. By the way, thank you for that."

"You're welcome." She took a deep breath. "That night, I kissed you without your permission. You were asleep, and you looked so tired. I felt so bad about how hard you'd been working. I was leaving in a couple of weeks and already missing you. I just got carried away."

"That's it? That's what you've been wanting to tell me?" Waves of pure relief flooded him.

She'd kissed him. That might explain why somehow subconsciously his brain had turned to thoughts of the two of them together. Because she'd made the first move and he'd reacted even in his sleep. He was still surprised a kiss hadn't woken him up but at the time he'd been working long hours on little sleep. Then again, in another way the kiss certainly had *woken him up.*

"That's not all."

He stood. "Wait. What else could have done that didn't wake me up? I'm not *that* heavy of a sleeper."

She went flush pink. "No, no. It's not that. It's just that... when I went into the kitchen, I looked out the window and saw the...the sunset."

"And?"

She popped up out of her seat, joining him. "Dylan! The sunset kiss. I kissed you at sunset, which wasn't fair to do without asking you. But I swear it was an accident!"

"An accidental kiss?"

"Well, no. The kiss wasn't an accident. I meant *that*. But the sunset part...that wasn't planned. It just happened. I swear." She held up her palm.

The thought was interesting if nothing else. Intriguing to

think that a myth had anything to do with his feelings for her when he understood that sunset or not, that kiss did change everything. Because he remembered. It hadn't been a dream at all.

"I'm glad you kissed me."

"You're not mad about the sunset?"

"The important part was that the kiss wasn't an accident." He hesitated. "And did you say anything to me after you kissed me?"

She hesitated. "No."

Interesting. That part, the "I love you" must have been added by his creative imagination. "You know what this means, don't you?"

"What?"

"*You* actually kissed me first." He grinned, feeling a little smug about this now.

"But mine didn't really count."

"Oh, it counts."

"How? You didn't even know until just now."

"Still counts. I'm counting it." He picked her up in his arms and carried her toward the bedroom.

"I guess we could table this argument for another time," she said, her eyes brightening.

He dumped her on the made bed and pulled off his shirt with one arm while with the other he started on his belt.

She stared at him, already removing her top and unzipping her jeans. "I love when you do that."

"Take my shirt off?" He grinned, unbuckling his belt.

"With one hand. Damn, it's so sexy. Do guys practice that when they're alone?" She tossed her bra and panties to the side, this time a shiny black set.

She was quite sexy herself, lying on the bed completely naked. Waiting for him. He had to stop and study her for a minute, simply enjoying her curves and creamy skin. She drove him out of his ever-loving mind, but it was her incredible heart that slayed him. A heart for her sister, such that she'd risk losing Milly so that she wouldn't have to be alone. A heart for him and his family. For their neighborhood.

The same heart that he'd always wanted to protect.

26

"Food is memories." ~ Kitchen magnet

The next morning Charley's internal clock woke her at four o'clock before her cellphone alarm. It was official. She'd become accustomed to baker's hours. But she'd never get used to waking up next to Dylan, lying naked next to her. His muscular arm slung possessively across her even in his sleep. His breaths slow and even. She took a moment just to enjoy the view. To let her fingers glide down the arm curled over her waist. To brush her hand slowly down his chest to his rock-hard abs.

He was so gorgeous, his tanned skin such a contrast to hers. His dark hair was tousled with an adorable morning look, and he had sexy bristle dusting his chin and jaw.

She managed to slide out from under Dylan's arm carefully so as not to wake him. If she planned this right, she'd be back here before he even woke up and leave the morning rush to Naomi. She'd bring coffee for Dylan and his favorite scone for when he woke up.

Checking in on Milly, who for once was sleeping, she fed Rufus and then headed downstairs. Naomi had already let herself in and started mixing in the giant industrial mixer.

"I got here early and started the coffee and the mixing."

"You're a lifesaver." Charley went for a cup of the magic beans. "I was up so late last night that I'm surprised I didn't sleep through my alarm."

"No problem. I—" Naomi stopped talking.

Charley turned to see the number one reason she'd been up so late. He must have gotten up seconds after she'd left him. His hair was wet from a shower, and he was dressed in yesterday's clothes.

"Hey," Charley said. "I was going to bring you coffee."

"I'll take it to go. Joe and I are going to meet for lunch and I need to head home for a change of clothes." He smiled at Naomi. "Hey."

"Hi, D-Dylan," Naomi said, still wide-eyed, jaw slackened.

Charley filled a Styrofoam cup, came out from behind the counter, and handed it to him.

He took the cup and tugged her in for a quick and tender kiss. Charley thought he was being sweet in front of teenage Naomi, all up until the moment he cupped and squeezed her bottom.

"I was going to come back up in a few minutes and make it worth your while," she whispered in his ear.

"Raincheck."

"Okay," she said, reluctantly letting him go. "Stay safe."

"See you soon." He slid her his tipped grin and was out the door.

"Wow." Naomi stared after him. "You and Dylan *Reyes*?"

Rather than join Naomi in the "let's see who can stare at Dylan's ass the longest contest," Charley decided to be the grown-up in the room. She got busy in the back by the large mixer and warming ovens, Naomi at her elbow waiting for Charley to give her the clean and wholesome version of last night. Problem being, there wasn't one.

"Yes, we're seeing each other."

"But I thought he was engaged to a seventy-year-old woman!"

Seriously, no one could keep their fake facts straight around here. Charley cleared her throat. "Ugly rumor."

"Tell me all about you two. And not just the PG version. Let me at least have the PG-13."

"See, we've known each other for a long time. He's a good guy, not just drop-dead handsome, because that's important. And we're both grown-ups. I feel *safe* with him. Do you know what I mean?"

Naomi gave a horrified look. "Omigod, you're not going to lecture me about safe sex, are you?"

She *was* going to do just that, in fact, but now Naomi had her second-guessing. "Do you *want* me to lecture you about safe sex?"

She covered her ears. "No!"

"Okay, then. All you have to do is say so." She moved to the giant bags of flour. "Glad we cleared that up."

"Actually," Naomi said. "If you're in the mood for advice, I kind of have this good friend of mine. A boy. He's really hot."

"Just say no," Charley said and then caught herself. She sounded way too much like Coral Monroe for her liking.

Oh, crap. It was much easier to avoid talking to a teenaged girl about complicated things like love. And sex. For the first time in her life, Charley felt actual sympathy for

Coral. She'd raised two teenage girls, both of them boy crazy, with one of them who didn't follow anyone's rules.

"I mean," Charley quickly corrected herself, "so, you have this friend. And...?"

"Here's the thing. I mean, I really think I want to kiss him."

"And the problem is?"

"He's my *friend*. I mean, he doesn't see me that way." At this, her shoulders drooped in misery.

How many times had this scenario played itself across the halls of high schools all over the country? The world? What she did know was that not all boys or men were Dylan Reyes. Not all boys would refrain from taking full advantage of the situation. The proximity. Hence the term friends with benefits, which she understood went both ways. But Charley *was* grateful that Dylan hadn't ever made a move when they were younger because timing was everything. She didn't think that teenage Charley would have been a good match for Dylan for anything more than friendship.

Of course, the jury was still out on whether she was a good match as a full-grown adult, either. She had to admit, though, she now had a pound of hope. And a stick of butter.

"How good of a friend?"

"Pretty good. I mean, he's in my tight circle of friends."

"Would you say he has your back whenever you're in trouble?"

"I don't get in trouble."

"Right." Charley took a different approach. "What's his family like?"

"Dude, I'm not going to marry the guy! I just want to go out with him."

"I know. You're far too young to think about getting married. *I'm* too young to think about it."

Naomi squinted. "You are?"

Charley scoffed. "Never mind, Naomi!"

"Well? What should I *do*?"

"Just tell him how you feel and see what happens. You could be surprised."

As the morning customers came and went, Charley came to terms with the obvious fact that she, Charlotte Rae Young, was plenty old enough to get married and maybe even old enough to...gulp...have kids. The thought made her grip the edge of the counter. But Dylan wasn't...he didn't seem ready to...okay, deep breaths. In and out. In and out. She was getting *way* ahead of herself. No need to worry. They were new, still trying this thing out which so far was going wonderfully.

Because if she'd been afraid for Milly to raise a child, Charley was simply terrified of the idea. What kind of a mother would she be? Would she be like Maggie or like Coral? Somewhere in between? The Google searches Charley had performed claimed a mother-to-be's wacked-out hormones made her, well, wacky. Crazy Town. Milly had (ahem) become psychic. Maybe Charley would become Maggie through the freaking magic of hormones. No, no. That wasn't possible. It didn't work that way. Pregnancy didn't change a woman *or* her brain. It didn't change who they were at their core. And Charley loved her family and her friends and wouldn't abandon a pet, much less a person.

Later that morning when Charley had gone to feed Milly lunch and then carried more trays filled with paninis downstairs, there was only one customer left in the shop.

"He's been here a while." Naomi nodded in the man's direction. "Just drinking coffee and using the free wifi."

"Well, if he's still here in a few minutes maybe we can talk him into having lunch."

Naomi eyed the covered trays. "What's all that?"

"The future." She peeled back the tin foil. "My paninis. Smoked salmon, sliced roasted turkey breast, prosciutto and marinated chicken breast. Help me move some of these pastries over so we can put these out."

"Milly said this was okay?"

"The crazy thing is, she did. She's okay with us trying something new."

"How's she doing? Since you guys stopped fighting, I never even see Milly anymore." Naomi nodded to the lone guy at the table. "Actually, that dude was asking about her."

"What did you tell him?"

"I told him she's not here today. I mean, he could be an ax murderer for all we know."

"*Seriously*?" Charley said.

Naomi just shrugged.

Once the set-up was complete, Charley wondered if it would be pushy to walk over to the guy and inform him they were now officially serving lunch. One thing she didn't like in bistros was a server who pushed a particular dish. Recommendations were one thing, but it should always be up to the customer. Always. No pressure. She glanced at the old-fashioned hand clock hanging on the wall. Milly had left it up in Coral's memory. Their mother had been worried people would eventually forget how to tell time. Five minutes. She'd give him five minutes. After all, free wifi was something no customer should take advantage of for too long.

Ten minutes later, Charley was kind of irritated with the guy. He hadn't so much as looked up from his laptop, earbuds firmly in place. What could be so fascinating? He had better not be watching porn in here. But no, he looked much too unhappy to be watching porn. Finally, the man caught her eye and smiled in her direction.

She motioned for him to remove the earbuds and flashed him a big grin. "If you're hungry, we're serving lunch now."

He stood and strode to the counter. Charley saw he was younger and thinner than she'd initially thought. Even though he was the picture of a Silicon Valley techie, dressed in jeans and a white polo shirt, she'd thought he might be older from a distance. But he looked to be right about her age with dark, closed-cropped hair, wearing half-rim eyeglasses over almond-shaped eyes.

In another reality she'd run upstairs to get Milly and do a little bit of old-fashioned matchmaking. Next to men in kilts, Milly loved techie nerdy guys. But, as Milly continually pointed out, she was a little busy at the moment.

"Specialty paninis." She swept her hand over the glass case. Did this seem pushy? She hoped not.

"Looks good." He pushed his eyeglasses up his nose, then pointed. "What's that one?"

"That's my personal favorite. Smoked salmon panini with crème fraiche over a bed of spring mix greens."

"Whoa. Okay, I'll have that one." He pulled out a wallet from his back pocket. "Didn't even know you guys were serving lunch now. Milly never did."

"How do you know Milly?"

She reached for a dish to plate and drizzled some of the olive oil across in a circular motion. Then she gently placed the panini in the middle and added a few more sprigs of green for décor. He went eyebrows up when she presented it to him. Frankly, too many food establishments didn't take enough pride in presentation. Shame. To some people this was just a sandwich, but every dish could and should be a work of art.

"Milly and I were pretty close for a while," he answered.

"I'm her sister, Charley."

"Oh, yeah. She talked about you a lot. You're a traveling chef. Right?"

"Right." Who *was* this guy? "And what's your name?"

"Henry Hunter. Milly and I lost touch when I moved down to San Diego for work, but we spent a lot of time together last November."

Last November? Charley sucked in a breath. Last. November. "Um. A-and you two haven't talked at all since you moved?"

"A few text messages and emails here and there, but Milly stopped responding after a while. I can't blame her. Long-distance relationships. I got busy and I imagine she got busy, too."

One might say that. "She did."

"What's she been up to?"

Oh boy. She wanted so badly to tell him all about Milly's "production." Tell him he was actually an executive producer without knowing it. Tell him everything. Drag him upstairs and just *show* him.

"She's...she's got a new project going on and it demands a lot of time away from the bakery."

"Ah. Well, tell her I said hi."

"Sure. You two should probably catch up sometime."

"We should. I've been in town, but I'm leaving early Sunday morning."

Charley managed to resist dragging him by his collar upstairs. But just barely. "Please stop by again. I'm sure she'd like to see you. I'll tell her you dropped by when I see her."

In about two minutes.

"Thanks." He paid and put his wallet away. "It would be good to catch up."

"How about Saturday?"

"Tomorrow?" He blinked. "Um, sure."

"I hope you enjoy." She jutted her chin at the panini.

"I don't see how this can fail me."

He went back to the table and his laptop to begin the last few hours before his entire world changed.

And as it turned out, Charley did feel sorry for him.

27

"Sometimes miracles just take a little time. Mine took about 13 years." ~ Charley Young

L unchtime customers continued to arrive. Padre Suarez, followed by Mrs. Luna, and unfortunately, Jenny and Sean. Padre Suarez could not be persuaded to try anything but his usual crème-filled Danish, Mrs. Perez said the panini's looked great, but she'd been saving up her calories all week for a Danish. Sean and Jenny were foaming at the mouth to try the Paninis. Sean to criticize them, no doubt, and Jenny to agree with him. But for the first time in a while Charley didn't care what Sean thought. He was a piece of...well. Coral had raised her not to even think such nasty names of anyone.

"I'll take the smoked salmon and Jenny will have the marinated chicken. We'll share and this way I get to try two of your creations." Sean smiled as he paid and didn't bat an eye when she handed over her presentation.

"Ooh, fancy." Jenny took her plate to a table.

"That thing you did the other night? Not cool," Charley hissed.

"I was trying to do you a favor."

"I know *exactly* what you're trying to do. You can see that I'm finally happy. Maybe this relationship will work out, and you won't have a back-up woman any longer. I've got news for you. I was never going to be your back-up woman."

"Ouch." He clutched his chest, like she'd just pierced him with a sword.

But he was still smiling which irritated her to no end. "And by the way, my butt is not too big, in any pants! I'm curvy, not a stick figure. Never trust a skinny cook! Sometimes, Sean, you're an ass, and I'm glad I can finally tell you that."

He flashed her a sly grin. "Should you really be telling me all this *before* I taste your paninis?"

She crossed her arms. "I don't care what you think."

He opened his mouth then closed it a couple of times.

"I know I'm a good chef, and so are you, okay? I get that, but I don't need *you* to like me. Sure, maybe desserts aren't my specialty, but I know food. I love food. And people are going to love my paninis. You'll see."

Henry raised his hand. "Big fan over here."

"Thanks, Henry."

"Well, well. I don't know how we got to this Charley Young but I think I like her," Sean said.

Oh, *sure* he did. Then again, it would be no time at all before he'd find someone else to intimidate. There were plenty of wide-eyed newbie sous chefs coming on board every week to learn the business. They, as she did, would see the much more experienced man of the world and think his opinion meant everything.

Thank goodness I'm over that.

"I'm headed to Paris as I planned," Sean said.

Charley nudged her chin in Jenny's direction, who was giving Sean a little finger wave. "Does she know that?"

"She will."

Charley almost felt sorry for Jenny. She wondered if Sean had already started criticizing. He found fault with everything. Except himself, of course. To think that she'd once found him attractive. Sexy. The only explanation was that she'd been Dylan-deprived for so long that she'd forgotten what a real man looked and behaved like. He certainly didn't get off making a woman feel small and...unnecessary.

And she was never going to let anyone make her feel that way again.

"I'm CALLING IT," Charley said, reaching inside to sell her very last sandwich. "Lunch is a resounding success!"

"Woohoo!" Naomi spun around in a circle and landed on her knees with her arms splayed wide. "Ta-da!"

She was met with applause, and a little hysterical laughter, from their remaining customers.

"Spread the word, everyone. Sunrise Bakery is now serving lunch." Charley turned to Naomi. "You can start cleaning up and I'll go check on Milly."

Charley found Milly in the kitchen by the French press. She wore her red bathrobe, belt loosely tied just above her protruding belly. *Star Wars* knee-high socks, plaid boxer shorts and a flowery tank top so tight on her now that it seemed to be squeezing the life out of her boobs.

"Um, okay." Charley joined her in the kitchen. "Did you *just* get up?"

"I sleep when I can." She scratched her head. "Once the baby comes, I'll never sleep again."

"You're exaggerating." Charley dug into the fridge. She needed to stock this better for Milly. "Do you want an...um, frittata for brunch?"

"Please don't talk to me in Italian before I've had the only drop of caffeine I'm allowed to have."

"It's an omelet."

"Sure. Whatever." Milly poured her decaf into a mug.

Charley whipped up eggs, adding basil, sliced grape tomatoes, half and half cream and mozzarella cheese.

While Milly sipped from her mug, Charley chose her next words carefully. "One of your friends dropped by today. I've never met him before but he introduced himself."

"Oh, yeah? Who was it?"

"Henry Hunter."

Milly dropped her coffee mug, the dark liquid spilling all over the hardwood floor.

"Milly! Are you okay?"

She winced. "I think I'm having a cramp."

"Go sit down, and I'll take care of this." Charley picked up the ceramic pieces of Milly's "Pilates? I thought you said pie and lattes" mug and mopped up the coffee.

She quickly put together the frittata and for once ignored presentation. She found Milly on the couch, eyes watery. "I'm not hungry."

"What's wrong? Is it the baby? Should I call Dylan? Should I call 911? Should I drive you to the hospital?"

"Calm down, that's what you should do." She gave the frittata a disgusted glimpse and Charley fought not to take offense. "As long as I don't have another cramp, I think I'm okay."

"Well, *think* isn't good enough." Charley went hands on hips. "I mean...I can't deliver a baby for you. I'll do a lot of things for you, but I refuse to deliver a baby. That's where I draw the line at this sisterhood thing."

Milly rolled her eyes. "You won't have to deliver the baby. I promise if it comes to that, we'll call Dylan. Or 911."

"Just call 911. Or I'll call 911." Her heart beat so fast she was fairly sure she was about to stroke out. "Who should call 911? Which *one* of us?"

"No one should right now!"

Charley let out a shallow breath and slumped down in a chair. "This all happened because I mentioned Henry."

Milly did the lip quiver thing and her eyes were far too shiny.

"He's the one, isn't he?" Charley spoke softly.

Milly nodded. "I didn't want him to know."

"Why? I mean, I don't really know him, but he seems like a super cool guy."

"He is."

"Then why? Why won't you *tell* him?"

"*Because* he's a good guy!" Milly rubbed her eyes. "He'd want to marry me out of obligation. But I don't want him to marry me because I'm pregnant, and besides I can't move to San Diego."

"Well, maybe he could move back here."

"No. I don't want him to do that. It's a really good career opportunity for him and he deserves it."

"But what about you? What do you deserve?"

"I know I don't want to leave Miracle Bay. Especially now that you're staying." She took a breath. "Wait. You are staying. Right?"

"Whether I stay or go doesn't matter. You have to tell him."

"I know."

Finally.

"You don't have to get married and you don't have to move. But you'll feel terrible if you don't tell him, or if he should find out some other way. If he comes back after the bean is born, he's bound to do the math. I bet math is kind of his thing."

"You're right. He's here so I'll tell him."

"He's leaving Sunday. But I have a feeling he'll be back tomorrow."

"You have a feeling?" Milly wrinkled her nose. "Are you psychic now, too?"

"Um, no. I used the great power of language. I asked him to come by."

"Great. I guess I should have expected that."

"I didn't tell him anything. That's up to you. If you liked him this much, why didn't you ever tell me about him?"

"Because I was happy for about five minutes. A month. That's all we dated, anyway. Something told me it wouldn't last."

"Aw, Milly." Charley reached over to squeeze her hand.

"That month we were together was like a dream. Stuff like that just doesn't happen to me. But I was such a dummy. One night, I...we...forgot all about protection."

Nope, that didn't sound like Milly at all. "I was wondering about that."

She quirked a brow. "That's how passionate he is."

Charley absorbed that knowledge and then decided she didn't want the picture in her head. "Sounds like he's worth another shot."

Milly's gaze swept over her humongous belly. "But I'm not at my best right now."

"If he loves you, he won't care about the big belly. That is *his* bean in there."

"Is he going to hate me forever for keeping this from him for so long?"

"I don't know, but I think that's a chance you're going to have to take."

28

"Each month has an average of 30-31 days, except the last month of pregnancy, which is 1,453 days." ~ meme

D ylan decided that the best place to celebrate his impending business venture with Joe was Juan's. They let Marco come along for kicks, because... the whole brotherhood thing. They were seated at a booth sharing a plate of nachos, Joe and Marco across from Dylan.

"Maybe you should change the name," Marco offered. "From Surf's Up to Reyes of the Sea or some such thing."

"Reyes mean royal, not king," Dylan corrected with a smirk. "And that doesn't have as nice a ring to it."

"Plus, there's Eddie. He's a big part of this," Joe said, digging into the nachos.

"How are you going to do this, bro?" Marco set his beer down and leaned back. "Fit it in between shifts at the station, home renovations, and work at the marina? And there's also Charley. I hear she's taking up a lot of your time."

"Joe, explain to our brother what silent partner means. And I'm not doing that many renos. Ty is traveling further and further south to find properties."

"And...Charley?" Joe leaned across the booth.

"Yeah, that's going...very well."

"Who would have thought it?" Marco said.

"I would," Joe said. "She's hot. Thought about it myself."

Marco nearly sprayed beer through his nose. "Dude."

"What?" Joe winced. "Like once, maybe."

Dylan straightened. "I don't want to hear about how hot you think my girlfriend is."

"Oh, so it's like that, is it?" Joe said.

"It's like that."

He was staking his claim. Not that Joe would have ever had a chance in hell, but Dylan was grateful it had never come to that. It would have killed him to see Charley with anyone else.

It would still kill him.

It was why he'd always found fault with any man interested in her. No one was ever good enough since his standard for her was perfection. But he wasn't perfect, either, so it obviously wasn't his desire to have her with the prince of perfection. It was his need to have her.

"This is going to be such a blast. I finally get you bozos to come down to Santa Cruz and hang with me. Get you on a board. You and Charley gotta come down this month." Joe pointed to Dylan.

"Yeah, we'll see. Milly having her baby might put a crimp in our plans." Jesus, listen to him. *Our* plans.

He'd never been in a serious committed relationship before and his longest relationship, other than family, was with Charley. As her best friend. It would be different now, and one of the ways it was different was that she wasn't going anywhere. Except Lake Tahoe. With him.

A pretty blonde, the same he'd seen with Joe the other night, came up to their booth, licking her lips. "Hey there, Joe."

"Hey, beautiful." He gave her his complete attention. "How you doing?"

His brother, the playboy. If he'd ever gone after Charley in earnest, he might have won her over, and then it would have come to blows.

"Lonely," she said, eyeing the room with the pool table. "You up for a game?"

"I'll be right with you, baby."

She walked away and Joe stood, clapping a hand on Dylan's back. "Bro, thanks for not talking me out of this. I know you haven't seen me as the most serious person in the world. I could have continued the Reyes legacy with you two, and you have no idea how close I've come. But I know I would have been miserable doing what someone else wanted for me instead of my own dream."

With a grin he strode away to join his lady friend.

"They grow up so fast," Marco said. "Would you look at our little Joey? He's got game."

"Not sure if you noticed, but you've got two different women staring holes into your backside," Dylan said.

Marco turned slightly, and the women quickly looked away. "Nope, don't know 'em. The woman at your three o'clock has been tossing hair and give you googly eyes since we got here."

"Looks like we've all got game," Dylan said, not even checking to see if Marc was correct.

Marco rubbed the bridge of his nose. "Yeah, but you're taken."

True. Taken about as much as any man alive could be. So wrapped up in her, and a possible future, that he hadn't seen the obvious. But Joe's little gratitude speech had made it abundantly clear. Charley wasn't leaving because she was trying to please him. Making him happy by sacrificing something she wanted.

She'd always wanted to see Paris. And though she claimed she didn't want to go now, eventually she'd be miserable at the lost chance. Maybe not now but a year from now. Five years from now. If he failed her in some way—and he was bound to do that at some point—she'd blame him. He'd blame himself. Whatever kind of ass Sean was, he was right in that Paris was a once-in-a-lifetime opportunity. It was what she'd always dreamed of. What kind of a friend would he be to Charley if he held her back from a dream?

She'd never once discouraged him from being a fire-fighter. It was as if she understood there was no other way for him. She'd always offered him the unconditional love and support a friend would do. What would happen if years from now they were married, and she blamed him for never getting to Paris? Whoa. Where the hell had that come from? Marriage? He swallowed hard and tugged at his collar.

But the obvious and rather pathetic truth was that for the first time in his life he was far more invested in a relationship than he'd ever been before. He wanted her to stay despite the fact that might not be the best thing for her. Either he was going to let her go, or he was going to tie her down. Neither were acceptable options.

She should have everything she wanted and had worked for. Which meant she'd leave, and he'd stay. Stagnant. Steady as always. Fantastic. He sounded like a clock, or a metronome. But the fact was he wasn't going to be able to pick and leave for Paris or anywhere else anytime soon. Or ever. And face it, Lake Tahoe was gorgeous, but it wasn't the culinary hub of the world.

"See you later." Dylan stood and pulled his wallet out, dropping several bills on the table. "Got to get to work."

"I'm not on till Sunday," Marco said. "See you then."

Dylan left Juan's, the sounds of laughter and good times fading into the background behind him.

29

"You only live once. Lick the bowl." ~ Charley Young

Milly spent all of Saturday morning driving Charley out of her mind asking how she should tell Henry the truth. In what *tone* of voice. Should she ask for forgiveness or not? How offended should she be if he asked for a paternity test? Should she allow him to be in the delivery room if he wanted to be or should she ask for privacy? Should she let him have some say in naming the baby or just assume he'd pick a horrible name and not give him the choice?

In the end, the final plan was that when Henry showed up and asked for Milly, Charley would simply lead him up the apartment stairs. She'd open the door, step aside, and Milly would be waiting for him on the couch, ready to do the rest.

Word was all over the neighborhood that Sunrise Bakery now offered lunch specials, and the entire fire department showed up to order. About half of the police department followed suit. Nothing like the residents of Miracle Bay supporting a new venture.

They'd developed a system where Charley would serve and Naomi would ring up. Charley wasn't sure she liked it as it had too much of a fast food air to it, but for now it would have to do.

"I will try one, my dear," Padre Suarez said. "In addition to my raspberry crème-filled Danish. You pick for me."

She served him the smoked salmon. "Let me know how you like it."

Henry was next. Look at that, he'd actually shown up. Smoked salmon. Charley was going to make more of them next time.

"Hey, did you tell Milly I dropped by?"

"Yes, I did, and she said to take you upstairs to her apartment."

Henry quirked a brow. "She's upstairs right now?"

"That special project I told you about? She's been working on that here. Upstairs."

"I see."

He so did not *see*. Henry had no idea how his life would change in a matter of—Charley glanced at the wall clock— ten, nine, eight, seven.... His life would be turned upside down and sideways and backward and inside out. The poor dude would probably need some antacids when all was said and done though certainly *not* because of her food.

"Naomi, I'm taking a quick break and I'll be right back." Charley took off her apron and crooked a finger toward Henry.

As he followed her up the creaky steps to the apartment, Charley wondered if she should tell him a little something to maybe ease the shock a little bit. Maybe if she simply told him that Milly had been on doctor-ordered bed rest that would give him a heads-up. Or maybe not.

Right before she opened the door, Charley turned to Henry. "Milly's had a rough time lately. I...just wanted you to know that. So, whatever she says or does, just go easy on her, okay?"

"I-I don't understand."

"You will. Everybody makes mistakes." She took a breath. "And everyone deserves a second chance."

"Are we talking about the project she's working on?"

"Sort of." Charley opened the door, and waved him in.

Milly sat on the couch, Rufus at her feet. Her long hair sat in a neat and tidy bun. Blue dangly earrings and a matching necklace. She wore her stretchy yoga pants and a blue maternity top. But her best accessory was the saintly and calm Madonna and child look on her face. And yes, it *was* true, pregnant women glowed.

Sometimes.

"Hi, Henry," Milly said.

Charley, still standing in the hallway, shut the door.

"My work here is done," she said to no one. "Now back to the bakery."

CHARLEY GAVE Henry and Milly their privacy for as long as possible. She'd been busy in the shop, but she'd never seen Henry leave so she assumed he was still with Milly hashing it out. She gave him props for not running away the moment he'd seen her baby bump. Charley assumed her own father had run when he'd heard Maggie was pregnant. At least, that's the implication she'd been given. Unless he'd never known about Charley at all.

Maggie had always said: "We don't need him."

But sometimes, even though she'd been afraid to tell Maggie, Charley had needed him. When Charley wanted to know who she could take to a father and daughter event at school, Maggie said she'd cross-dress if that would make Charley happy. She'd laughed, although she hadn't understood the joke. Then Maggie laughed too, and Charley knew. She'd never have a father because Maggie had made the choice for her. She didn't want him around, whoever he'd been.

Charley pressed her ear up against the door to Milly's apartment and heard soft voices, so she went back to her apartment and cleaned, otherwise known as stalling. Because, c'mon! She wanted to know how Henry had taken the news. She was bored with all this waiting and cleaning two seconds after she started.

Her phone finally pinged. Milly.

"Hey, how'd it go? Is he still there?"

"No, he left two hours ago. Where are you?"

"Next door giving you privacy!"

Hanging up, Charley crossed the hallway and let herself in. "What happened? Tell me everything!"

Milly smiled. "He was so understanding. I mean, after the initial shock. He stared off into space and needed a drink of water but after that he started talking and everything."

"What did he say?"

"Well, first he simply stared at me for several seconds which felt like hours. My big belly. Then my face. Then my big belly."

Charley nodded. "Putting it all together. Processing."

"Exactly. All I had to do was nod and say, 'Yes, it's your baby.' And then he plopped down on the couch and nearly sat on Rufus."

"Poor dude."

"I know. But after all the initial awkward stuff he wanted to know how I've been. I told him about the bed rest. He wants to be in the delivery room."

"Are you going to let him?"

"I think so." She cocked her head to the side. "But jury's still out."

"So, what happens now?"

"He goes back to San Diego."

"That's it?"

"He's going to ask for some time off."

"Did he, you know..." Charley's voice drifted, waiting for Milly to fill in.

"Ask me to marry him?"

"Yes, that's exactly where I was going. Did he ask you?"

"No," she said. "And I'm glad he didn't. It would have been too much for one day."

Charley couldn't argue with that. But now Milly would have support. The bean would have two parents.

Why did she feel so sad? "Guess you won't be needing me anymore."

"Oh, stop it. You weren't excited about this anyway. Diapers? Formula? Middle of the night feedings? Crying? Screaming? Tantrums?"

"You're describing a typical night working for the head chef."

Milly cocked her head. "And why do you put up with that, again?"

"Because I don't have my own bistro. Yet." She took a deep breath. "I had a chance to go to Paris this September."

Milly gasped. "What you mean *had*? You turned it down?"

"It was through Sean's connections. And I don't think he likes me very much right now. Plus, I don't like him."

"I thought he was a friend."

Charley shook her head. "Fair weather friend. He told Dylan about Paris before I had a chance to tell him. Also, he told him we'd slept together. I never told Dylan that."

"Lord of the Rings! What an ass. But what about Paris? Don't you want to go?"

"Well, now that you've got Henry I *could* go."

"You could. And I don't want to stop you."

"Funny, that's what Dylan said."

"A good friend wants the best for you."

"And I always thought that was Paris. The world. That was my dream, right along with having my own bistro. But the real dream was having anything that was mine. I never felt like the bakery was ever mine. It was yours, and I went off to get something of my own. I never even thought you'd want my input or want to make a change. I should have asked but you've already given me so much."

"Funny, because I got tired of being in charge. Mama left you half the bakery for a reason. She saw what you loved and she wanted you to have a piece of that. The only real thing she could give you."

The thought that Coral had known what Charley needed, a place to work and cook, a place to find herself, was more than she'd ever expected. But she'd been lucky enough to have Coral in her life for a short time and would have never thought to ask for anything more. Too greedy.

Huh. Maybe she was Coral's daughter after all. "I'm coming in for a hug."

Milly rolled her eyes. "Alright, get it over with already."

This time Milly hugged back.

30

"You touch the bump, I punch the throat." ~ Maternity T-shirt

The next morning, the Miracle Sunday rush passed, with everyone asking whether Charley planned on offering the lunch menu at the same "buy one, second half off" price. But she refused to discount her quality ingredient paninis. Coral would probably agree. For one thing, Charley couldn't keep up with the demand. But most importantly, offering a Panini half off meant that in order to break even she'd have to use less expensive ingredients and sacrifice quality.

And Charley Young did not sacrifice quality.

"I'll come up with a special Miracle Sunday panini. That's the best I can do." Charley explained to Padre Suarez, who'd now become a huge fan of the smoked salmon Panini.

Creature of habit that man.

"Isn't Milly due any day now?" Mrs. Luna asked.

"That's right. But you know her. She's determined to make it to her due date."

"The baby will have something to say about that," said Mrs. Perez.

Lunch rush passed in a flash, Charley barely aware of the fact that the line snaked out the door this time.

Sean had the gall to show up again. "I'm leaving early. Got a few things to settle before I head to Paris. Thought I'd say goodbye."

"Goodbye."

"That's it?" Sean made a motion as though she'd greatly wounded him, clutching at his chest.

"What do you want from me?" She drizzled olive oil on the plate, and added an extra sprig of garnish, hoping Sean would choke on it.

"How about a little bit of gratitude for one."

"Excuse me?"

"I did you a favor. Two people who are together shouldn't keep each other from their dreams. Anyway, you're welcome."

"I didn't *say* thank you."

"You didn't have to." He shoved hands in his pockets, not a care in the world as he waited to stuff his blowhole.

She pictured shoving the entire panini down his throat, while everyone in the shop watched. Probably not good for business, and Coral had raised her to be a better person than that. Tried to, anyway. She handed his plate over to him without comment, and her best attempt at a look that could physically kill someone. It made her right eye twitch.

"Hope to see you in Paris if you've got any sense left at all." He paid and saluted her. "Call me when you change your mind, and all's forgiven. No hard feelings. Hannigan out."

Charley removed her plastic gloves after she and Naomi had taken care of the last lunch customer. "I'm going to check on Milly and feed her lunch."

Charley found Milly in the kitchen, clinging to the edge of the counter so tightly that her fingers seemed to be losing circulation.

"What's up? Another cramp?"

Milly didn't speak, apparently so involved with that counter edge that it seemed to be taking all of her concentration.

A moment later, she turned to Charley and gave her a smile through what appeared to be gritted teeth. "I'm good."

"You don't *look* so good."

"Speak for yourself. I'm really rocking this pregnancy thing, I think we can all agree." She gripped the counter edge again and made a sound a bit like a wolf howling.

"It looks like it's time to go to the hospital." Charley ran into the bedroom and grabbed the overnight bag.

They'd rehearsed this a couple of times, and Charley knew what to do. Call the doctor, grab the bag. Or grab the bag, call the doctor? Go get the car and get Milly to the hospital. This all had to be done with the utmost swiftness, as the baby might come quickly considering Milly's incompetence.

Charley grabbed her phone. "Calling the doctor."

"No!" Milly cried out. "I can't have my baby on Miracle Sunday."

"Why not?"

"Everyone's going to call her a miracle baby. That's too high of a standard for anyone, even my baby."

"Sorry. You don't get to choose the day she's born."

"I'm going to cross my legs. Maybe if I don't move. Just one more day is all I'm asking. I can do this."

Charley dialed the doctor anyway, and the woman told her to get Milly over to San Francisco General immediately.

"We have to go now."

"I'm not ready. I have to change into my 'go to the hospital clothes.' It's such an ow, holy shitake mushroom, cute outfit I don't want to, son of a biscuit, waste it."

She was gasping now. Rufus meowed loudly, apparently having sympathy pains, and walked in circles around the couch.

"No time to change. The baby could be here any minute. Do you want me to call 911?" Dylan, or another paramedic from the station, would deliver the baby. *Not* Charley. "I can't deliver the baby. We made a deal, remember?"

"Yeah, I remember." Milly lay on the bed. "But don't worry, because I don't think I'm going to do this. I changed my mind."

"About *what*?"

She shook her head, hair plastered to her perspiring forehead. "Having a baby. You were right. It's going to be hard."

"Too late!"

"Maybe if I'm really super still and quiet, she won't come out."

"No!" Charley pulled on Milly's elbow and tried to lift her, but she weighed as much as an orca. Not that she would ever say that to Milly. "Get up."

Not listening, Milly did something terrifying. She started removing her clothes.

"W-what are you doing?" Charley screamed at her. "You don't have time to change."

"I'm hot," she said and removed her bathrobe.

Her shorts went next. It was as if she were getting ready for Charley to catch the baby. Which was not happening in a gazillion years. Charley wanted to kiss Dylan for having her put 911 on speed dial.

"I'm afraid we don't have time to get to the hospital and my sister is in labor," she told the 911 operator.

The woman advised she'd send help, then said she'd stay on the line until they arrived. "Do you see the baby's head crowning?"

"Um," Charley said. "I hope not. Remind me what that means?"

Milly rose up on her elbows and gave Charley a wild-eyed look. "My water broke!"

The little clothes she still wore were soaked. So were the bed's sheets.

"Her water broke! Help us!" Charley didn't know much, but she did know that this was very, very bad.

"Go find some clean towels," the operator advised. "And make sure your door is unlocked so they can come right in. They're already on their way."

Charley did both those things then rushed back to Milly, still carrying the phone in one hand to keep her connection to a human being who wasn't behaving like a crazy person. Milly now appeared to be in a type of trance, half moaning and half dozing as if this might be a good time to catch a nap.

"Now you've done it! We're not getting to the hospital on time. Thanks a lot!"

Milly didn't seem to hear. She made a little mewl type sound. It sent Rufus skittering back into the room where he hissed at Charley.

"I do not have time for you!" Charley told him.

"How is she doing?" the operator asked.

"She seems to be napping," Charley said, "and moaning. What do I do? Ma'am, listen. I really can't deliver this baby. I just can't. You don't know me, so you're going to have to trust me on this."

"You'll be fine," the woman's calm voice assured her. "Just breathe. And then tell her to breathe."

"When will they get here?"

"Soon. How is the mother doing now?"

Trying to get Milly's attention, she poked her shoulder and got right up in her face. "Are you okay?"

She opened one eye. "Oh sure. Yeah, fine thanks. This is actually so much fun I might do it again tomorrow."

"She's her regular smartass self, so yeah, she's doing alright."

"They've arrived," the operator said. "Good luck to you all!"

"In here," Charley shouted, and a moment later Marco strode in with a blonde guy she didn't recognize, and Dylan.

They all slipped on gloves and went straight to work.

"Milly, honey, how are you doing?" Dylan kneeled beside the bed.

She spoke through gritted teeth. "Not so good. I think I'm having a baby on Miracle Sunday."

"I think you're right."

A moment later Dylan was at the foot of the bed, while the other guys were doing stuff with what looked like a blood pressure cuff.

"Charley, how long has she been like this?" Dylan said.

"I came up to feed her lunch and she was in pain. I got everything ready to go, called the doctor, but she wouldn't move and then...it all happened so fast."

Dylan grabbed a towel and positioned one under Milly's lower half. "Okay, let's have a birthday party."

Milly opened one eye. "Now?"

"When were you thinking? Next week?" Charley said.

"But I wanted Henry to be here," she whined. "This isn't supposed to happen for another three weeks."

"This baby doesn't want to wait for anyone," Dylan said.

"Oh, geez already being a pain in the ass," Milly cried out. "This isn't fun!"

"I've heard," Dylan said.

It seemed like Charley should *do* something. She'd had her duties outlined and prepared and had launched into them. But now everything had changed. Should she say a prayer or a rosary? She should *do* something. For lack of anything better to do, she wrung her hands together. Very helpful.

"Milly, I need you to push," Dylan said. "The baby's crowning. This one is in a huge hurry to be born. It won't be long now."

Milly rose up on her elbows and pushed, her face contorted with effort.

"Good job!" Dylan turned to Charley. "Go help her now."

Oh, that's right. She'd seen the birth videos and read up on Lamaze. She knelt beside Milly at the head of the bed and grabbed her hand.

"It's okay. Breathe. We can do this."

She quirked a brow. "*We*?"

"You know what I mean."

"Seriously? Because I hoped you were offering to take over for me."

"I wish I could."

"Liar." She grunted and tried the staggered breathing along with Charley for about two seconds before giving up. "The breathing isn't *working*."

"Try again," Dylan instructed like a freaking drill sergeant.

This time Charley actually felt useful as she helped Milly lean forward so she could push. Marco and the younger dude were now both on either side of Dylan, equally as intent. Marco held another towel in his hands.

After several seconds of effort, Milly ran out of steam and fell back.

"The baby's almost here. I can see the head," Dylan said.

"I can't do this anymore," Milly sputtered, out of breath. "I'm too tired."

"Charley," Dylan called. She met his gaze which was not at all the soft warm gaze she'd become accustomed to. All business. He mouthed the words to her: *help her.*

How she wanted to, but Charley had nothing. If anything, Milly had always been *her* cheerleader. "Okay. Milly, you can do this. You're the stronger sister, and we all know that."

"No, I'm not. And stop trying to butter me up. You're not even good at it."

"Look, Milly, maybe you're not the stronger sister but you're the *better* sister. You were always there for me just like you're going to be for your baby." She took hold of Milly by the nape of her neck. "Now push. Her. Out!"

"You're not the boss of me! Aayeeeee!" Milly leaned forward and if effort counted for anything, her baby should be out in a second.

"Good job," Dylan said.

When Charley turned to look, she saw a little head protruding out of Milly. A head of dark and wet hair.

"One more push," Dylan said.

"You people don't ask for much, do you?" Milly gave one more push.

The baby was out, and a loud cry filled the room.

"It's a girl," Dylan said.

Charley had always been a sympathy crier but right now only one thought ran through her mind. How wonderful and amazing and bright and glorious it was to see a baby take her first breath. It was a miracle and the first one she'd actually witnessed.

"You did it, Milly," Charley said.

"My baby," Milly blubbered. "Is she okay?"

Dylan and his crew got busy. Marco wrapped the baby in a towel and Dylan used some kind of syringe in the baby's mouth. She then let out another even louder scream that demonstrated her lungs were fully developed, thank you very much. Dylan cut the cord and some EMTs came in moments later. They helped Milly onto the stretcher and handed her the baby.

"Where are you taking them?" Charley asked.

"They're taking her to General," Dylan said without looking at Charley, "They both need to get checked out. The baby looks a little small."

"That was amazing," Charley said. "I don't know how you did it."

"Milly did most of the work. I just caught the baby."

"Just caught the baby? Seriously? *Just* caught the baby?"

"Yep."

"Well, thank you for doing that because I couldn't have."

"I've been trained."

There was something else going on. She could feel it in her bones. In her heart. Something was *wrong*. The baby was three weeks premature, after all. Fear gripped her gut because she could sense the anxiety and regret in Dylan, who was pulling away, refusing to look at Charley. That always meant bad news. It meant something he didn't want to tell her but would anyway.

My mother has cancer.

I hate to tell you this, Chuck, but Coral isn't going to make it.

Hand on Dylan's forearm, she forced him to turn to her. "What's wrong? Please tell me. Is it the baby? Is there something you're not telling me?"

"I told you. She needs to get checked out because she's premature." His eyes were hooded and unreadable.

There *was* something else, and her body knew it as her brain attempted to catch up. Her stomach churned, and her throat closed up. "Why won't you look at me?"

He met her gaze. "What do you mean?"

But it was far worse when he locked gazes with hers. "I'm worried. I—"

"Don't worry. The baby is going to be in good hands. I'll be back tomorrow night when I end my shift. But now I've got to go. Okay?" He gave her a quick light kiss on the lips.

Then he was gone.

31

"Cooking is like love. It should be done with passion, or not at all." ~ Apron

Dylan wasn't ready to talk. Milly's delivery was unexpected, and he wasn't prepared to face Charley yet. He'd made a decision, much as he hated it, and she'd obviously sensed something had changed because he felt the insecurity in her. He saw the raw pain in her amber eyes and it was killing him.

He and Marco followed the EMTs into the emergency room where Dylan spoke briefly to the doctor and told him about the delivery.

Then he rubbed Milly's shoulder. "They're going to take care of you both. Congratulations."

He was about to leave when Milly grasped his hand. "Thank you. Please do something for me."

He gave her a playful wink. "You haven't already asked enough?"

"You were doing your job, as you always say. This one is for me."

"Name it."

"Please get her to stay."

"Milly." Dylan felt a line of tension and anger ride up his spine. "I can't do that."

"I know what you're thinking. But Charley has done a lot of growing up and I think it's all because she fell in love."

The words hit him hard. They sliced right through him with a swift cut, because he didn't know how to fix this. How to make them both happy.

"Charley should have whatever she needs even if it takes her away from us."

"You can't mean that. I want her to stay and you can *get* her to stay. If anyone can, it's you. Please think about it."

"Right You take care, Milly."

He walked outside the electric double doors of the ER, joining Marco and Johnny. They all climbed in the rig to drive back to the station.

Johnny seemed to be on a high. "That was so cool. I think I might want to be a doctor."

"You should," Dylan said. "Better pay."

"Worse hours," Marco added. "And a lot more years of studying."

"But nurses love doctors," Johnny said. "Cute ones, like Ashley."

"Ahem." Marco cleared his throat and slid a glance at Dylan. "She is cute, isn't she?"

"Hey, pull in here." Johnny gestured to the Safeway. "It's my turn to cook."

Marco pulled in and parked at the back. It was common for the fire department to shop at this local grocery store.

"Actually, if you're interested in picking someone up, go to the vegetable aisle. The single women will flock to you like vultures to a dead carcass."

"Great analogy." Dylan snorted.

Johnny brightened and hooked his thumb toward the store. "Come be my wingman."

"Show him the way, oh wise one," Dylan said.

"Nah, I'm taking a break." He leaned back in his seat and folded his arms behind his neck.

"From *women*?" Dylan asked as Johnny hopped out of the truck and went on his merry way to score fresh vegetables and the heart of a woman.

"Donna broke up with me." He shut his eyes, apparently unconcerned with this. "I'm not serious enough for her."

"Sorry."

"She's right. I'm not ready to settle down by a long shot." He elbowed Dylan. "Not like you. You've been ready to settle down for like...what, ten years?"

Dylan scowled. "How do you figure?"

"It's been ten years, give or take. I don't know, how long ago did you meet Charley again?"

"Look, we've been friends for years. We tried something different and it isn't going to work. She has an opportunity to go to Paris and I'm not standing in the way of that. Now we need to take a step back and re-evaluate."

Marco snorted. "You mean *you're* taking a step back."

Dylan didn't answer. For the past few days he'd been on a high, but he was back to reality. Love was risky and the risk couldn't be calculated. He'd given Charley his whole heart on a platter and now he would need to take it back. Sacrifice was something with which he was far too familiar.

"She wasn't looking at you any differently today than she

always has. Like you're the center of the universe. Like you're the one who makes the sun come up every morning. Man, I tell ya, if a girl ever looked at me like that, I might re-think this commitment thing."

This wasn't about commitment. They'd both invested in each other long ago. But since he was now both friend and lover, he had to think about more than what he wanted. He had to think of the best outcome for all concerned.

"Joe said something that made me think twice about Charley."

"Joe did? About the surf shop?"

"No, genius. I tried to push Joe into firefighting which was stupid. But I wanted him to have a direction. You were right. He had to want it. Now that he's found something that excites him, he's got a purpose and he's willing to work hard. And Charley...she has a chance to go to Paris like she's always wanted to do."

"Oh crap. Even I know how much she's wanted that."

"She's telling me she doesn't want to go now."

"You don't believe her."

"She's only telling me what I want to hear. It's not true. If she doesn't go when she has the chance, someday she'll blame me."

"Or maybe not."

"Yeah. I can't take that chance." He rubbed his constricted chest.

"Sounds like you need a break. Time off to think. Take the sailboat out. They're not just for Sunset Kiss."

"Don't remind me. Charley made me feel like Bernie Madoff for wanting to make a quick buck off the couples who want to sail that weekend. When she saw me working on the boat to get it ready, she got ideas."

"That doesn't surprise me." Marco chuckled. "You should have seen that coming."

Just then Johnny opened the passenger door and climbed in with a paper bag. "Guess who's got a date for Sunset Kiss? You guys want to tell me what that is?"

Marco howled in laughter, while Dylan started the truck up and drove them back to the station.

32

"Never trust a skinny cook ~ Apron"

E arly Monday morning, Charley closed up the bakery, annoying some of the regulars who were waiting. She hastily wrote up a handwritten sign and taped it to the entrance:

Closed today due to baby. Please come again tomorrow.

"I heard Milly had her baby," Mrs. Sorrento said. "I wanted a dozen donut holes and all the latest news."

"I'm headed to the hospital right now. Tomorrow I'll give a full report."

She went to the garage and fired up the Vespa to drive to the hospital. Sure, Bean was a girl as they'd suspected, and that was great. Super. But was she going to be okay being born so fast and on Milly's bed which they'd never thought to disinfect first? When she had to be wrapped in a couple of warm towels and taken by ambulance to the hospital?

If only Milly had stopped stalling and listened to

Charley, she might have made it to the hospital. Then both mom and baby would have received the best of care. Carrying her helmet once she reached the hospital, she was directed to the maternity ward on the second floor where she asked a nurse for Milly's room number.

"Visiting hours aren't until five o'clock," the nurse said. "Now is family only."

"I'm family," Charley explained and felt her stomach tighten. She did a chin lift when the nurse hesitated and gave her a doubtful look. "I know we don't look much alike, because she looks like our mother and I look like my father."

Hell, maybe it was even true.

The nurse gave her an odd look. "Room 220."

Charley found Milly's room. The curtain around her bed was drawn, so she cleared her throat. "Milly? You here?"

"I'm here," came Milly's voice. "Open the curtain."

Charley did and found Milly with little bean in her arms, her boob hanging out. "Oh, geez."

"Sorry, I had the nurse draw the curtain so I could have some privacy. It's just a boob."

"Is she healthy?" Charley came closer to peek. She hadn't had much of a look at her before they'd both been wheeled away.

"She's perfect."

And she was. Beautiful dark hair like Milly's and a healthy pink color. "I'm sorry I yelled at you. I just..."

"Didn't want to deliver her?"

"Well, yeah."

"That's okay. I'm sorry I was being so weird and lost my mind for a bit. I should have listened to you and gotten dressed right away."

"She could have been born in the hospital instead of on your bed."

"Or she might have been born in the backseat of the car on the way. Anyway, Dylan did all right."

"What are you going to name her?"

"I've been thinking about it, and I have the perfect name."

"Coral," they both said at once.

"Jinx!" Charley pointed. "But what about her middle name?"

Milly scrunched up her nose. "Not sure. Maybe I'll let Henry have a say."

"Coral Henrietta?" Charley bit her lower lip to keep from laughing.

"Don't even joke about that."

"He's a smart man. He won't suggest it. I am nominating Charlotte for a middle name, though. You know, C.C. Pretty cool, and it's even a good nickname. Up to you."

Milly smiled. "I already called Henry, and he's really bummed he missed being here, but he hopped on a plane and should be here in a few hours."

"That's good." Charley took a seat on the one chair nearby. "I'll stay until he gets here."

"That's so sweet. You don't have to, though. There are plenty of nurses here to take care of us."

"I want to." She settled in, placing her helmet on the ground nearby. She might as well make herself useful.

But Milly really wasn't kidding about the nurses. They came in every ten minutes. A few hours later, the baby had a bunch of tests and the little overachiever passed every single one. She was already Milly's mini-me. Milly's doctor came in to check on her stitches. Milly had ripped a little during the delivery. Charley thought it wise not to ask what or where she'd ripped and decided this was as good a time as any to take a walk around the hospital. In the gift shop, she bought a lovely bouquet of mums for Milly and a little pink teddy bear for baby Coral. She took the long way back, just to make sure all the stitches and ripping talk would be done when she got back.

The curtain was closed again, but this time Charley heard Henry's voice behind it.

"Will you at least think about it?"

"That's so sweet but my sister has this amazing chance to go to Paris. Pretty sure she's going to take it so I'm not going anywhere for a while."

"If you moved in with me, we could really give this thing a fair shot. You and Coral could have the spare bedroom and we'll take this slow."

"I'd love to but maybe some other time."

"Well, I could quit my job and come back. I can always find work in Silicon Valley."

"I don't want you to do that."

"But—"

The argument went on, and Charley disappeared back into the hallway to give them their privacy. She found a chair and sat holding her yellow mums in one hand and the plush pink teddy bear in the other.

Another stone lodged itself in her throat. Clearly, she was the most selfish person on earth. Even Milly expected that she would leave immediately because the baby had been born. Because she'd been trying to find the father so that she could feel better about leaving again. Maybe that was true at one time, but she'd changed. If she didn't believe her, it was because of her history and the fact that nothing had ever kept her from traveling for long. Now there was Paris, a dream she'd had forever. But for the first time in her life she didn't want to go. This time it was Paris that could wait. It wasn't going anywhere. She'd rather stay in Miracle Bay and never see another city for as long as she lived than to live even one day in Paris without Dylan.

Charley saw Henry emerge from Milly's room a while later and head in the opposite direction, walking with his shoulders hunched, hands in his pockets. Milly's eyes were closed when Charley walked back in the room. The curtain was open and little Coral slept in the bassinette next to the bed.

"Asleep on the job?"

Milly opened her eyes half-mast. "Oh, Henry just left. He wouldn't stop talking. How beautiful Coral is, what a great birth weight for a baby three weeks early, blah, blah, blah."

"Proud papa."

"He's great," Milly sighed. "Just as I suspected he would be."

"But now you have another problem."

"He's not going to push it. He knows I can't go with him, and I'm not going to let him give up the great opportunity he has in San Diego. Such is life. Our daughter is perfect. Maybe we get only one perfect thing."

She sounded so much like Coral. *I'm not greedy.*

"But you *can* go with him and you should. I'm not leaving Miracle Bay, so I'll stay here and run the bakery."

"Trying to get rid of me?"

Charley shook her head. "Not trying to get rid of you. Trying to set you free. You were the one who stuck around and ran our bakery while I traveled. You've always been the perfect daughter and the perfect sister. It's your turn to have an adventure. I want you to reach for your dream, just like you always wanted me to reach for mine."

"But Pa—"

"Look, I don't care anymore. I have the bakery and the new lunch menu is going well, and I have lots of other ideas. I've never had this kind of creative control. It's exciting."

"But...Paris! I can't let you give that up. I just can't."

"I've already given it up. Dreams change, you know?"

"But if *I* move, you'll still miss seeing little Coral grow up." Milly's eyes got watery and her lower lip quivered. "Oh, these damned hormones! Whether you go to Paris, or whether I go to San Diego, we're not going to be together anymore, are we? Life is changing for both of us."

Heart in her throat, Charley had to nod because for a moment she didn't trust herself to speak. "You'll come visit often, right?"

"Of course. And...you never know, it might not work out with me and Henry."

"Don't say that. You hope it will."

"Yeah, of course I do. That would be kind of ideal." Milly grabbed Charley's hand in a rare gesture and squeezed. "I'm scared. This happened so fast and I haven't had time to get use to the idea. Henry and I are parents."

"You've had nine months to get used to the idea."

"To get used to the idea of having a baby. *Not* to get used to the idea of living with a man and sharing my life with him. Sharing a bathroom, not to mention a baby. Being together all the time. I've never done that before. I mean, what if we don't get along? What if I *hate* him eventually?"

"Maybe, maybe, maybe. Isn't little Coral a good enough reason to try?"

33

"Bra off. Hair up. Belly out." ~ Meme

L ater that night, while Charley waited for Dylan she cooked. Always good therapy. Tonight, a flourless quiche made with eggs, milk, butter and salt because eggs were highly underrated. Sort of a breakfast for dinner. Maggie used to feed Charley breakfast for dinner often, except it was a bowl of sugared cereal and milk. Like any six-year-old kid, Charley had loved it. But there were some days when the cereal she ate three times a day ran out and Maggie was either not home or asleep when Charley got hungry.

She'd found a neighbor lady who gave her cookies when she rang her doorbell. So, Charley had ramped it up a bit and asked for eggs one day. As a child, she'd loved eggs. Scrambled, sunny side up, any way she could get them they were a rare treat.

That same nice lady brought her inside and fed Charley

at her table. Pretty much a feast. Eggs, bacon, buttered biscuits, jam. Whatever she wanted. After that, Charley came every day that Maggie didn't have time to feed her. The kind lady watched Charley eat and one day when she left the room she spoke in hushed tones to someone over the phone. That really wasn't unusual to Charley. All the grown-ups in her life spoke in hushed tones around her. "Grown-up stuff" Maggie called it.

Unfortunately for Charley, the kind lady had been speaking with Child Protective Services. The next day some more grown-ups she didn't recognize showed up and asked for Maggie. Charley had no idea where she was, but knew she'd be back. She always came back. She asked them to come inside and wait. Keep her company.

Even though she swore she'd never ask anyone for food again, those people took her away from Maggie Young. As a full-grown adult, Charley realized it had been the right thing to do. But as a child, they might as well have gutted her like a fish. It had taken some time, but she'd found the right family with Coral and Milly Monroe. Two women who never gave up on her. She still had Milly and now little Coral.

And Dylan, of course. Because terrified though she was by the thought, she was in love with him. She loved him in a soul-harvesting, bone-crushing way that she'd never loved anyone before.

When she heard a knock on the door, she opened it to Dylan. Her basil. They were tomato and basil, a combination meant to be together. He looked amazing, wearing a black denim type jacket and still dressed in his blue BDUs. A little tired, his dark eyes took on that edgy look when he was worried about his family. Or about her.

"Hey, you." She folded into his arms.

He tugged her in tight, so much so that she had trouble taking in a breath for a second. When he let her go, he tucked a hair behind her ear and gave her an anguished look that kicked her in the heart.

Her voice came out sounding shaky and small. "What happened?"

It couldn't be Coral. She'd just seen mother and baby this afternoon and they were fine. Irrationally, she considered the eggs she'd cooked tonight would bring her devastating news again. Her heart rate kicked up and her breathing became shallow.

"Is it the baby?"

"No." He shook his head.

She allowed herself to breathe again. "I went to visit them earlier. Her name is Coral. Isn't that perfect?"

"Wherever she is, Coral is honored." He pressed his forehead to hers. "Hey. You know I'd do anything for you, right?"

"I know. Now tell me what's wrong."

He took her hand and led her to the couch. "Sit down."

"No. I won't sit. Not until you tell me what's wrong."

"Fine. *I'll* sit down." Then he pulled her onto his lap and his hands tightened around her wrists. "You need to go to Paris."

"What? Oh, is that what this is about? That's why you've been so weird? I'm not going anywhere. Did Sean say something? You shouldn't listen to Sean."

"I'm not. I still think he's an ass. But he was right about one thing. It's the opportunity of a lifetime."

"All that can wait."

"For how long?"

"I don't know, does it matter?"

"It does to me. Chances like this one don't always come up. God knows I can't take you to Paris."

She wrenched herself from out of his lap and stood up. This would be adorable if it wasn't so damned infuriating right now. Once again, he was making a sacrifice and being the hero.

"But you do *want* me to stay. You asked me to stay."

"I said that before I knew you had this opportunity."

"For years I've wanted adventure and I thought traveling would do that for me. I thought Paris would be exciting and all I ever wanted. But these past two weeks, I've been on the greatest adventure of all. I don't want to go and you're the reason."

"That's just it, Charley. I'm not ready to be the only reason you stay."

Her heart dropped feeling from roughly the distance of the Empire State Building to hell itself. "You're...not ready?"

"I can't be the reason you stay when I don't even know if I'll be around tomorrow. Or the next day. I didn't tell you this, but the night of the fire I almost didn't make it out of that building."

"Oh. Dylan."

"And I can't have you losing more than you've already lost in your life. I don't want you to invest any more time in me or fall in love with me."

Too late, buddy. Too late.

"I think," he said, without meeting her eyes, "that we rushed into this without thinking."

"Rushed, Dylan? *Rushed*? It's been thirteen years for me!" Trying to find regulate her breathing, she fought to keep her balance while the entire world was tipping over. "You said you were in. You were all in."

Eyes closed, he pinched the bridge of his nose. "I thought I was. Now I know it's my heart that's all in. Not my head."

She was about to tell him that she'd take his heart and he could forget about the rest, but Dylan made all decisions with his head. Never with his heart and she'd known this about him for as long as she'd known him.

"We'll always be best friends." He tipped her chin to meet his gaze. She saw shimmering dark eyes that were unreadable. This meant she couldn't even tell if he was as heartbroken as she felt.

He was breaking up with her.

She pushed against his chest, feeling like a hollowed-out dead tree. "But not...not naked friends."

"No." He loosened his hold on her. "Not anymore."

She shook her head, feeling tears wet her lashes. It was too much. Love and pain and grief and longing mixed together so that she could barely breathe or stand on buttery legs. She heard Maggie's voice in her head.

We don't need him.

And for the first time she understood. Understood why Maggie kept her from a father and why Milly came close to doing the same with Coral. Loving someone deeply was too scary. Too risky. It was easier to keep people away. Maggie had chosen not to love or need anyone that much, not even her own daughter. But it was too late for Charley. She'd never really been given a choice. She needed the man who'd loaned her his strength when she didn't have enough of her own. She needed the flawed and infuriating man with a huge heart.

He was hers. He'd always been hers.

"This is the biggest cop-out I've ever seen, and I've seen and heard some doozies. This isn't about me. It's about you! *You're* the one afraid to risk your heart. You're the one who's running. For the first time, you can't pin this one me. You are the one who's leaving."

"Okay, maybe you're right." He released her, his hands gliding up her arms and back down again. "Maybe I don't trust that you'd be happy here forever. Maybe I don't think that's really who you are."

"That's so unfair. How can I prove it to you?"

"That's it. I don't know if you can." He stood. "I've got to go."

"Why? We're not done here."

"Talking more isn't going to help either one of us."

"Don't you leave right now. Don't go."

"Someday you'll see I was right about this."

"No, I won't! You are wrong. I won't ever agree."

"I get to be right occasionally." He gave her a sad mile. "And this time, I know I am."

Without another word, he was out the door.

34

"A party without cake is just a meeting." ~ *Julia Child*

Dylan spent the next few days keeping busy while feeling sorry for himself. His was a sad state of affairs and he was already sick of himself. At least both the sailboat, and now Joe's new business, were a welcome distraction. The loan papers were prepared for the board shop in Santa Cruz and the loan would be funded within thirty days. He'd be a silent partner in a venture which would hopefully turn his youngest brother into a regular business man.

A couple of days before Sunset Kiss, Dylan was putting the last touches on the sailboat when both of his brothers showed up. Marco had a six-pack of Corona with him.

"We need to talk," Marco said as he hopped on board. Joe followed, and the combined weight of his two tall brothers made the boat rock.

"What's up?" Dylan picked up the rag he'd been using to make this baby shine and accepted a beer from Marco.

"Wondering if you're tired of yourself yet," Marco said.

"Excuse me?" Dylan scowled.

"You told me once that you'd *want* someone to tell you if you were being an idiot," Joe said, grinning. "And it's taken me a hell of a long time, but brother, I can now tell you: you're being an idiot."

Marco nodded. "I concur."

"If I wanted your advice, I'd ask for it. There's nothing here for you to worry about."

"Right, right," Marco said. "Because you're the only one allowed to worry about your brothers."

"I'm worried, D," Joe said, his brow creased.

"What? Why? I'm doing good. I just invested in a promising new business, and I'm about to make a killing over a few misguided people wanting to take a sailboat at sunset. Work is good, family is good." He took a swig of the cold beer. "I'm good."

"Denial," both Marco and Joe said at once.

"I think it's the first stage," Marco said.

"Bro, I've seen you break up with a lot of women over the years, but I've never seen you more miserable than you are now," Joe said.

"Same," Marco said.

They were right. Charley might think that he'd fallen for her because she'd accidentally kissed him at sunset. He knew better. She was strong, funny, beautiful and brave and he was deeply in love with her.

Not much he could do about it now.

"I hate talking about this," Dylan said.

"We know," Joe said.

"I kept quiet as long as I could, believe me," Marco said.

"I don't like talking any more than you do. But I'm tired of watching you mope around the house like someone tore your heart out."

He'd been slayed to the core by his own decision. Torn up by the fact that he'd hurt her without intending to. Hurt both of them. Worse, he'd done it intentionally and preemptively to avoid a greater hurt later on.

Who the hell did that? There was no way this could hurt *any* worse. No way in hell.

"I can only imagine what it must be like to love someone that much, but you do love her and you can't change it now. Maybe it's time to take that risk." This from Joe, risk-taker extraordinaire.

Risk equals reward. Yeah, but Dylan only took calculated risks in business. And if he took a chance on Charley, she was taking one on him. "What about her risk?"

"Dude, she's the biggest risk-taker of all of us," Marco said. "She was born into it. If Charley hadn't taken any risks, she might not even be alive today."

"And you can't make the decision for her," Joe said. "If she's ready to stick around for good, to love someone who might not come home from his job one night, then you need to be ready to let her. Because maybe it's better to take whatever time you're given together than nothing at all."

There was silence, other than the rolling sounds of the tide and the seagulls squawking overhead.

Marco fist bumped with Joe. "Damn, bro. That was some seriously good shit."

Joe beamed, his bright smile lighting up his face. "What do you think Dylan? Good shit?"

Yeah. His little brother had just schooled him. Maybe it was high time to take a risk. No point in protecting his heart when he'd already lost it to Charley. If she was willing to give up Paris for now, he was willing to trust that she'd never regret it. What's more, he was willing to work to make sure she'd never have the smallest regret.

"Guess I've got some planning to do."

This would be all for her, and all about her. Because she was everything to him and if it meant swallowing his pride, he was willing to do far more than that to get her back.

"Can we help?" Marco said.

"Glad you asked," Dylan said. "Because I'm going to need all the help I can get."

He had one day to get this right.

One day to say the right words.

One day to ask her to forgive him.

One day, and then hopefully, the rest of his life.

35

"You're my favorite mistake." ~ Meme

Charley cried for three days.

She cried so much that her eyes were almost swollen shut and Naomi thought she'd had an allergy attack.

"Antihistamines really work for me," Naomi said brightly, completely oblivious.

Charley wanted that kind of oblivion. She wanted to evaporate like water, or a good reduction sauce. Mostly she wanted the pain to stop for a few minutes. And of course, she wished for Naomi that she'd always live in a bubble and never feel pain, or loss, or her heart lying shattered in pieces.

But by the fourth day, all the crying was done. Now she was just royally pissed.

Dylan was wrong about her and if it took to her dying day she'd prove it to him. He didn't trust her. Well, she wasn't going anywhere ever again. Not Paris. Not New York City or New Orleans. Then he'd have to eat his own words. Before the DNA debacle and the search for Milly's baby daddy, Dylan hadn't won one of their arguments in years. In fact, he'd once joked about the fact. Said he looked forward to the day she'd agree with him and admit he'd been right. Well, she had already admitted he'd been right about Milly. That was enough for the rest of her life.

Because he wouldn't get to be right about this. Never! Because oh hell yes, she was staying. She'd decided, and it wasn't just because Dylan was here. Miracle Bay was her home, it had always been home, and all the residents were her extended family. She was planting down roots in Miracle Bay once and for all. Just call her Miss Tree, spreading her branches.

When Milly and Coral were discharged from the hospital, they'd come home with Henry, who stayed with them the first couple of nights. Then he had to get back to work and Charley stayed in Milly's apartment for days. Easier that way. Charley didn't need privacy anymore and Milly certainly didn't. She loved the extra help.

And with Milly in the room, Charley was less likely to sit for hours with her thumb hovering above "send" on a text message to Dylan that read simply:

I'm going to prove you wrong.

She would send it, but she wasn't speaking to him right now. Twice a day she deleted the text. Recently she'd revised her previous text message. This one read simply:

You should realize that you've already lost this argument.

The plain and simple truth. She hadn't sent that one, either.

Something else tugged at her heart. Another Sunset Kiss weekend was wrapping up. On Miracle Sunday, the last day, the bakery did their greatest business. She'd already served many couples on their way to a rented sailboat to launch just before sunset. Lucky people, all of them, on an adventure of a lifetime.

The shop door opened, and Marco swaggered up to the counter. "Hey, Charley."

"I've got your order ready."

Health nut Marco had become a regular. She pulled the bag out she'd carefully packed him with the cheese encrusted paninis with her chicken salad. It was made with Kalani olives and walnuts tossed in an olive oil vinaigrette and Marco was its biggest fan.

"On my way to the marina," he said, paying for his sandwich.

"Are you going on any of the sailboats later?"

"Ha! Hell, no. It's just fun watching the dummies from the sidelines."

And it was true that couples and families made a day out of Sunset Kiss. Packing picnics and hanging out.

"Dylan is going to be there," Marco said.

"Oh, right." He'd obviously be a part of the festivities. "How's he doing?"

"He made a killing this weekend. You should come down. His boat is booked solid." He leaned in close. "You could come with me. Like, right now. It's fun to watch all the hopeless romantics."

Charley tried not to take that personally. "Sure, I will. If I have time."

"Seriously? You can't leave for a few minutes?"

She gave Marco a patient smile and gestured around the shop. "As you can see, we're quite popular."

"That's the best I can do," Marco muttered as if he didn't

think Charley could hear him. "Come or don't come but I've done my part."

Alrighty then. Charley waved to Marco as he went out the door.

"You look tired," Padre Suarez said as he placed his order. "Have you been sleeping?"

"Sure."

Liar. She hadn't been sleeping. Or eating. Two basic life sustenance requirements. She was doing okay on the breathing, though frankly, some days were better than others.

"Then there must be some other reason why your eyes are so swollen." This was from Mrs. Perez.

"It's allergies," Naomi called out helpfully.

"I'll say a rosary," Padre Suarez said and paid for his doughnut and panini. "When's Milly bringing that baby down?"

Little Coral was a week old but still hadn't met everyone.

"She's bringing her down today."

"Well, it's about time. Miracle Bay's very own miracle baby. We all want to meet her."

"Shhh," Charley said. "Don't call her that. Milly doesn't like it. High expectations or some such thing."

She glanced up at the clock. The shop was filling with their regular patrons, and they'd all want to see baby Coral aka the Miracle Baby.

"I'll call her and tell her to come down." She pulled the cellphone she kept in her apron at all times (in case Dylan called or texted because, face it, she was *hopeless*.) "Oh, no! No!"

"What is it?" Padre Suarez asked, hand to his heart.

No. It couldn't be. She thought she'd closed that screen,

but somehow, in a similar way to a butt dial she'd just apron texted Dylan!

You realize you've already lost this argument, right?

"I sent a text message and I didn't mean to do it."

"My dear, you really have to stop overreacting." Padre Suarez shook his head and shuffled to a table.

Charley slipped the phone back in her apron. He'd told her in so many words that he didn't want to be the only reason she stayed. That she couldn't be trusted. Only time would prove that she *could* be trusted to stay. Beyond that, there was little left to say.

Five seconds later her phone buzzed in her apron and she was almost afraid to look.

Red Hot Heartbreaker:

Nothing new. I always lose arguments with you. Here's my secret: it's because I let you win.

Oh no he didn't! Was he joking? Because it was not funny.

Ha! Just ha!

Okay, not all that brilliant but the best she could come up with in a pinch. Charley typed her answer back furiously, her thumbs flying. "You wouldn't believe what Dylan just texted me!"

"What? You two are talking again?" Naomi asked.

"Arguing again, you mean. Boy, he has some nerve! He *lets* me win arguments? The ego on him!"

Naomi crossed her arms. "I hate guys."

"Hey, everybody!" Milly appeared in the bakery, holding baby Coral wrapped like a burrito in a pink blanket.

Within seconds, Milly and her baby were surrounded.

"What an adorable baby!"

"Just look at those cheeks!"

"She looks just like you, Milly!"

"Coral would be so proud!"

"I'm going to say a rosary."

"Our Miracle child!"

Milly didn't seem to mind the reference today. She smiled and glowed with pride. "If you want to hold her, wash your hands first."

There was a mad dash for the restroom and Charley took the moment to text Dylan:

You don't let me win. I win because I'm right. I'm never leaving because this is my home. You'll see.

Red Hot Heartbreaker:

You're still here? Not texting me from Paris?

She couldn't text back fast enough:

That's not funny!

Red Hot Heartbreaker:

It is a little bit funny.

Charley could haul out a long list of times when she'd won an argument, though she wasn't sure how she could prove he hadn't let her win. Either way, this was a conversation better had in person.

"Naomi, take over for a while?" Charley pulled off her apron. "I've got to go."

"Why? What happened?" Milly asked. "Everything okay?"

"She's very upset about a text message she didn't mean to send," Padre Suarez explained, shaking his head and waving a hand dismissively.

"I'm going to the marina to win an argument." She handed her apron to Naomi. "I'll be back."

"Take your time." Milly gave Charley a huge smile. "We've got this."

Charley hopped on the Vespa and drove, a light bay breeze whipping around the long hairs that stuck out of her helmet. She arrived and got lost again down the rows of boats that all looked so similar among the throngs of couples. Then she heard Dylan's low whistle. As she redirected and turned toward the sound, she saw Dylan onboard the *Miracle One*. The sailboat gleamed in the bright patches of sunlight breaking through the fog, looking brand new.

Dylan hopped off the boat. It was so good to see him again that her anger faded, and it took everything in her not to run and jump into his arms. But she stayed planted several feet away from him on the pier. Her knees knocked together, so loud she thought they could be heard over the sounds of the seals' barking.

"We don't talk or text for a whole week and the first thing you do is pick an argument with me?" Her breath hitched.

"Sorry about that, but I had to get you down here. I was going to call you just before you texted me."

"That was an apron text. Kind of like a butt text. An accident."

He slid her that boyishly one-sided grin, and her heart threatened to bust out of her chest because she loved him so much. She loved seeing that easy smile on his face, the worry lines gone from his dark eyes. He looked happy and that was all she'd ever really wanted.

"Still, I'm glad you sent it. Saves me the trouble of sending Joe to kidnap you. Marco was supposed to bring you here with him. He failed." Dylan waved toward the sailboat. "What do you think?"

"It's beautiful. I guess you've made a killing this weekend."

"It could have been more."

She snorted. "What, you couldn't find enough desperate people to fill each day?"

Hands stuffed in the pockets of his jeans, he cocked his head. "I found one guy, and he's pretty desperate because he was an idiot. He walked away from the best girl he ever had because he was too scared."

Oh, my. That sounded vaguely familiar, but she didn't dare hope that Dylan was the idiot guy. But when he walked toward her and stood only inches from her, the small hope she had left grew like a wildfire in her heart.

He pulled her to him the rest of the way. "Forgive me, baby. You're right. I was running. Running from something stronger than I've ever felt before. If you want to know the truth, I'm terrified. But I can't lie to myself anymore. Right or wrong, I'm not going to be able to let you go. I'm no hero, something I've been trying to tell people for a long time."

"*You*? Y-you're the idiot?"

He gazed at her from under hooded eyelids. "So, what do you say? Want to go on this sailboat at sunset? It's available because I wouldn't let anyone else rent it today."

There went her heart. It was just a gooey mess inside her. He hadn't rented the boat to anyone else today. "Are you sure you want to do this? You don't even believe."

"Here's the thing. I'm in love with you, so in love with you that if this is what you want, then you're getting a ride on a sailboat and a kiss at sunset."

"Dylan—"

"But let's get this straight. I don't need a sunset kiss, and I don't need a miracle. Because you're the love of my life, and you're all I need."

Her heart swelling and tears wetting her eyelashes, she kissed him right then and there as couples bustled about them. Miracles happened often in Miracle Bay, but some took a little more time than others. Hers had taken thirteen years and it was worth every minute.

"I'm one lucky miracle bastard. You chose me."

She went into his arms and wrapped her hands around his neck. "I choose you. I always will."

"I love you, Charley."

"I love you too. So much. I know where I belong, where I always have. With you. No matter where I am, it has to be with you."

He tugged on a lock of her hair. "I want you to know that I'm going to work hard so you never regret staying in Miracle Bay."

"This is my city and I'm staying here. Besides, I'm finally going to open up my own bistro."

"Yeah?"

"And I already have the location. Sunrise Bakery and Bistro."

"You got your dream."

"I sure did, but it's not the bistro." She curled her fingers around his strong neck. "I claimed you a long time ago. You just didn't know it."

She rose to the balls of her Chucks and met his kiss. Tender. Sweet and long and hot and lingering. A salty breeze kicked up and rocked the boat, causing her to cling to him even tighter.

The seals could be heard barking and celebrating.

Welcome home, girl!

Because this time Charley Young was home to stay.

EPILOGUE

"Cupcakes are muffins that believed in miracles." ~ Bakery plaque

Six months later on Miracle Sunday, and the grand opening of Sunrise Bistro

Charley adjusted her chef's apron three times. She took off her chef's hat. Put it back on again.

"I don't know. Is the hat too much?"

Dylan, who'd been responsible for the remodeling that had taken place in the Sunrise Bistro in the past few weeks, came up behind her and lowered his head to her shoulder. "We've gone over this."

"I know *you* like the hat."

His breath tickled her neck. "Because it's sexy."

"Sexy is not what I'm going for. And you just think that because the first time I tried it on for you I wasn't wearing anything else."

"That didn't hurt."

"Fiancé privileges."

He'd proposed to her last month in front of his entire family. At sunset. It seemed too fast to some people, if you wanted to call thirteen years fast.

"We're ready." Naomi popped her head into the remodeled kitchen. "And we've got quite a crowd."

"This is it." She turned in Dylan's arms. "I'm really doing this."

"Yes, you are."

In the past two months, the bakery had been enlarged and remodeled into a small bistro where she and her small crew would serve lunch and dinner. There were now white cloth-covered tables and real silverware. A few tables were available for outdoor seating, with parasols for shade. The only things remaining from before were the red brick wall and Coral's clock. There were memories in this place that tugged on her heart and made the bistro alive with her family history. And even though she'd changed so much about the bakery Coral ran for so many years, Charley felt certain that Coral was watching over her now giving her blessing. Proud that her hard work had paid off, all because she'd never given up on a hostile and hurting fifteen-year-old girl.

Dylan took Charley's hand and pulled her toward the swinging doors that separated the kitchen from the eating area. "Ready?"

She adjusted her hat again, ignoring Dylan's tipped grin. "Oh, wait a second." She bent down to tie a shoelace on her pink Chuck Taylors. "Ready."

Charley would greet everyone on their grand opening. The tables were already set up with hors d'oeuvres: cream cheese and olive biscuits with olive parsley spread; marinated chicken satays; pepper jelly goat cheese cakes. They also had tables set up with their usual pastries for the regulars who had supported them all these years.

She'd been experimenting with Julia Child classic recipes, putting her on spin on them, Dylan her willing guinea pig. Bruschetta, beef Bourgogne and, of course, ratatouille. But now that they would finally open their doors, she wondered once again just how smoothly the regulars would take to this transition. Hopefully they'd stick with her and not call her a culinary snob.

Naomi, Marco, who was filling in as a waiter today, and the sous chef she'd hired were standing by dressed in black pants and white shirts, ready to greet the crowd and ply them with trays of champagne and food.

"The line winds all the way around the block," Naomi said. "I checked."

Charley swallowed and squeezed Dylan's hand. "Open the doors."

Naomi flipped the sign from "closed" to "open."

"It's about time. I've been waiting," said Mrs. Perez, filing inside.

"You haven't been waiting any longer than I've been. And I've got about a decade on you," Abuelita said.

Alice walked in with Joe, whose surf shop had just made a list of one of the top ten places to visit while in Santa Cruz.

Padre Suarez was also near the front of the line. "Will you still be requiring my blessing every week?"

"I would really appreciate it. New restaurants need all the help they can get."

A little knowledge was a dangerous thing, and Charley had too much knowledge on the success rates of new restaurants. Honestly, they were rather dismal. But she reminded herself that she was starting with existing customers she had no intention of chasing away. All the wonderful residents of Miracle Bay.

"Is Milly coming?" Alice asked, giving both Charley and Dylan a hug.

"She'll be here a little later with Henry and Coral. They're driving up."

Their little family was doing so well that Milly had only called Charley once a day for the past week. Usually the calls came three times a day with at least a dozen texts and photos of Coral. Milly wanted Charley to know about every new and magical thing Coral had done.

The pastries were gone within minutes, but she was pleasantly pleased that Naomi and Marco were re-filling the hors d'oeuvres trays, too.

"Is this...jelly?" Padre Suarez asked, taking a bite out of a goat cheese cake.

"Red pepper jelly," Charley said, and held her breath. She wasn't sure Padre would think that jelly and red pepper belonged in the same sentence, much less together on a cake.

"Delicious."

Dylan pulled her into his arms. "See? You were worried for no reason. Everyone loves your food just as much as I do."

"Okay. You were right, and I was wrong." She kissed him. He gave great advice. Most of the time.

"Wait. I was right? Can I get that in writing?"

A RECIPE FOR PASTA CARBONARA

Ingredients:
   Salt and pepper to taste
   1 pound of rigatoni
   1/4 c. extra-virgin olive oil
   1/4 pound of pancetta, chopped
   1 tsp. crushed red pepper flakes (optional)
   5 garlic cloves, chopped
   1/2 c. dry white wine (optional)
   2 large egg yolks
   1/2 c. grated Romano cheese

Put a large pot of water to boil. Add salt and rigatoni, cook about 8 minutes (al dente.)

Heat a large skillet over medium heat. Add olive oil and pancetta. Brown for 2 minutes. Add red pepper flakes and garlic, cook 2-3 minutes longer. Add wine and stir.

Beat yolks, and temper them by adding some of the water from the pot boiling the pasta. Drain pasta and add to the skillet with pancetta and oil. Pour egg mixture over pasta. Toss to coat quickly, without cooking the egg mixture. Remove from heat and add a handful of cheese. Toss until egg mix thickens, about 1-2 minutes.

Eat with your true love, straight out of the pan.

ABOUT THE AUTHOR

Heatherly Bell is the author of twenty-seven published contemporary romances under two different pen names.

She lives for coffee, craves cupcakes, and occasionally wears real pants. She lives in Northern California with her family.

ALSO BY HEATHERLY BELL

Wildfire Ridge with Harlequin Special Edition:

More than One Night

Reluctant Hometown Hero

The Right Moment

The Wilder Sisters:

Country Gold

She's Country Strong

A Country Wedding

Heroes of Fortune Valley with Harlequin:

Breaking Emily's Rules

Airman to the Rescue

This Baby Business

Starlight Hill:

All of Me

Somebody like You

Until there was You

Anywhere with You

Unforgettable You

Forever with You

Crazy for You, Christmas in Starlight Hill

Only You

Made in the USA
Middletown, DE
27 March 2022